The Scent of Gardenia:

A Killing in Princeville

Based on a true event -- the devastation of Hurricane Floyd upon Princeville, NC where caskets washed from the ground -- this book is otherwise a work of fiction. Any similarity to a real person is purely coincidental.

Cover Design: Sherrye Alves
salves47@yahoo.com

ISBN 978-0-578-03548-2

WARNING: This book contains material not intended for readers under 18 years of age.

Printed
In the
United States
By

Frog's Hair Press
PO Box 34483
Charlotte, NC 28234
www.frogshairpress.com

Third Edition
February 2016

Forward

Malice Able, a forensic specialist with a special department of the government, is at emotional and professional crossroads. His work demands secrecy that has kept him from relationships of any kind – a decision that demands reconciliation. But he's discovered a secret kept even from him. Experiments conducted on abandoned children had two unexpected results: it healed birth defects, but turned them into serial killers. One has come of age and is cutting off hands and feet, nailing them to a cross.

While deciding what to do, Malice is asked to identify bodies that washed up in one of the worst hurricanes in decades. He discovers one of those bodies is a white woman pregnant with a black child, secretly buried in a black cemetery over thirty years before.

Her murder becomes the intersection for a ritual killer who thinks himself sent by God; the death of a local bisexual who knew her identity, and the downfall of the accomplice who unknowingly put her in the grave. The estranged family Able protected with his own lies is in the killer's path.

The Scent of Gardenia begins as a tale of murder, secrets and lies. It evolves as a story of belonging, sacrifice, and love. Throughout, it is a search for Truth.

Acknowledgment
~Q~

Every writer must have a friend who suffers through the beginning of a new creation – when every word is sacred script. Jacqueline Dove-Miller was that for me. Girlfriend, I am sooo sorry. Your encouragement was felt in every grammatical correction. Judith Garmon and Gail Patterson helped me trim away pages. Ladies of "Reading of the Mind" book club: thank you for my first review! Yvonne Jackson, Emma Pemberton, and David Cole: thank you, thank you.

Lastly, special gratitude to Chuck Collins. Your honest, thought-filled comments helped crystallize details that otherwise were not even considered. Thank you Chuck! That critical mind was exacting and exactly what this story needed.

Those who were inspirations for characters and events will remain anonymous for my protection!

Thank you my sisters, Tina and Toni. Telling me that I should publish "something" kept this goal before me.

How many friends will sit through a class to show support? Only the real ones. Marlene Cox did that for me. Tina, Toni, and Marlene - your belief in me did not go unnoticed. Love you beyond words.

Lastly, to my daughters, Nikki and Manetta. I hope I have made you proud. It all began with "Speedy The Caterpillar", and a little boy named MoonPie. I continue to write for you.

3

The Scent of Gardenia
A Killing in Princeville

The sky went dark. A violent storm whirled towards the eastern shore. In Princeville, North Carolina rain fell hard from a sky soaked with bad intentions. Water fell from everything into everything. Drenching, washing, destroying, remaking.

The first day, workers hurried to their cars from the mills and factories, and made their way home crouched over steering wheels, eyes wide. Windshield wipers swished pounds of water to permit seconds of clarity. Radios on various stations throughout the factory warned them. Get Out. Go Home. Take cover.

Within hours, everyone looked into a sky that demanded they pray. And each one said, to no one in particular, "I have never seen nothing like this."

Another said, "Something ain't right." Others worried that God was angry, that the sky was about to do something unnatural. It didn't take long for worry to settle deep in their bones, wear on their faces, be felt in the touch of their children.

By the next day, every street looked like a stage of drunken dancers. Outdoor furniture swam frantically through flooded byways. Defiant trees leaned.

It wasn't long before reservoirs spilled. Houses perched on cinder blocks fell to their knees. Nature's water forced everything into surrender. Nothing spared. Not even the dead. Caskets oozed up through six feet of clay and joined the frantic tide of limbs and cars coursing bewildered and anxious through Princeville.

Early the fourth day the plummeting stopped. The gashing winds calmed down. The clouds had changed from fierce to flannel gray. But the faces looking through mud-smeared windows bore the same horror-filled eyes as when they entered the shelter. The fear that had gripped everyone for days turned to tears.

Cleanup was into its seventh day by the time Lucas found all the caskets and put them in an old barn spared from destruction. He called the medical examiner in Greenville; spoke with Dr. Ben Riley, pronunciations revealing his southern roots.

"They're nine of 'em Doc, the recently buried, most likely. With everything these folks been through and lost, I wanna make sure they at least get back their dead. We could use your help."

Ben shook his head. Lucas had graduated high school with him, could speak impeccable English, but often chose a dialect the people in his town found comforting.

"Lucas, I understand the problem you got there and I respect what you're trying to do, but I can't get away; we're overflowing with bodies ourselves."

"From the storm?" Lucas asked.

"A few. One fool thought he could drive through three feet of water, an elderly lady from a heart attack. But most of them came the old fashioned way: people killing each other. Got deadlines to meet for the DA." Ben hoped this would get him off the hook, but Lucas' silence said it hadn't. "Look, Let me make a call; I'll hit you back."

Ben sat down hard in the well-worn sofa on which he catnapped when the workload didn't let him go home. He dialed and got voicemail. "Hey old man, I hear you're retiring. Who retires at forty-six? I'm gonna be like you when I grow up. Anyway, man, I need a favor. Has to do with Princeville. Give me a call A.S.A.P. I'm at work." As he hung up Ben heard his name over the intercom. No time to reminisce, just enough to believe Malice would call. He'd said the magic word: Princeville.

Chapter 2.

He pushed the blade deep into the earth. The South Carolina clay moved easily. Another foot would be enough. The moon clouds hindered his vision but did not impede his task. He dug the spade into earth's flesh once more for surety she would accept his gift.

The spade fell onto the warm mound with barely a sound. It didn't matter; no one would hear. He opened the tote size cooler and lifted the hands. As he nailed them to the cross, the words he had seen repeatedly etched in bronze beneath the feet of a crucified Jesus, he imagined on his rendition: 'Do This in Remembrance of Me'. The soft flesh of the palms yielded with each blow. He returned to the cooler for the feet and placed them in the imagined footprint of the Savior.

The hands knew not the feet and no body laid claim to either. He raised the offerings and tilted the cross as it found its place in the ground. He lifted his face and offered his first prayer.

When it comes to pass
They will believe that I am He that sent me
By my hands, I render your deed
My feet, I concede.

Chapter 3.

"Willa. You came back."

"Hello Ray," she said. "What happened to you? Looks like someone played rough."

"Nothing to get excited about." Raymond Solder pressed his hand against the bruise on his waist. "Small disagreement."

"May I come in?" Willa asked.

"I guess you want to talk more about my offer."

"Sounded like blackmail to me," she said. "No, we've talked enough. I came back for you."

Raymond Solder stood aside as the woman in the trench coat walked in and straight down the hall to his bedroom. With her back to him, Willa removed the coat to reveal only a garter, tightly gripping black stockings. She tossed the coat onto the side chair and waited. Her expectation of what he would do was confirmed when she felt Ray's finger trail from her neck down her back.

Ray turned his guest around and kissed her chest, biting the tiny nipples until he heard her gasp. Before long, his naked body surrendered to the woman behind him. Willa's long brown hair brushed his skin as she trailed kisses down his spine. Shortly, the wooden bed rocked against the floor, the springs clacked and whined.

When she was done with him, Willa went to the kitchen, leaving her lover in the arms of satisfaction. She returned to find him as she left him, face down, arms stretched wide. She straddled his back on her knees, lifted his head, and kissed the side of his lips. She slid the other hand underneath his throat. Raymond could not see the knife with the blade facing his neck. Nor did he expect the violent force that slammed his head down on it. She slid the blade sideways through the warm flesh until it withdrew.

Chapter 4.

As he'd hoped, Malice was certain Fawks Belnais had not seen it coming.

"Look, Mal, I know we disagree on a lot of things, but you can't be serious." Fawks sprang from the leather chair, slapping the handwritten letter on the desk as he stood.

Malice was sure this was why Fawks was an administrator. His outbursts were often inappropriate, a vice for the line of work he'd chosen. Perhaps he didn't choose. Maybe the work chose him just like it chose me, Malice thought. Now, all he can do is feel what he's lost. Malice turned his eyes from Fawks just enough to lose contact but still appear to be listening. The smoke brown tinted window gave a warm, calming quality to his boss's stylish suite.

Fawks continued. "I woke up this morning, made love to my wife, jogged five miles, and then here to get the details of your mission. Your resignation was not in my day."

Malice looked back at Fawks. Even though he no longer did field assignments, Fawks trained as if he expected to be called back any day. His body was a testament to that hope. But Malice was sure that would never happen. A brilliant strategist, but whatever demon had him was stronger than his will to control it.

"We are on the verge of something life-changing here, and you want to walk away now!" Fawks strolled to the window of Malice's attention, his hands fumbling at the keys and coins in the pockets of an expensive jogging suit. He looked out the fifty-eighth story window and shut his eyes against the morning sun. "I believe we were at this same juncture not that long ago. I asked if you knew why we don't bother with the Ivy Leagues. Do you remember that, Malice?"

"Yeah, you said they were populated with privileged whiners."

Fawks turned around. "Think whatever they have or want they deserve. Hell, some will tell you they *earned* their inheritance by putting up with their parents. We leave those assholes to aspire to public office and run the companies that finance what we do. We let them play secret agent with their checkbooks."

"So you go to state colleges to find expendables."

"That's bullshit. We're all expendable, Malice. MENSA didn't select you because you're stupid. That means you're smart enough to know we didn't pick you to die in some fuck hole on the other side of democracy. We read your theory on DNA Physiological Mutation and were intrigued. We said 'Holy shit, what if he's right,' when you documented parallels between your theory and serial killers. We saw the implications, Malice. The possibilities.

10

Don't tell me you didn't know what you were doing twenty feet underground."

Fawks grabbed the letter from his desk. "So what's the real reason you walked in here with this piece of crap?"

Malice stood and brushed the legs of his jeans. He picked up his brown felt Indiana Jones hat and tapped it into place on his head. "It's there, in your hand. Personal conflict. I'll stay to tie up loose ends, go through SCRUB. Wasn't that one of your acronyms? Systematic Containment and Removal of Unauthorized Benefit'. Cute. Unauthorized Benefit... real cute. The timeline is up to you, but sooner is better."

Fawks watched the solid mahogany door close behind Malice. He pinched the bridge of his nose with his fingers and moved them upward to smooth his salted brown hair. He picked up the blue phone on his desk and spoke into the handset without dialing. "Misletoe."

Chapter 5.

Malice stepped into his Reston, Virginia condo as the answering machine beeped. He removed his vintage hat and the weapon from his shoulder harness. He poured a shot of scotch and swallowed as he listened to Ben's call. He leaned back in the leather recliner, savored the warm burn to his stomach, and the comfort of it settling in.

"Princeville," he said out loud. His mother was born there. He glanced at the only photograph in the house. Anyone curious about its connection to him would find ends as dead as his father.

Thoughts of his mother brought stories of Princeville that she'd told him as a child, stories he insisted she tell.

About men and women who built a town from nothing and named for who they were—princes and princesses—descendants of Kings. And, as a child, he believed. Even now, when the ugliness became too much, he wrapped himself in her stories. Kings whispered in his ear.

Malice took another swallow of his scotch and picked up the phone. He heard the signal that said his line was secure.

"Dr. Riley," the voice on the other end answered.

"You got my attention ... what's up?"

Ben grinned. "I knew you'd call."

"Yeah, you're the master of crypt-tease."

"Not this time, I promise." Ben blew tired air from his lungs. "Unless you've been in some god-forsaken spot, you know about the hurricane that hit us. Practically washed away Princeville."

"Yes, I saw." He *was* out of the country, in western Africa, where Hurricane Floyd had gotten its start, but no need to share that. "One of the deadliest since Agnes, I understand," Malice replied.

"Thirty-five dead across North Carolina. Eighteen in the area. Could have been worse."

"What's up, Ben?"

Ben breathed harder. "Remember Lucas? The sheriff there? I've mentioned him before. Anyway, he has a little problem. And since you're retiring, I thought you could use a little diversion while you decide what next."

"How's that?" Malice asked.

"The storm was hard—practically washed up everything. Even some caskets." Ben waited for Malice to respond. He didn't. "I know what you're thinking, why not just put them back in the ground, right?"

"Well?"

"Lucas tries to do the right thing. Families in Princeville visit their dead like going to Sunday dinner. Lucas wants the right body in the right place. Family's important in Princeville, Malice, even after you're dead."

It's a small town, Malice thought. Everybody has to be related to each other, so what difference would it make?

"We need to bury them again as soon as the ground permits. I thought we could interview the families who buried someone in the last ten years, run a few tests and see who's who. Wha'd'ya say?"

When Malice still didn't answer, Ben gave his second pitch. "Look Mal, you're always asking me about the town, here's a perfect opportunity to come see for yourself. You've avoided every other invitation. Think of it as a job rather than a homecoming if you want. You can do what I'm asking in your sleep."

Ben waited again. "Damn, they trained you good, man." Out of steam, he said, "Think about it; I'll be here late." He didn't wait for a reply, nor offer the 'right-oh' that signaled his good-bye.

Malice took another swallow from his glass. He went to the bookcase and pulled out a small handmade book. *The Keepers of Carifa.* His mother had made it for him when he'd asked her to tell the story again and again. This, and his father's photograph were his only sentimentalities. Inside the book, a black bar covered what use to be his name on the dedication page. He didn't have a birth certificate on record anywhere any longer so it hardly mattered. He turned the page and read.

~Q~

"Once upon a time, on an island in the middle of the Atlantic Ocean, lived a noble race who brought the world into being. They were artists and musicians. Others were

13

teachers of knowledge and skill. And some were farmers
who grew exotic plants, foods and flowers.
 *The Unknowns had powers to control everything around
them. But the people lived simple lives, respecting the
earth and all living things..."*

Malice passed through the middle of the story where the
children of Carifa forgot who they were and caused all
kinds of strife as a result. He drank the last of his drink and
read the end:

*"... Carifa's children reclaimed their freedom. In Arecima, a
small group of these new Keepers of Knowledge found their
way to a small valley in a beautiful land with clear blue
skies. There, they practiced the skills of their mothers and
fathers. Remembering their instructions, they built a city
named for who they were—strong, resilient, noble and
brave: Princes and Princesses of Carifa.
In honor of their mothers and fathers, who sacrificed love
and life, they named the valley Princeville. And they are
there to this day, living as Mother-Father-Sun-Moon
taught them, thousands of years ago."*

GR

As he basked in the story's lessons, a reporter's voice on
CNN grabbed him back.
 "Police in South Carolina are baffled by a mysterious
 murder. In the little town of Wylie, a farmer discovered
 human hands and feet nailed to a cross, crucifixion style;
 except, there was no body. Even more baffling, the hands
 and feet appear to be from different people. A four-county
 Search is underway for at least two mutilated bodies."

Malice stared at the television. A chill hit his spine and spread throughout his limbs. He surfed through channels in search of further details. Finding none, he clicked off the television. He'd know soon enough. Ben's call may as well been the too much garlic salt he put on his steak; both stayed with him. To restore his mood, he turned on the stereo. Vanessa Williams' smooth melodies would keep him company through dinner. After putting away the dishes, Malice picked up the phone and left a simple message on Ben's answering machine. "I'll be there."

෪

In Temple Hills, Maryland, far from South Carolina, another man heard the same CNN report. He sat calmly on the side of his bed and changed his shoes. This man knew what had happened to the bodies, and why. The crucified hands had tied four women to trees in various positions. One's back against the bark with her knees to her chest. Another's face lined with grooves she was tied to the tree so tightly. Each had been drugged into submission.

The hands that took them had gotten into an old pickup truck and seized the steering wheel. Those hands rammed the truck into these women. Backed up and rammed again. And again, until the broken bones were fragments picked from skin and muscle like splinters from the lion's paw. Eventually caught, those hands gripped the ageless bars of Coleman Penitentiary.

Like so many others before and after, those hands had been given a Bible. Those fingers had turned the pages, and on the thin sheets of black instructions and red promises had found God. Those fingers fervently clutched each other in mercy.

The highest priest of God had judged unworthy the wayward sheep whose hands lay nailed to the cross. But the feet that accompanied the hands on that cross in the South Carolina field he sanctified.

Chapter 6.

Malice settled into Home Town Suites in Greenville, North Carolina. As expected, the room was nothing memorable. Shortly, he greeted his cousin and loaded Ben's company car with a small leather satchel: a repository for the tools of his trade. Some innocent, like his cameras and laptop, others that could kill within seconds. Not so innocent. They headed west to Princeville.

"I see you shaved that shaggy rat you had growing under your nose," Ben said.

"Didn't want to be mistaken for you while I'm here."

"Riight," Ben laughed.

"By the way, Billie D called. He wants his moustache back," Malice added.

"That's because he's jealous."

"So, who is the rest of it suppose to be," Malice teased.

"Man, don't hate on the goatee."

When their laughter subsided, Ben said, "Lucas will meet us at the barn where the bodies are stored. I didn't tell anyone except Lucas that you were coming. He knows you're a forensic scientist. Told him you were like Henry Lee from the OJ case; that you hold down the east coast while Mr. Lee keeps out of your way in the west. He was blown away. Watched that trial everyday," Ben laughed. "Anyway, like you asked, I haven't told anyone about my hot shit relative. I doubt anyone from cousin Dee's family will recognize you since you don't use her name. You were what, eight, last time you were here?"

"The department suggested I change my name to keep my family safe. My work is delicate, and some of the people I meet are not mankind's best work."

"I know, man. I know. I've had some threats myself from people wanting a different version of the truth than what I find on the table. I don't want to imagine what you deal with. Maybe when you hang up that beaver hat, you can tell me," Ben said.

Malice thumped the brim of the black Indiana Jones from his collection. "Not even then, little cuz. Not even then."

Ben drove the last three miles in silence as both took in the carnage left by Floyd. Lucas stood in the doorway of Talbot's barn, his head nearly touching the frame, when Ben pulled up beside his ten-year-old sedan with "To Protect and Serve" written along the side panels. Malice grabbed his bag and stepped out of the newer, Greenville city car. A puddle formed where the cars were stopped and water spewed from underneath their steps all the way to the barn. Lucas reached for Ben's outstretched hand and the two patted each other's back.

"This is Dr. Malice Able. I attended a seminar that he taught at American University. We were the only Blacks in the room. I knew he had it going on since he was teaching the class."

Malice remembered that meeting. He had been impressed with the young man on the front row whose eyes darted with curiosity. He'd learned that Benjamin Adair Riley was from Princeville, North Carolina. And later learned, through his mother, that he and Ben were cousins. The two connected as quickly through friendship as they had in blood.

Lucas reached for Malice's hand and shook it firmly. "Can't tell you how much we appreciate your help, Doctor Able."

"What happened here is beyond words. I think the world of Ben; couldn't refuse." Malice took stock of the large hand that gripped his like a vise. The strength clearly came from the broad chest and muscled shoulders of this man who stood a few inches above him. There was a stillness in his face that reminded Malice of burnt embers. It was a look that told him Lucas could be fierce if required. Malice offered a tentative smile of assurance.

One of the worries on Lucas' face seemed to disappear. "Here, let me show you where the bodies are," as he led the two inside. "I don't know if Ben told you, but one of these caskets might be a problem."

"Yes, he did," Malice answered.

"I'll tell you both right now that I haven't had the nerve to open these boxes on my own. I've seen an accident victim here and there, but never anything that's been buried."

The caskets were positioned in an orderly fashion. Most still showed markings of their original design. "I see what you mean," Ben said. "This one didn't come from the economy room."

Malice set his bag on a shelf in the barn and removed two cameras. He gave the Polaroid to Ben. Within seconds, the barn echoed with mechanical wheezes. Malice picked up a more expensive camera, so small, the spray of its bright flash appeared to come directly from his eye. Turning to Ben, he said, "Call the wagon. Let's get these transported to Greenville."

Ben drove through more of the ruin to give Malice a deeper view of what had happened to Princeville. Houses were scattered in broken pieces like Lego blocks. Roofs missing. Trees torn from the ground. Crumbled brick where a building used to be. Malice had seen some of it coming in, but after seeing the caskets, the destruction took on new meaning.

"The storm was unforgiving," Malice said.

"Made its presence known," Ben said, "Even to the dead."

In the days that followed, five of the nine cases were completed. With luck, three more were settled. It was time to take Lucas up on his dinner invitation.

While waiting for their drinks, each grabbed peanuts from the bucket on the table, tossed the shells to the floor, and munched. The music was country, but decent.

With no prelude, Malice began. "Lucas, eight bodies have been identified, marked, and checked off your list."

"Wow," Lucas smiled. All in a week."

"Malice even found out Steller's Funeral Home is switching caskets," Ben shared.

"Don't surprise me none. I never trusted those people. Do anything to make a dollar and twice as much to keep it."

Malice interrupted Lucas' disdain for the mortuary. "As you suspected, one body is different. It was buried much longer than the others. My guess is it wasn't buried as deep as it should have been."

Ben sat enrapt, hearing this for the first time.

Malice continued. "The remaining names on your list of possibilities are men."

"What are you saying?" Lucas asked.

"The last skeleton is female."

"If the body was dead longer than the twenty years we went back, that might explain why it's not on the list," Ben offered.

"Yes, it might," Malice agreed, "but this woman was pregnant when she died. I traced the records of deaths thirty years back. There is no medical record, or death certificate of a woman dying during pregnancy that I could find."

"Maybe she died at home. Back then, no one was particular about keeping records on Blacks," Lucas said.

"Maybe," Malice replied and paused. "Lucas, you said all these bodies were from the cemetery in town?"

"Yeah, it's the only cemetery for miles."

"There's more, isn't there, Malice?" Ben asked, just as their dinners arrived.

"Later. Right now, I'm starving." With knife and fork in hand , he looked across the table. He had their attention. Good, he thought. If I'm right, more than a hurricane has hit this town.

Chapter 7.

Sweat rolled slowly from his temple to the crumpled pillow and made tiny spots that outlined the shape of his head. Through the valley of dreams he ran, barely escaping the realm of nightmares. Consciousness woke and informed that the water baptizing his sleep was not sweat but tears. He lay still, hoping the specter that provoked him, the one whose wisdom he both favored and despised, would fade into sanity's shadow. But Nietzsche's words stayed with him through the rushed counting of specks on his ceiling. But counting did not keep him from falling into the darkness. He shouted aloud. Why do you mock me!

I only suggest you be done with God. Your belief causes your sickness, not I. Your God says you cannot serve two masters.

20

Who will believe me!

Of what importance is that to the one who has been chosen?

No! No! What I've done is evil.

The world is full of evil and cruelty, and man's their greatest instrument. So, follow your holy epileptics or denounce them. As my words speak to you, be assured. You are beyond good and evil.

The man shut his eyes tight against the darkness as if the pain in his eyelids would stop his deeper descent and drown the voice. The thousands of spackles on the ceiling did nothing to help him. Each speck became an echo. You are beyond good and evil. Beyond good. Beyond... evil. Beyond... The mantra lulled him.

He turned his face back to the pillow of his baptism and surrendered. Nothingness seeped into the follicle of every pore; the torment hushed. Like a caterpillar weaving its own cocoon, he gave himself to the dark unknown. With the preordained calls of morning, he awoke reborn, complete. The call to give with one hand, and take with the other, to balance justice and reward, to offer vengeance and solace, had begun its reign to judge the deeds of his subjects.

Chapter 8.

Ben stood beside Malice looking at the tiny fragments of a full term fetus. "What have you learned?"

"Tested mom and child as much as the equipment will allow. A faint fragrance permeates the bones. Was there ever a time when bodies were perfumed, or buried with live flowers in the casket?"

"You mean like in ancient times?"

"Something like that. Was it a custom around here?"

"Not that I recall. But I can't say it never happened?"

Malice laid a cloth over the baby bones. "I have to go to Virginia for a couple of days. Can you make sure nothing here is disturbed? No one is to touch this body."

"Is something wrong?" Ben asked.

"I just need to wrap-up some ends there."

"When you're back, maybe you can take time from the mystery lady there, and let me show you around. Time to look at some women who can stand up," Ben teased, "Unless that's why you're headed back to V-A."

"Nothing like that," Malice smiled. "But you're on."

Ben winked, laughed his perfunctory "right-oh," and left. Malice collected the plastic bags he'd prepared, looked at each before placing it into the satchel, and said, "Let's go put some billion dollar equipment to better use."

It was less than an hour flight; just long enough for peanuts and a cup of ginger ale. The drive into Manassas felt good. He turned the car onto Highway 267 towards the laboratory that had been more home than office for the last six years.

His work resulted in the ERC, the Etogenic Re-imagining Computer. He was one of only seven people who knew of its existence, and one of three with access to its magic. The computer could recreate a person's physical identity. In 1963, working with cadavers, a team named Zeus discovered the physical characteristics code in humans. It looked like a star burst with millions of soft luminescent rays. They had thought it simply a staining of brain fluid on the skull, but discovered each ray actually contained, and delivered, the body's physical imprints to the base of the cranium.

22

Later, Zeus II questioned whether they could locate the compound in living subjects. It would take another three years, but they did. Eventually, the ERC could recreate the appearance of any person at any point in the aging process. Hundreds of unclaimed Does from morgues across the country showed up in Virginia as if this had been their purpose. Using them had not concerned Malice; he was too intellectually invested. Now, the thought of people who went unnoticed, unknown, unmourned bothered him.

A News brief on the radio interrupted his reflection. The mutilated victims with the missing hands and feet had been identified. That aching feeling he'd gotten when he'd first heard the story came back. It stuck in his brain like the nail driven in those hands and feet on that cross in South Carolina.

Chapter 9.

"Dr. Riley, this is Regina Bailey with *The Rocky Mount Tribune.* Can you elaborate on the unidentified body in Princeville?"

Her question caught Ben off guard. "I'm not sure I know what you mean. A body has yet to be identified. But we expect to have a name in a few days. I'm afraid the deceased didn't have a wallet on her."

"So, it was a female?"

Crap. Ben thought to himself. "How much attention did you pay in biology class?"

"Why?"

"While the size of the body, and pelvic bones suggest the corpse is female, it could just as easily be a young man."

"I understand a forensic pathologist from Washington is in charge of the case."

As Ben hoped, she wasn't prepared to challenge him on human anatomy, but her recovery impressed him. "There is no *case*, Ms. Bailey. But yes, a friend is helping. Given the need to rebury, and because we're swamped, he's lending a hand."

"Since you think it might be a female, is it true there is no record of a pregnant woman dying?"

He didn't see that one coming. She'd absolutely gotten information from someone. And now she was stirring his Kool-Aid.

"Look, Ms. Bailey, it's highly likely there is no record of a pregnant woman dying. Maybe no pregnant woman died; maybe documents were lost or misplaced. I can't say. You want Records and Deeds; this is the morgue. Now, if you'll excuse me, despite popular belief, it's not true that the dead can wait."

Chapter 10.

"What? What's going on?" Fawks demanded. The words came out of his mouth in chunks. "Fuck the protocol! I will NOT treat this like a scenario from a goddamn fucking manual!"

"We have a situation," the man standing at Fawks' window replied. "This is a courtesy call, not a debt I'm paying." The younger man reached into his pocket, and withdrew a Q-Tip. He broke it in two, and lightly swabbed the folds in his ear. Something he'd learned from his veterinary work. A relaxation technique he, himself, found calming. He put the other half of the swab in his pocket.

"Yes, but–"

"Look, Fawks. All I can tell you is I got a call. You, of all people know that call is not open to debate."

"What is this about, Dingo?"

Seeing enough of the bustle fifty-eight stories below, the lithe man turned to face Fawks.

"It's about Mistletoe."

Dingo did not wear the dark blue suit and muted tie that conveyed their profession. He spent no time pondering a dress code because he only wore two colors: black and denim. Its only variation was the length of the sleeve or the pattern in the weave. Today, it was all black. His incurious, beach bum demeanor would have been all wrong in a suit anyway. Incidental was the best way Fawks could describe Dingo's appearance. Still, something in his presence made others take him seriously. His eyes, Fawks concluded.

"You made one call; someone else made another."

"No, no," Fawks answered. "That call does not warrant you. Something else is going on here. If you didn't want me to know about this, I wouldn't. And—"

"And it changes nothing," Dingo added.

Fawks looked his friend in those evasive eyes. Searching, pleading. He met orbs that knew unspeakable things but would never convey the slightest detail.

Six months before college graduation, Fawks had handed Christian Dingo a business card that said: 'National Defense Administration' in small print across the US Government Seal in the background. The name, 'Fawks Belnais,' appeared in smaller print beneath the seal, with only a phone number. "I'm also told you could have gone into medicine. Why not?"

Dingo studied the card. "I want to travel. Study obscure languages. Can't do that with a stethoscope stuck to some-body's chest." He put the card in his pocket and added: "Besides, what's the point? Death knocks on every door; nothing to be done about that."

Fawks had been convinced on the spot that this young man had a disposition the Department considered *special*. "I'm prepared to offer you a job, Mr. Dingo. You'll see parts of the world you can't even find on the map." He then stared into eyes that would elude him years into the future.

Twelve years later, a thirty-four year old Christian Dingo stood in Fawks' office with the confidence that comes from having done something well, repeatedly. The past twelve years of competency had crystallized, and polished what was Christian Dingo like water smoothing rock.

Unable to see what he'd hoped for in Dingo's eyes, Fawks laid two fingers across his mouth briefly, then ran the same hand through his hair as if the name of something escaped him. "Thanks, Chris." As the men shook hands, for an instant, Fawks was certain he saw something in Chris' eyes that wasn't there before.

Chapter 11.

"Mister, what did I ever do to you?" the man cried out. Tears filled the pockets of his eyes and rolled from the corners with each troubled blink.

"You did nothing to me," the captor replied.

"Why? Why are you doing this!"

As the man in the dark robe poured a black-red liquid into a golden cup and put it to the bound man's lips, he answered, "I'm doing it for your salvation."

The freightened man's blurry eyes stayed locked onto the silvery blade of the machete that lay on the table nearby. "For God's sake, please don't!"

Who shall serve My God but me?
I am chosen amongst the many
To bring home the few.

"Drink," he told the man. When the warm fluid was safely past the man's throat, the monk reached for the worn mahogany handled machete and spoke the last words the man would ever hear.

My Lord, I am Your Will.

Chapter 12.

Why do people kill? Assistant District Attorney Brooklyn Beaudeau tapped her desk with the folder and tossed it back in the pile. She opened the red file labeled 'Solder: Laceration. Deceased'. "Another one," she said. "Over something stupid."

"Another what?" The paralegal asked, as she walked casually into her boss's office.

"Another black man, dead, is what."

"And your point?" Connor asked.

Brooklyn looked up as the fuller-figured young woman plopped in the chair in front of her desk. "What is it with our brothers? Every argument is settled with a knife or a gun." Brooklyn read the next file. "Seems some sisters handle business the same way. There are two here with reservations for a dirt row condo."

"Nothing says I love you like a bullet," Connor said.

A laugh escaped Brooklyn's lips. "What do you want, Annie Oakley?"

"Judge Pascal's office phoned. He wants to see you. Would you like me to reschedule with Dr. Riley since Michelle is away from her desk?"

"Just spoke with him myself. Did Vanessa say what Judge Pascal wants?"

"You mean Ms. Fort Knox? Wouldn't surprise me none if the man made up something just to look at you." Connor paused for a second. "Speaking of Dr. Riley..."

"Don't start, Connor."

"About which one—the judge, or the doc?"

"Neither. Judge Pascal is a reputable man. Besides, the fact that he's never married should tell you something."

"I ain't assuming nothing about nobody's sex life."

"Girl, who taught you English?" Brooklyn teased.

Connor waved her off. "That still leaves the doc, and since you don't want him, help a sister get an after-hour exam."

"I stay clear of breathing people's messy business. And romance is as messy as it gets."

"Damn BB, just let me call the man. If he hears my voice enough, he might get curious enough to ask me out."

"He could also get a restraining order."

"Now that is cold. Just tell me when the doc is coming? Let me interrupt with something, or give me this file to bring back."

"How did someone as young as you get to be so manipulative?"

"Learned it at my mama's knee," Connor kidded. "Before we forget, what time shall I tell Vanessa you can meet with Judge Pascal?"

Brooklyn studied her young assistant, knowing how much truth was wrapped in Connor's joke. "See if five o'clock works, and give me that file. Besides, have you ever thought Judge Pascal never married because he's a player?"

28

"Could be, but nobody with his credentials gets away that long. The man might be jaded about women, Brooklyn, but he ain't blind. If you ask me, that blue-eyed, silver spoon has discovered Godiva chocolate."

"After three years, Connor?"

"Five years ago, some things I wouldn't put in my mouth. Now, let's just say…I've developed a taste."

"Girl, get out of here," Brooklyn laughed. and shook her head as Connor closed the door behind her. She returned her attention back to the file. Raymond Solder. Black Male. 52. Homicide. Over a woman. Good a cause as any I guess, but a piss-poor reason to die.

Chapter 13.

Ben Riley collected his notes and x-rays on Raymond Solder and walked the block to the judicial complex housing the courthouse and the DA's office. Michelle buzzed Brooklyn, and motioned Ben in with a smile.

Each time he entered her sanctum, Ben was struck by the contrast, even after three years. The room did not reflect Brooklyn's courtroom persona. Her office displayed comfort, a place designed to help victims feel at ease, to trust her, to believe she would serve them justice with tea. That easiness stopped here. In the courtroom, she was single-minded, one of the best legal strategists he'd witnessed anywhere. Order was the commonality, her trademark, in both places. He was about to read the needlepoint he'd read countless times that spoke about surrender, when Brooklyn looked up and drew his attention.

"Hi, Ben. Thanks for adjusting your schedule." Brooklyn directed him to the sofa while she moved to the recliner.

He'd thought this was a power play the first time to her office, but later learned she liked to rock while she talked through difficult material. Medical matters were that for her.

"There's no place I'd rather end my day," Ben said. The blank stare on her face made him sit forward on the sofa. He opened his file on the coffee table. He would wait on her hand and foot if she asked but hated his desire for her at that moment.

Brooklyn let her file open to the place she'd inserted her finger. "Apart from the obvious, what can you tell me about Mr. Solder's death?"

Ben followed her lead. "He took a pretty bad beating."

"Yeah, the defendant is messed up, too. Probably why he resorted to the knife. Solder was not a lame duck."

"No. Unfortunately, in this case, he took better than he gave. Solder was in great shape, physically. But just as scissors cut paper, knife cuts flesh."

"Mr. Purdue admits to fighting with the victim, but denies the murder even though two witnesses put him at Solder's house. They're sketchy on the timing but–"

The secretary buzzed in the middle of her sentence. "Yes, Michelle?"

"Connor is here. Says she has some information you need for your meeting. Should I bring it in?"

"No, Michelle, ask her to join us."

Connor walked confidently into the room. She spoke to Dr. Riley, and gave Brooklyn a wink. "I wasn't sure I would get this to you today, but got lucky. If this is a bad time, I'm happy to come back."

"No, we're just starting." Brooklyn leaned back in the rocker to see if Connor would back-peddle or pull a rabbit. She watched as the young woman slid gracefully into the side chair, crossed her shapely legs arched by three-inch heels, and began a tale that ended with startling information that was not in the report.

"Where did you get that?" Brooklyn asked.

"Can't tell you that just yet, but you might want to put the detectives back in the field." Connor turned to Dr. Riley. "Did you find old wounds on Solder's body?"

"Yes. Some appear to be self-inflicted. There are also, some, uh, modifications."

Brooklyn looked at Ben. "Modifications?"

"Yes, two. I didn't think much of the first until I saw the second. One is fairly common with younger people—a tongue ring. Well, it's actually a metal bead," Ben said tentatively.

"And the other," Brooklyn asked, her voice rising a little at Ben's hesitation.

"The other was a ring of tiny pearls implanted in the sheath of Mr. Solder's foreskin."

A look of curiosity and disgust mingled with the implication of pain contorted Brooklyn's face.

"Exactly," Connor said. "Pain would be one of the benefits."

"And this means..."

"It means," Ben offered, "That, at the very least, Solder's sex life was intense."

Connor took over, hoping to head off Brooklyn's sideglance at Ben. "My source tells me that Raymond Solder never had a woman of his own. He liked playing the field with OPP—other people's pu...uh...property—married women in particular. The more jealous the husband, the better. The body enhancements were for the women. Their pleasure was his pain, in more ways than one, seeing as how he's now permanently stiff."

Connor continued, "It's pure speculation at this point, but a theory worth exploring as we develop the prosecution's case, don't you think?"

"Despite whether any of what you've said is true, the man *was* killed," Brooklyn said.

"No doubt about that," the younger woman chimed, "but when you consider a man who likes pain, add old wounds, his sexual instrumentations, mix in a few pissed-off husbands, you get something from the booth-in-the-corner-on-the-dark side. I'd want to know everything the defense might offer for reasonable doubt."

"She's right," Ben said. "I'll go back and look at the physical evidence personally. Great work, Connor," he added, and stood to leave.

Connor followed. Brooklyn stopped her. "Would you wait for me?" Brooklyn walked Ben to the door. "Thanks, Dr. Riley. Let me know what you find."

When she'd shut the door, Brooklyn spun around. "What from hell was that? Was it your intention to impress the man with some wild theory, or to make me look like a fool?"

Connor's eyebrows raised. "Neither! When I was here earlier, I noticed that small tattoo on Solder's front shoulder and saw a tongue ring mentioned in the report. I didn't say anything because I wanted to make sure. I called a friend who manages a…uh… very private…sex club. That tattoo is their calling card. He knew Solder."

"And you just happened to share this now, without discussing it with me first?"

"Brooklyn, I'm sorry. I got off the phone with my contact minutes before showing up at your door. Yes, I admit I wanted to impress Dr. Riley, but I never meant to disparage you in the process. You know me better than that."

"I know you get twisted when it comes to Ben Riley. But never do that again." Brooklyn solidified the reprimand with a look of authority. She let the young charge take in its full effect before moving to her desk. She pressed the intercom. "Michelle, would you get Detectives Martin and Wash. Tell them it's about the Solder case, and it's urgent. I want them in my office immediately."

Connor pointed to her watch. "Judge Pascal."

"Michelle, Ask them to see me first thing tomorrow." Brooklyn turned to Connor. She crossed her arms. A look of motherly query replaced the managerial. "Now. Exactly how do you know about some underground sex club?"

CR

My voice echoes as before
Words cut clean through the bones of sin.
No scream.
Quiet surrender.
A gift by hand and feet.

Chapter 14.

Mava stomped around the cafeteria giving orders, mumbling under her breath when she heard the door shut. "Boy, that sneaking's gon' attack my heart one of these days. Then where your old aunt gon' be? Out there with your uncle, that's where. And I ain't ready to see Ferris again too soon."

Lucas watched her drag wearily to the pantry. The bulk in her arms lobbed, the whistle-getting figure she'd carried into her fifties had given way to the round creature moving away from him. As Mava's memory of Ferris faded, so did something about her.

"Why'd you want to see me, Aunt Mava? The Mayor's got a mess out there, and you know who he thinks should keep it from stinking."

"Too late there, baby boy. You been on the west side lately? Them pig pens throwing stank from ten years deep."

The look on Lucas' face made her pause. "Pity," she said. "The art of conversation is as dead as Ferris. Sit down boy; let me get rid of them old hags in the kitchen. Don't need 'em in my business."

Returning, she sat down across from Lucas. Mava held a deep breath, and let it go. "I had a dream. Your uncle came to me. God rest his soul, been dead fourteen years, but there he stood. Naturally, I ignored that old fool. But he brought a woman with him. I thought the old goat found somebody on the other side to flaunt at me, but Ferris would never do that.

"She had a baby in each arm. Got my dander up for a second seeing as we was never able to have children." Mava mourned that fact for a second. "She didn't say nothing; just reached one of them babies out to me."

Lucas considered she was conjuring because of the bodies that washed up. Or maybe it was loneliness.

"I don't go telling every dream just like you don't arrest everybody who breaks the law. Some things you just let be. We ain't meant to meddle in all God's business. But when I get that feeling, I know He's giving me permission. That woman in my dream keeping one child and showing me the other, there's something I'm supposed to do about it. Since you're in charge I'm telling you."

Believing her, Lucas went into police mode. "Tell me about the woman."

34

Chapter 15.

Malice stopped at the laboratory entrance and inserted his clearance card at the first gate. It allowed him passage to retinal clearance, where he placed his eye to the electronic scanner that slid gracefully along a mechanical arm. Last came the visual checkpoint where an armed security agent watched as he swabbed a stiff strip across the inside of his mouth and place it in a machine that verified the DNA matched that on file. Not until then did the guard greet Malice and invite him to have a good evening.

Things were quiet inside; staff didn't stay beyond four-thirty, security reasons no one ever explained. After checking messages and electronic mail, Malice washed his hands, and put on a pair of latex gloves. He took samples from the bones: the lining of the skull and nasal passages, the bone cavity, and vertebra. He sealed the samples in air-tight containers. The floral fragrance was faint, but still present. He lifted the strands of hair he'd found in the woman's clothing, and a sample of her own.

Machines spat and dragged, whirled and hummed, clicked and turned. Computers flashed alphanumeric symbols on an eighteen-inch screen while printers shared data in long and short codes. As the machines did their work, Malice cleaned up and reset everything to default. When the machines stopped, the printouts confirmed what he had hoped not to find.

ભ

My God, my God.
No will have I than your will.
My hands and feet
Surrender.

Chapter 16.

Your sin is but a memory
Washed away in tears.
Praying hands are deliverance.
Gladly offered to our Lord.

ભ

The sharp burst of her ringing phone startled Connor but not as much as the voice on the other end.

"This is Dr. Riley. I was impressed with your report. You should work with me. I'll run it by Brooklyn if you're interested."

Connor was glad Ben was not standing in front of her. She tested her voice to make sure it wouldn't give her away. "Thank you, Dr. Riley." It sounded okay; she was safe to go on. "I'm flattered; but I'm not assigned to the case. I just happened to see the file on Brooklyn's desk and made a call."

"Then I'll see that you are. You have talent."

More than you know, she thought to herself, but out loud she said, "Thank you."

"Then you're interested?"

"I'd love to work under you."

"Great. Be prepared to meet me at the lab at nine tomorrow morning." Ben ended with his trademark, 'right-oh.'

Hearing the dial tone, Connor raised an arm into the air and let out a victorious "yes!"

ભ

Vanessa was packing to leave as Brooklyn entered Judge Pascal's suite. "He's expecting you, Ms. Beaudeau. Have a good evening."

"You too, Vanessa." Brooklyn paused. "Can you tell me what this is about?"

"The Judge didn't say." Vanessa smiled, retrieved her purse from the bottom drawer of her desk, and left.

Brooklyn's curiosity rose. Vanessa always knew who, what, when, how and why anyone entered her boss' sanctum, and generally stayed until they left. She remembered what Connor had said earlier. What if this was personal? She agreed with Connor that the man was GQ material. Intelligent, traveled, powerful. But he'd never come on to her before. Word was Pascal had a lover in Raleigh, a word whispered rather than spoken so no one knew for sure. Outside his door, she rapped twice and turned the antique brass knob. "Judge Pascal?"

The silver around his temples caught the evening sun as Pascal looked up from his desk. The rest of his full auburn locks lay in soft waves away from his face. He had taken off his suit coat and undone two of the buttons on his linen shirt. A merlot colored tie with blue detail and vivid gold arches, like sunflower petals, rested on a masculine chest. Standing by the door, Brooklyn spoke. "Vanessa left."

Pascal half-smiled. "Yes, some church function. Come in. Have a seat," he said, as he redid the buttons on his shirt, leaving loose the tie.

Definitely not a come on, Brooklyn thought, unsure whether to be relieved or disappointed. She looked around the room. The same lone plant that Vanessa had added when she came to work for him sat on the sill, its slick broad leaves drenched in evening light.

William Pascal served on several local boards, was a generous philanthropist, and respected adjunct professor at East Carolina University. Nothing in his office conveyed any of that. The plant was the only personal item in his space, and that didn't belong to him. Brooklyn sat in the standard wing chair and bound her ego between interlocking fingers pressed against her belly.

"Thank you for stopping by." Pascal spoke as if reciting from a transcript. "Since coming to the DA's office, you've learned the system, and your work has been exemplary."

An uneasy feeling crept into Brooklyn's legs, moved up her spine, and licked her armpits. She had learned enough to know that her skillful maneuvering to stay clear of the system was about to be tested. Brooklyn translated everything Judge Pascal said in her head, and it sounded like: 'you've been here long enough to know how the game is played. If you want to move up, it's time to meet the piper and that would be me'. Mentally, she searched her political handbook and found the only appropriate response: 'Thank you."

"You know Judge Sloan is retiring at the end of the year. You also know we don't have a female presence on the bench. The one black judge is controversial—to say the least. We're looking for Sloan's replacement. The successful candidate will assume Sloan's caseload January first."

She thought he was about to tell her to wait her turn and not muck the water.

"I'd like to nominate you."

Brooklyn's brain went from first to fourth gear in seconds, breezing past the obvious question, then skipped to fifth gear where it calculated the odds of her selection against equally qualified candidates. I've tried high profile cases, by Greenville standards, but they weren't the kind that made judges, she thought. So, she went back to the obvious question: Why? Brooklyn's eyes went to Judge Pascal, and saw that he was waiting for a response.

"This is unexpected," is all she could manage. She assumed his offer carried a price tag and she'd have to figure out what it was before accepting. "When should I give you my answer?"

Judge Pascal leaned back in his chair. "Is there some reason you can't answer now?"

As some have in the judge's courtroom, Brooklyn did not quake. "Judge Pascal, I never expected this. Being a superior court judge is a huge responsibility. And I hope you selected me, in part, because I do not rush to judgment."

Pascal was impressed. She did not leave room for an argument that he had not expected to give.

Brooklyn stood and reached out her hand, "Thanks for your confidence in me. I promise to give you my decision very soon."

Outside his office, excitement found its way to her face and smiled as she pondered a new title. Judge Beaudeau. Her jubilation was brief. Questions engulfed her brain like ants on newly found candy. Why me? More than any other, that question lingered. Brooklyn headed back to her office to call the one person whose judgment she trusted.

ଔ

Judge Pascal picked up his phone and dialed. The other end rang several times before he heard the baritone voice that didn't bother with a greeting. "Yes?"

"She didn't jump on the offer, Vincent. Are you sure; maybe we should use someone else."

"She'll have direct access to anything Dr. Able comes across through Dr. Riley. As her mentor, she'll be inclined to please you. You'll just have to manipulate that without her knowledge. And should anything come to light, I'm counting on her feelings for me to intervene. We have a lot to lose if we're wrong."

Fear put its hand on Pascal's shoulder, and dug in its talons. "Yes, we do, *Senator*."

Vincent Haiger was silent for a moment. "That was a long time ago, William."

"And yet, the past seems to be coming back to haunt us," Pascal replied.

"Does Brooklyn know of our relationship?"

"Only if you told her. But she must know that you've had a hand in her career. She has to be asking herself what I want, and if it has anything to do with you."

"Yes, you're right. I expect she'll call to ask that very question. She can't know our history. And neither you nor I can probe about that casket without raising suspicion."

Pascal breathed out loud. "We don't even know if it's her."

"Able is in Virginia right now figuring that out. If it's not, we don't have a problem; Brooklyn will make a good judge. If it is, that secret must go back to the grave. I can survive my past. But there is no statute of limitation on murder, William. Are you ready to join the convicts you've locked away over the years? Are you ready to destroy your family's name? To die in prison, or worse—live there?"

The senator's words sank into Pascal's brain like an anchor in water. While it wasn't proved who the woman was that lay in Greenville's morgue, he knew it was Joy Marie as strongly as he knew the burden of thirty-two years of guilt. He hung up the phone, leaving Haiger to ponder his own loss should they fail.

Vincent Haiger clicked off his cell phone and pressed three numbers on the keypad. "What have you learned?"

Christian Dingo answered. "Dr. Able is at the laboratory. The machines he used last night will forward me a copy of his reports."

"Good. Meet me at 9AM. I want to know what he knows."

Walk in grace my brother
Your steps are set in faith
Tread no more in suffering
For you have been judged and blessed.

Chapter 17.

"I don't know if the woman in my dream is dead or alive," Mava told Lucas. "I ain't got that much yet. I called you because of the child she was holding. They're in trouble. Maybe the child needs help."

"That could be, Aunt Mava, but I have to know more. Was there something about the woman, or the background that you remember? How was she dressed?"

"Hold on boy; give me a minute." Mava pushed the small chair back with her heavy body. It only moved an inch, but was enough to satisfy her given that it moved at all. "I need to get comfortable. Come on." She stood up, and walked to the back of the cafeteria. Lucas followed and sat on a folding metal chair. Mava plopped down on the sagging sofa, and let the heavy smell of cooking fumes escape her lungs. "Ohhh, that's better," she said. "Now, let's try again."

Mava closed her eyes and regulated her breathing. Lucas did not interrupt even after it appeared she had fallen asleep. He glanced at his watch. He was to meet Ben in forty-five minutes and she'd just dozed off twelve of them.

Just as he leaned back in his chair to wait her out, Mava opened her eyes.

"That was a good question about the clothes Lucas. I focused on that. She was well dressed; wearing what we use to call an empire dress. The ones that had a seam under the bosom." Mava moved her floppy arms underneath her even floppier breast to demonstrate for Lucas.

He wished she hadn't.

"Call 'em sundresses now," she finished. "And she was wearing a button on one of the straps. Said JFK, but there's a shadow across her face. The baby was wrapped up. It's a tiny bundle so I'm guessing it was new born."

"What about the scenery, Aunt Mava? Is there anything that might tell you where she is?"

Mava frowned. "Well, that's the funny thing. I can't see much of anything else. Guess my eyesight's no better on the other side. But there was a strong odor. Some kind of flower. Humph. What do you make of that?" Mava put her hands flat on the old sofa to push herself up. "That's all I got right now, Lucas. But I'll think on it some more."

Chapter 18.

Ben arrived for dinner just as Sandra was taking fresh biscuits from the oven. He reached into the pan and picked out a fluffy golden wafer. "Girl, took you ten years, but you're getting good at this cooking thing."

Sandra patted her biscuits thin so they cooked into little ovals slightly thicker than cookies, then brushed them with real butter. She slapped his fingers. "You forget; I know where those hands have been." She yelled to the back of the house. "Ben's here."

Lucas rounded the corner as Sandra headed to the table with a bowl of fried corn. "The boys can eat in the den. I need to talk to Ben about some things they don't need to hear."

"And do you think they'll complain?" Sandra smiled. "Batman is on. They'll be going Ka-Pow any minute."

Bowing over wafting aromas of mashed potatoes, fried corn, pot roast with mushroom gravy, biscuits and lemonade, Lucas said grace. "Thank you, God, for our home, health, and family. Give us wisdom to do the right thing. Please share your peace with those burdened with the loss caused by the storm."

Into their third and fourth spoonful, and small talk satisfied, a southern requirement before anything else, Ben got down to business. "So, Lucas, seeing your beautiful wife, and this great meal aside, why am I here?"

Lucas swallowed, and ran his tongue around his jaw. "I'm worried about my neighbors, Ben." He took a drink of lemonade to clear his mouth. "I sat with Mrs. Galebrey the other day while making my rounds. She still doesn't have running water so I bring her enough to cook and wash up every other day. She asked me when I thought things would be okay again. She wasn't talking about the water, or the town. The look on her face, the sound in her voice… That storm took something from these people, Ben. It broke something in them just like it shattered every window in the AME Zion Church."

Sandra and Ben stopped eating. "Lucas." Sandra's voice was that of a wife comforting her husband. "I had no idea. Why didn't you say something?"

Without a doubt, Ben knew this was why Sandra loved her husband, why Sheriff Wade hand-selected Lucas to replace him. Why he, himself, counted Lucas his dearest friend. "What is it you need from me, Lucas?"

43

Lucas pushed his plate to the side and rested his hands in its place. "These people need more than their homes rebuilt and the streets cleaned. They're grieving, confused, and angry. I haven't talked to anyone about this; I wanted to see what you think."

"About what?" Ben asked.

"Well, I'd like to get a couple of counselors to donate some time to the community. We can set up in the Baptist Church, or evenings in the schoolhouse. Get a van from somewhere. I'll talk to the mayor about a few dollars for refreshments, maybe travel expenses, things like that."

"You've given this a lot of thought. Not sure why you need me, though."

"To be honest, I was hoping you could pull it together. You speak their language, and you know the people here. You can help the doctors understand how much we need their help. I wouldn't know where to start."

Ben sat back in his chair and lightly rapped his fingertips on the table. Sandra went to check on the boys. She returned with peach cobbler. Both men sat quietly absorbing the enormity of what Lucas wanted—for people who earned their money counseling to give their service away. And for how long? Months certainly. Years, maybe.

Sandra saw the uncertainty on Ben's face. "Lucas, I can talk to my brother. The dealership where he works might donate a van for a few months." Sandra looked at her husband. "How long do you think we should ask for?" She glanced at Ben and held him in her stare.

"Okay, But it'll take a while. I have a big case that just got more complicated. Add to that Regina Bailey, the reporter from *The Rocky Mount Tribune,* is asking questions. Somebody's feeding her information about that body."

Chapter 19.

Judge Pascal leaned back in his chair. Like everyone, he'd read about the caskets washing up in Princeville. *The East Carolina Herald* and the *Greenville Gazette* carried the story on the front page for weeks after the storm. He studied them for the fiftieth time. Zoom cameras had captured the pain on people's faces. Aerial shots showing shattered homes, up-rooted trees and overturned cars eerily reflected the same pain.

Those same cameras captured resolve in the face of one woman comforting another. A four-year-old child wrapped himself around his mother's leg, afraid to let go. That photo became the image the country would associate with Princeville's misfortune.

He studied the first paper again, staring at the two caskets in the photograph. An overturned tree had stopped one of the boxes and held it protectively. He knew it was she. The shot was taken from a distance; so nothing distinguished this casket from the other; still, he knew.

Pascal walked to the credenza and poured himself a scotch. The golden liquid warmed the back of his throat and hurried towards his stomach. He put the newspapers back and closed the desk drawer. Until he'd seen that photograph, the memory had only sneaked into his dreams.

CR

To forgive is a perfect gift
Given and received.
An instrument of God
On the glorious path to redemption.

Chapter 20.

The reports confirmed what Malice already knew. Something was very wrong. He reached for the skull to do a second test. Down the corridor, the familiar thump of security cameras activating made him look at the clock. Anyone in the lab had one hour to leave the building. The second set of heat sensory cameras would come on at precisely eight o'clock. At nine, infrared beams would crisscross the floor in continuous random patterns. He didn't have time to do another test.

Twenty miles away, Christian Dingo studied the same printouts that Malice had collected. Dingo took a Q-Tip from his shirt pocket and swabbed his ear while he read. He came upon a line in the report that gave him pause. He threw the Q-Tip into the wastebasket and picked up the phone. "I'm stopping by."

"But it's nine-thirty, Christian. Can it wait?"

"Sure it can wait. You can attend my nine o'clock and tell the man why I had to cancel. Maybe you can convince him to reschedule because now was a bad time for you."

Fugama had no idea who Chris was meeting tomorrow morning, and wouldn't ask. Whoever it was could have him working at an all night pharmacy by daybreak.

"Dammit, Chris," is all Fugama could say.

Baru Fugama had listened with one ear to Christian Dingo, and directed the other to the CNN anchor retelling the story of body parts nailed to crosses. He turned up the volume on the television, but the segment on the mutilated bodies was done.

Doctor Fugama answered the door twenty minutes later. "What is this about?" he asked, following Dingo to the den.

Chris was always taken aback by the stereotype that was Fugama. He accepted that it was an imprint, a cultural idiom. People in certain professions had certain looks. Even as he thought it, the observation was lost on himself. Chris pulled the report from his jacket. "Tell me what you see."

Baru Fugama put on the glasses hanging from his neck. He was a biochemist, the product of a Chinese mother and a Russian father—two other prodigious scientists. His parents had made critical discoveries in Genomics. Baru followed them into the field, but had not proven to be the procreated genius everyone expected. Still, he was acclaimed, having made revolutionary strides in cloning. Chris surmised the man's bar had been set too high. No matter how much he accomplished, it wouldn't have met expectations. At sixty-three, the best he had left was information.

Baru studied the report and looked at Dingo. "I taught you this stuff. What am I to tell you that you can't see for yourself?"

Dingo thought he saw relief on the old man's face. "Just tell me what *you* see," he said calmly.

Baru deciphered the reports. "You have a white female in her twenties. Her body was going through changes consistent with pregnancy at the time of death. It appears she died from a chemical overdose. We have a fetus showing a disposition for sickle cell anemia had it survived."

"What can you tell me about the chemical?"

"Nothing from this. A full toxicology is needed. But if this is correct, she has been dead for over thirty years. It might be hard to determine what chemical was induced."

47

"Just one other thing. Do you see any connection between the woman and the child?"

Baru's immediate reaction was towards sarcasm, but dismissed the notion as he was ethnically mixed as they come. He put the DNA markers side by side. After several minutes, he said, "They have markers in common and the child shows traces of the same chemical. Since the baby was unborn it had to come though the mother's bloodstream. If you are asking me if they are mother and child, I say, highly probable."

"Probable?" Chris sucked his teeth. "Is that a word they roll up in your PhD?"

Chapter 21.

As day was breaking, Malice programmed the computer to tell him what toxins were present in the bones of the unidentified woman and at what levels. The computer would calculate the dosage, taking into account the chemical properties and dissipation over thirty years.

The last act was to give the woman a face. He prepared the solution using the fine sand-like particles he'd scraped from the skull. Because the fetus was not fully developed, it was not a good candidate for the ERC. But Malice couldn't resist; he programmed it for a second image anyway. In the meantime, he'd know what killed them.

Shortly, he had the cause of death. So did Christian Dingo. Chris would not know the result of the Etogenic Re-imaging process. That computer could not be linked to any outside source for any reason. That information, he'd have to find some other way.

Chapter 22.

Senator Vincent Haiger sat alone in his DC office on Connecticut Avenue. Security cameras announced Chris' presence. Haiger buzzed him in. Having been here after hours a few days ago, Chris knew the way. He took the cup of coffee Haiger handed him, warming his hands before sipping. Haiger did not speak, not even to say good morning. Chris was equally reserved; in his opinion, talking was over rated and often problematic. He reached inside the pocket of the black jacket that matched his black trousers, and pulled out the report.

Haiger locked his fingers in his lap across his charcoal gray suit. It picked up the newly grown silver in his hair. "Just tell me what you know."

Chris put back the report and wondered if the red stripped tie Haiger wore came with the election of every politician. He guessed Haiger's age at mid-fifties. "Dr. Able is working on a body that washed up from the hurricane in Princeville. So far, he's learned it's a young woman who died some thirty years ago from a poison resembling strychnine."

Haiger showed no reaction to Chris' summation. "Anything else?"

"It appears the woman was pregnant at the time of death, and very close to term. The child showed signs of a condition called sickle cell anemia. It's a–"

"I know what it is," the Senator interrupted. He leaned back in his chair. "Why is that significant? Many African Americans as well as other ethnic groups, including some whites, are afflicted with that particular blood disorder."

"Yes, sir." Chris agreed. "Ordinarily, it wouldn't stand out given the body came from a black cemetery. I mention it, and it may be significant because, according to the tests, the woman was of European descent."

"You mean she was white?"

"It would appear so, Senator."

"And you're saying the child had black ancestry."

"That would be a logical conclusion. The father could be Greek or Hispanic or even Asian, but when you consider the racial demographics of the area during the time of death..."

Haiger didn't let him finish. He stood. "Keep me apprised. There's a shredder in the office two doors up."

Alone again, in the back room of his office, Haiger pressed his forehead with the heel of both hands and let them slide downward. The heat of his breath warmed his palms and passed through his fingers. He dialed on his private line and put in a code that routed the call directly to Pascal's chamber. When Pascal picked up, Haiger spoke into the mouthpiece calmly. "We have a problem."

What is there left to do my God?
There is no righteousness save thee.
He, who has been called by name
I shall render.

Chapter 23.

Connor stretched in bed and smiled. Today began her quest to become Mrs. Benjamin Riley if all went well. His lover if nothing else. She showered quickly and made a cup of tea to rinse her eagerness.

Against the cool November morning, Connor wore a light trench coat. The storm had left the days overcast and cooler than normal. Rather than three-inch heels, low rubber-soled pumps carried her quietly to Dr. Riley's door where she knocked briskly. Her mood was interrupted by the appearance of Detectives Martin and Wash. Though different in age and ethnicity, each smiled at the young woman, offering his hand in order to touch her.

"Nice to see you, Ms. Crawford," Detective Martin said. "Ms. Beaudeau says you've come across something."

Connor applied her best professional smile and sat in the empty chair near Dr. Riley's desk. "Mr. Solder was a member of a sex group that would make de Sade look sideways."

"Dr. Riley was just explaining some of the victim's uh… unusual features," Detective Martin offered.

Ben was relieved by the older man's discretion. Dory Martin was a product of the old south and soulfully ascribed to the notion of polite conversation in a woman's presence, even if she didn't.

Detective Wash, around the same age as Connor, blushed. "So what leads you to believe that's relevant?"

"I don't know if it's relevant, or not, Detective." Connor kept her voice moderate so that her words did not further rattle his young sensibilities. "That's why you're here. I suspect Mr. Purdue's lawyer will parade Solder's lifestyle to induce reasonable doubt. Purdue admits to the fight; this was not their first run-in. Says Solder was sleeping with his wife. Given word on the street, that's likely true. It can also be true for a number of other husbands. Purdue has no alibi other than he was driving around to clear his head so that he wouldn't deliver the leftover whup-ass to his wife."

Realizing she'd blown gentility, Connor tried softening her delivery with southern charm. "Our case is circumstantial, at best."

But the young detective shot back. "The evidence points to Purdue. Solder was shagging the man's wife; that's motive. Witnesses put him there."

Ben shook his head. Like most of his generation, Detective Ethan Wash had no schooling in the fine art of decorum. He was like an untrained pup nipping at their ankles. And Connor didn't make it easier yanking his chain. He refereed. "All of which can be explained." Ben looked to Detective Martin. "What about the woman the witnesses reported seeing at Solder's house? Have you found her?"

"No, we assumed it was Mrs. Purdue. Our witness must be eighty-five years old. The description she gave doesn't match Mrs. Purdue." Detective Martin pulled the notebook from his shirt pocket and flipped to the page dedicated to the witness and her description. "Taller than usual. Long brown hair, wearing a black trench coat with the collar up."

Connor interrupted. "Did this witness say if the woman was white or black?"

"White," the young detective said, putting himself back into the conversation.

"Did you come to any conclusion about that?" she asked.

"This is the twenty-first century. Mixing ain't new," young Wash answered.

"No, it ain't *new*, detective, but if she was white, she couldn't have been Mrs. Purdue."

Detective Wash smiled at Connor. "You're wrong there. Mrs. Purdue can barely call herself black. Unlike you or me, if she were wearing a wig, she could walk into the Governor's mansion, ask for a mint julep, and get it."

"I've been to the Governor's mansions. The mint julep is delicious," Connor countered.

Detective Martin interrupted their sparring. "We assumed it was Mrs. Pudue. She admitted to being at Solder's the day before. We figure the witness, given her age, got the day mixed up."

"But Mrs. Purdue is just over five feet tall with a short cut. Any woman half blind in one eye who can't see out the other can tell the difference between a short woman and one taller than usual. Even one eighty-five years old." Connor was failing Southern Belle 101. "I'm equally sure ADA Beaudeau will want statements from the women in Mr. Solder's life. Perhaps you can find them... *Detective.*"

Ben cleared his throat. "According to other bruises on Solder, it would appear he....played rough. I'm guessing he left bruises on the women as well, so there are bound to be other husbands who wanted him dead."

Martin followed Ben's lead. "We'll question the neighbors again. Solder lived in Winston-Salem for a few years; we'll poke around there." Martin stood up and arranged his tie. "Pleasure to see you again, ma'am... Dr. Riley."

When the officers had closed the door behind them and Ben was certain they'd rounded the corner, he cracked a smile at Connor. "Wow, you're gonna make a hell'uva lawyer. Come on. One of my associates found something. Since you like poking around in dark places, you might find this interesting."

At the lab, Dr. Riley directed Connor to the projection wall. "My assistant combed Solder's body. We found strands of hair, not Solder's, in the lower regions of his body. Some are longer, straight strands, others short."

You mean someone polished the band of beads?"

Ben almost blushed. "I was about to see if they are human or synthetic, and from where on the body they came."

"Why didn't you say something to the detectives just now?"

"Because there's nothing to tell, yet. If the hair is synthetic, we know the woman seen at Solder's house was wearing a wig. If it's human, we can test it against the DNA we have on Mr. Purdue, and maybe match to any other suspects the detectives might find. We can also match the compounds of the synthetic against a wig, if they find one. We might be looking at new evidence."

"Doc, you're overlooking one thing."

"What's that?"

"Wigs can be made of human hair."

"Yes, but that hair would have been treated, no roots. Some of the ones we found have follicles," Ben smiled.

Connor looked over Ben's shoulder as he finished his tests. It didn't take long before he announced, "It's European."

"Then my contact was right."

"About what?" Ben asked.

"That old Raymond satisfied sisters of all persuasions."

"This guy sure knows a lot. He didn't happen to know a name? Could save us a lot of time here."

"No," Connor smiled. "No names. Against the freakazoid code. He did say Solder worked both sides of the equation, if you get my drift. Any way to tell whether those shorties belong to a man or a woman?"

Ben shook his head in amazement. "Have to send these off for that."

"You're cute when you blush," she teased.

He was about to respond but remembered she could be his little sister, if he had one. "Your contact was right about Solder's non-preferences. He was bisexual."

"A giver or a taker?" she asked.

"Both," Ben laughed.

"And just how did you find that out, doc?" Conner smiled. "I should be so lucky."

54

"Well, I guess you'll have to open your options." The words, once out of Ben's mouth, embarrassed him.

"Doc!" Unable to resist her next comment, Connor said, "I'm *open* to suggestions."

Ben threw up his hands in surrender. "Lets get back to something I can handle. Do you recall my saying I was bothered by the blood splatters?"

Connor let him retreat. "Any more thoughts?"

"Yep. But we have to revisit the crime scene."

Conner put on her coat. "What do you expect to find?"

"Why Solder lost the fight."

Chapter 24.

Brooklyn knocked on Judge Pascal's door after getting clearance from Vanessa. His back was to her, a cup of coffee in hand. Brooklyn spoke softly, "Good morning, your Honor. Beautiful day." She moved to stare with him out of the three-story window. "The rain washed away the leaves we'd see this time of year, but there is still something very calming about the scenery."

"Yes. There's something special about this time of year."

The words were there, but Brooklyn didn't hear the conviction in his voice. In fact, the words were flat and indifferent. His staring out the window wasn't for the view.

"How's the Solder case coming?" he asked, turning to freshen his coffee, offering her a cup which she decined.

"We may have come across new information that's being explored as we speak," she said.

"New information?"

"Yes, we should know something today."

"You're being evasive."

"Well, I know you like to stay objective. Especially when you might pull the docket."

"You're right. It's just that rumors abound. Just wondered which were true and which were embellishments to an already sensational case. Guess I got caught up." Judge Pascal checked his watch. "I have to prepare for my eleven o'clock. You have an answer for me, I presume?"

Brooklyn extended her hand to shake his in gratitude. "I'd be honored to have your endorsement for Judge Sloan's seat."

Judge Pascal held her hand and half-smiled. "Excellent. See Vanessa on the way out. I already cleared two hours on Wednesday. We can talk strategy for putting you in one of these," he said, reaching for his robe.

Again, the right words, but Brooklyn had expected more. Whatever was on his mind didn't include her decision. "I look forward to your guidance."

Pascal picked up the phone. "Vincent, She's in. She must have called you."

"Yes, just as I expected."

"What did you say to her?"

"Nothing that wasn't true. She's ambitious, William, like all attorneys. I just pointed out the next vacant seat could be years away, and even if another came tomorrow her refusal now might affect future consideration."

"Your niece is idealistic, Vincent. She believes in fairness; she'd expect to wait her turn."

"She also knows there is a price on the seeming good will of honorable intentions," Haiger said. "She asked what this seat might cost her. I talked her through the downside, told her it was her career, her decision."

"So, it went smoothly?" Pascal asked.

"She was worried about how it would look, her uncle being a senator. But I reminded her, you folk have made nepotism a cultural commandment."

Pascal ignored the racial criticism. "What if—"

Senator Haiger lowered his voice. "We have enough to deal with William; let's focus, shall we."

Pascal dismissed the reprimand. "Has something happened?"

"Dr. Able has a picture. He knows she was poisoned. I've sent someone to Greenville to intercept."

"A picture? How in hell did he get a picture? There are no pictures; I made sure of that thirty-two years ago." He lied. One was left he couldn't bring himself to destroy. He'd taken it the day she died. He could see it in his mind. She was smiling down on her swollen belly, loving what was inside. "What are you talking about, Vincent?"

"I can't go into details. But rest assured, he has put a face to the bones he brought to Virginia."

"Vincent, Raymond Solder is dead."

Haiger had not anticipated this news. His mind flashed through time and brought back memories. When the images stopped, he began the inquisition. "When?"

"Four days ago."

"Where?"

"Here, in Greenville."

A new anxiety registered in Haiger's voice. "What was he doing there? I thought he was in Winston-Salem?"

"He moved here a few months ago."

"William..." is all Haiger allowed himself to say. He paused, letting questions pass that he chose not to ask.

Pascal spoke. "Brooklyn is handling his case."

"Which means what?"

"Brooklyn can not find the connection between Raymond Solder and those bones."

Haiger quickly laid out the strategy. "We have to make sure Dr. Able loses that picture. Without it, he has nothing. His access to the lab here is terminated. All his files have been confiscated. Someone is searching his home and removing every scrap of paper down to his grocery receipts as we speak. I'm taking care of my end, William. You have to do the same."

"Won't that raise his suspicion?"

"Not necessarily. He's given notice and might assume it's part of the game we play. If he doesn't, it's a risk I'll take." Haiger ended the conversation. "Handle your end, William."

Pascal hung up the phone just as Vanessa rapped on the door. "Five minutes, sir."

"Thank you, Vanessa." The memory of Raymond Solder's last breath covered him like wet cement on his way to judge someone else's deed.

Chapter 25.

Malice drove casually on Highway 11 towards the hotel in Greenville. Sun-coated air brushed his face. The subject on the radio was Princeville. 'Worst flooding in the area in 100 years. Help from around the country for one of the oldest black incorporated towns in America'.

Malice had no reason to watch his back, but his hand went to the mirror and he looked anyway. A feeling. Habit. The green SUV he'd noticed when he turned out of the airport was there. It turned off when he turned and stopped at the hotel entrance when he pulled into the parking lot. At the registration desk, he announced himself.

"Nice to have you back, Dr. Able" the college student answered. She pecked on the keyboard and found his entry. "Do you have a departure date yet, Dr. Able?"

"Not yet. Put me down for another week."

"Excellent. Will there be anything else?"

"Yes, the woman who was just here, did she register?" He saw hesitation cross the young woman's face. "I think we were on the same flight. I lost contact at the airport and kicked myself all the way here for not introducing myself when I had the chance. When I saw her here, I couldn't believe it."

The young woman knew about missed opportunities. The romance books she read while on duty were full of them. "Yes sir, but I'm afraid that's all I can tell you."

He touched her hand to seal their conspiracy. "I can take it from here." He winked and the receptionist smiled. Malice looked past the front door. The sport utility vehicle was gone, but he was certain he'd see her again.

In his room, Malice called Ben. "Meet me at the restaurant in ten minutes."

"But I'm in the middle—"

"Ten minutes," Malice repeated calmly, and hung up. He put on his hat, packed up his laptop, collected his briefcase, black bag and the car keys. As he was leaving, 'Breaking News' stopped him. The reporter's head filled the television screen.

"The mutilated body of a young man has been found in Texarkana, Texas. Police say the unidentified man is missing both hands and feet. Several days ago, in Wylie, South Carolina, the hands and feet of two unknown persons were found nailed to a cross."

The story would have to wait. Malice took the side door back to the rental car and sped off. Ben pulled into the restaurant parking lot within minutes. With his bags and laptop in hand, Malice got into Ben's car. "Drive."

Ben stepped on the gas and moved the car towards the exit. "What's going on?"

"I need a private car. Here are the keys to the rental. Get it back to the airport for me."

"You couldn't come to the lab for this? What's going on, Malice?"

"Could be my agency playing its games."

Malice sounded as if he were picking lint from his sweater. But the tone had not set well in Ben's stomach. He pulled the car into the garage at the Medical Examiner's Building. He reached into his pocket and handed Malice the keys to his car. "It's the blue one at the end over there."

"We'll have to communicate by cell phone."

"But cell phones can be traced, too," Ben reminded him.

"Not this one. Memorize this number. Do not write it anywhere. Do not give it to anyone else. Give me your hand." Malice wrote the number with his finger in Ben's palm.

"But that was only six digits."

"Exactly," Malice replied. He got out and proceeded to Ben's luxury car. "I'll call you later. Keep your evening free."

"Yeah, welcome back. Good to see you, too," Ben yelled.

Malice drove west and pulled into a gas station to think. Someone had been assigned to him. Why? He started the car again and headed south where he checked into the Comfort Inn Hotel in Snow Hill. There was one person he could call. If anyone knew anything, it would be Chris.

Chapter 26.

Judge Pascal sat in his office at the end of the day, his robe still on, a shot of whiskey in hand. The *Greenville Gazette* stared back from his desk. He read the caption:

A casket floats in a flooded yard in Princeville, NC. Several caskets from the cemetery floated through town on Wednesday Sept. 22. Officials say Hurricane Floyd's floodwaters spawned the worst environmental, agricultural, and human disasters in state history.

Pascal tossed his head back and swallowed hard. He folded the paper and returned it to the drawer. Barely audible, two words crossed his lips. "Joy Marie."

🚲

No child is ever lost to God
Reach your hand to salvation
Even in the dark
Speak my name
And hear my trumpet's reply.

Chapter 27.

Brooklyn sipped her sweetened tea while waiting for Judge Pascal. She looked around the restaurant he'd selected wondering why she'd never been here before. Upscale. Pretentious, but not arrogant. An air of quality wafted through the room and melded with budding magnolias on wallpaper so gentle they looked like wishes.

Judge Pascal interrupted Brooklyn's submergence into the Magnolia Room. "Charming, isn't it," he smiled. "Since

I've never seen you here, it felt like the right place for new beginnings."

"Seems my late hours have caused me to miss a few of Greenville's amenities," she replied.

"It has been our loss." He'd barely positioned himself in the seat when the waitress appeared with his favorite cocktail and a smile.

Amanda lifted the napkin from the center of Brooklyn's plate, let the fabric unfold, and laid it expertly in her new ward's lap. She did the same with Judge Pascal and left so quietly she could have been mist. She returned just as quietly with their appetizers and bread wrapped in linen.

"Have we decided on lunch?" she asked. "If not, may I recommend the Magnolia Salad topped with our seasoned grilled salmon, generously sprinkled with roasted pecans. Raspberry vinaigrette on the side."

Brooklyn's smile signaled her choice. "Yes, for the lady," Pascal said. Handing over his menu, he added, "I'll have the seafood fettuccini in that wonderful wine sauce, Amanda. And would you bring us a bottle of champagne?"

"Would the Judge like his favorite?"

"Perfect, Amanda. Thank you."

"Champagne?" Brooklyn questioned.

"I invited you here for good news. The buffet at Denny's just wouldn't do."

Chapter 28.

The Comfort Inn was nothing like Home-Town Suites. No conference room, no corner kitchenette faking a semblance of home. Malice pressed two keys on his cell phone and listened to the scrambler activate before connecting.

"Okay, I saw her; why is she here?"

Chris heard no concern in the question. "Always the direct approach."

"Yep. A straight line, and all that."

"Her name is Charlene; one of my best. I figured you'd spot her soon enough; the least I could do was make it worthwhile. So, what'd you think? Nice view?"

Malice could hear the smile on Chris' face. Any other time, the comment might have been amusing. From what he saw, Charlene could disarm any man just by saying hello. "You haven't answered my question."

Chris conceded. "You know how they enjoy their games."

"Uh-huh. So, SCRUB is your department now?"

"No, it's not, and yet you called me. Why is that?"

"I figured you miss me."

"All I know is I gotta keep an eye on ya," Chris said.

"And then what?" Malice was certain Chris understood the question. He waited through Chris' long pause.

"Don't know. But consider Charlene my only warning."

"Thanks for the gift."

The secure connection ended from Chris' side. Malice considered the conversation and decided his evasive maneuver was enough for now. He pressed another button and waited for Ben to answer. "Get Lucas. Meet me at the hotel."

"And which one would that be?" Ben asked.

"The one you're paying for. Six-thirty." He decided to let Charlene confirm what whoever sent her most likely already knew.

છ

Lucas showed up first and milled around the lobby. His police jacket proudly announced his position in Princeville. The desk clerk invited him to coffee or tea from the complimentary table where huge chocolate chip cookies awaited guests. Ben arrived next, and sat on the edge of the armchair for fear of sinking into its sluggish basin. Lucas joined him by taking a side chair. Small talk led to the request Lucas had made for counselors.

"I put the idea to a colleague, a psychologist with the Greenville Police Department," Ben said. "He thinks it's a good idea, but has reservations about how successful it will be."

"Why is that?"

"Lucas, you know as well as I do, black people don't do psychiatry. We don't go round telling what's in our heads, or behind our doors. Mistrust is still deep. And if you get over that hurdle, there's the time involved."

"We're not asking them to tell their business. All I want is for people to have somebody to talk to about their grief. This thing shook people more than you see; but I see it, Ben, every day."

Ben forgot and sat back in the chair. The cushion folded up around him, confirming its tired appearance. He pried himself up and propped again on the edge of the frame. "I hear you, Lucas. I'd hate to get doctors to give up their time and nobody show up. But a minister might sell."

"I'm not sure about that. Princeville's two ministers don't have much formal training; all they got is a calling. Ordinarily, that's enough, but they can't handle what's happened any better than their congregation."

Ben countered. "And those two would be insulted, then what have you got?"

"Okay, I hear you. Any ideas on a minister with a psychology degree?" Lucas said, smiling.

"You ain't letting me off this big ass hook, are you, brother?"

As Lucas lowered his head to chuckle, Malice walked through the lobby door. He carried the same black satchel Ben and Lucas had seen on his first visit.

Malice stopped at the desk. "Would you send some ice tea and sandwiches to my room? Thanks." He turned towards the two men waiting. "Good to see you again, Lucas."

"Same here, doc."

"Come on. We'll meet in my room."

Ben looked at his cousin. "Are you sure that's a good idea? Maybe we should go someplace more private."

"No, it's exactly where we need to be. But the matter you and I discussed earlier still holds." There would be no talk of his car, where Malice went with it, or why.

The three made themselves comfortable in his room. Malice turned on the radio. The jazz station sent comfortable background noise throughout the suite. Without prelude, he began. "You know I had suspicions about the last body."

"You gave us the impression there was more to this case than no record of her death. So, what is it?"

"Let him tell it, Ben," Lucas said, taken aback by Ben's terse remark.

"I learned something that might be more problematic than finding out who she is. I knew she was white before I left. She was full term into a pregnancy when she died. According to my tests, the child had African ancestry."

Ben and Lucas looked at each other.

Malice continued. "In addition to some other qualifiers, the child had the sickle cell anemia trait. It's a disorder found prominently in people of African heritage, but not exclusively."

"So what?" Ben questioned. "Nothing strange about white women tipping to our side of town. Happens more than you think."

"That's true, but I've never heard of one getting buried here," Lucas added.

"Well, it might have cost this one her life. She was poisoned." Malice got up and pulled a document from his brief case while that little bomb rolled around the table. He handed the papers to Ben.

"What does it say?" Lucas asked.

Ben flipped through the three pages, settling on the last. "It says there was a high concentration of a toxin I'm not familiar with. It was very potent given the trace compounds present after thirty-two years."

"Gelsemium," Malice said. "It's a depressant which acts on the anterior cornus of gray matter in the spinal cord. It was tested once upon a time as a treatment for migraines, severe asthma, rheumatism, epilepsy, and nerve-related disorders such as pleurisy and trigeminal neuralgia."

"Wow," Ben said.

"Speak English, please, " Lucas said.

Ben had the look of a child in a fun house for the first time. He quickly decoded the conversation for Lucas. "Trigeminal neuralgia is a condition causing shooting pain in the area of the facial nerves, around the lips, gums, cheeks, and sometimes the eyes."

"Malice helped. "Gelsemium is so powerful, that as it relaxes the muscles, it suspends all sense of pain. Respiration slows; in high dosages, death occurs from centric respiratory failure. The heart stops almost simultaneously. Death can occur anywhere from one to seven hours after ingestion."

"So, are you saying she was murdered!" Lucas asked.

"No, I'm not, though other elements point to that likely conclusion. The woman could have tried to medicate herself. She could even have committed suicide. But set that aside for a minute."

Malice reached into his briefcase and retrieved another document. "I found strands of hair embedded in her clothing and a lace cloth." He handed the results to Ben.

After speed-reading the document, Ben translated for Lucas. "It says that the woman and whoever those other strands belong to are related. The unknown hair is male."

Lucas wasn't there yet. He looked from Malice to Ben. "So what? All that means is she was with a relative the day she died."

Ben shared his conclusion. "A white woman was buried in a black cemetery. She was well into the pregnancy of a child with the sickle cell trait. She's been dead over thirty years. There is no record of her death, or being reported missing. You're the policeman; what does that tell you?"

The bomb on the table exploded. Lucas didn't speak right away. Rather than affirm Ben's conclusion, he said, "We still don't know who she is."

"Not yet. But we know what she looked like when she died," Malice offered.

"What?" Ben asked. "How?"

Malice pulled out the ERC-generated picture. The child's image was inconclusive. "Had one of our artists reconstruct her face. He fed the features into a computer that says this is what she most probably looked like." He could tell his lie was believed.

Lucas studied the face of a twenty-something year old woman. She'd died during the era of flower power, when the earth, and all things natural was the religion of the day. The photograph reflected that. "She was pretty, I'll give her that."

"No lie," Ben added. He then raised the question he was certain the others were thinking. "What now?"

Lucas took a deep breath and let it out as if a doctor had said 'slowly'. All three were silent for several minutes.

"I guess it's up to me," Lucas finally admitted. "I'm the one got this started. Problem is, I'm not equipped to solve a thirty-year-old murder, especially this one." He looked at his best friend. "Jesus. What have I got on my hands?"

Lucas returned his friend's gaze. "We know what you've got Lucas. The question is what are you gonna do with it?"

Chapter 29.

"Men are chug-a-lugs. Mistakes of nature, like the hyena. Vicious deviants, every one. Gotta be master to everything. Devour their own to do it. Defile even their mother's womb."

"Carrie, what on earth are you fussing about?" Rae Lee York poured her house guest another cup of coffee. Carrie Agnes had lost everything in the flood. Rae Lee took her in; it was a natural thing to do since Carrie Agnes spent most of her days there anyway.

"I'm talking about evil, Rae Lee. That horn of the devil stuck between a man's legs. Hiding till it's ready to do its nasty business."

"God is a man, Carrie Agnes," Rae Lee pointed out.

"So they say. Got my doubts about that. But if he is, that puts him in the vicious category, too. Just look outside."

"Are you blaspheming at my table, Carrie Agnes!"

"I'm eighty-six years old. Will be meeting God personally real soon. If I'm wrong, I'll apologize. Just ask forgiveness is all."

68

"I don't think heaven is where you're headed, talking like that."

"Well, a man runs that show, too. I'm sure of that."

Rae Lee York looked at Carrie Agnes sideways and shook her head. "What on earth has you so riled? The day ain't shook the sleep from its eyes and here you are, all fussed up before you've even seen your shadow."

"Did you hear the news last night? Heard it again this morning. Some man over in Greenville done got himself kilt."

"People get themselves killed all the time over there."

"Not like this one. Sarah Louise heard her grandson telling some other boys about it. Say he went and fixed up his worm."

"Lord, Carrie Agnes, what on earth are you talking about? What's in your head?"

"I'm just telling. You asked. So you hear. The boys were laughing about some beads the man put in his worm. Wonder if they was sterling silver or gold? Anything else might have been what kilt him."

"Old woman, what are you talking about?"

"Sarah Louise's boy and them others were speculating on it. Of course they made mention on how them beads must pleasure a woman. Sarah Louise don't stop 'em from talking, I know, because she tramped herself into old age, and nobody wants her now. Use to sit up in them clubs trying to feel on young boys. She probably had to pay 'em to let her."

"Carrie Agnes!" Rae Lee York exclaimed. Still, she laughed, but tilted her cup to her lips to hide her guilt.

"That's what they say. Man done fooled with hisself, probably for his own satisfaction. But lord, can you imagine?" A look crossed Carrie Agne's face that took her back

69

some forty years, a memory upon which she laid her wonder.

Rae Lee took notice from behind her coffee cup. "My lord! And you got nerve to talk about Sarah Louise."

"I'm just wondering is all. It ain't like Sarah Louise doing. Besides, tell me one good thing a man ever done that wasn't for his own satisfaction?"

"One gave you Mava and Davis." Rae Lee knew she'd made a mistake soon as the words left her mouth. Carrie's husband had been a terrible drunk with a temper as hot as Alabama in the sixties. He'd beaten seventeen-year-old Carrie, and raped her on the same day her father had given her over to marriage. Mava had been born from that.

Carrie Agnes showed no recognition of the affront. "They say the police looking for a woman. Ain't no woman kilt that man. Another man done that!"

Rae Lee tried changing the subject. "Was good to hear from Denise last night, wasn't it? She's called a lot since the storm. Said a surprise was gonna show up on my doorstep any day now. Wouldn't say what it was."

"I wonder what that man was doing to get himself kilt like that," Carrie Agnes inquired.

Rae Lee shook her head and refilled her friend's cup. She wished for a conversation that didn't involve a dead man and his privates. "Didn't Mava say she was gonna stop by today? She sure kept things together during that storm, didn't she?" When Carrie Agnes showed a tiny smile of pride, Rae Lee thought she'd succeeded.

"You know Davis works down at the courthouse. I wonder if he knows anything about that man who got kilt? Dial down there for me, Rae Lee."

"Davis is working, Carrie Agnes. He ain't near no phone."

"Go ahead. I call him all the time; talk to whoever answers, I say, 'tell Davis to call his mother. You know I'm eighty-eight years old, so tell him not to be too long.'" Carrie Agnes laughed at herself.

"But you're not eighty-eight; why do you lie to those people?"

"Cause it sounds better than eighty-six."

Rae Lee bobbled her head. Carrie hadn't had even a cold as long as she'd known her. "What do you want with Davis? I thought he works in the mail room?"

"He does. Supervisor. Davis knows what's going on before the judges do. Now go ahead, call him. Here's the number," she said, pulling a little book from her purse.

Davis' name was written in big letters on the first page. She had called him once and was told there was no Davis there. When she'd fussed at him for not calling back, he made her the book. Forgetting a number, she was entitled. But on the chance it was ever an emergency, he wanted her to dial correctly.

Rae Lee listened to the rings until the call connected. To her surprise, he answered. "Hello, Davis. I didn't expect to get you. Your mother wants to talk to you. Hold on."

Carrie Agnes motioned. "No; ask him about the man that got kilt. The one we been talking about."

"Lord, lord. Here, Carrie Agnes, take this phone. I'm not asking that boy no such thing."

Carrie Agnes wiped the mouthpiece. "Davis. Hey. Sarah Louise was telling me about the man in Greenville that got himself kilt. You know anything about that?"

"Mama, I can't talk about that here."

"Then come this evening. You know I'm at Rae Lee's."

"I know, Mama. You wouldn't come live with me."

"No. I'm just fine right here. Me and Rae Lee understand each other. You and me don't. That's all."

Had Rae Lee and Davis been in the same room, they would have seen the smirk on the other's face. They knew it was partly because Davis lived in Fountain, and that was just too far from Princeville for Carrie Agnes, all eight miles from one town to the other. It was not wanting to be a constant babysitter for her grandchildren. Most of all, it was because of friendship. She and Rae Lee had been through life and death together. And would face it again, together.

"Davis is gonna come by this evening." While hanging up the phone, another thought crossed Carrie's lips. "Rae Lee, Did you see the News last night? Somebody chopping off people's hands and feet. What in the world! Who would do such a thing as that?"

Chapter 30.

Connor closed her laptop where she worked in Ben's office when he walked in. "Who ate your cheese?"

"What?"

"What's the matter? Did something happen to the case?"

"Didn't sleep much last night. Guess it's showing," Ben said. He dropped into one of the side chairs and stretched the knots from his shoulders.

"Whatever you wrestled with obviously won." Connor zipped her carrying case and set it in her seat. "Can't wait to compare notes with Martin and Wash. We're meeting at ten o'clock, remember?"

"Wouldn't miss it."

Connor looked at Ben, "You sure there's nothing I can help with?"

Ben looked at the wall clock. "I appreciate your offer, but I'm fine. Besides, I have about forty minutes to keep you from showing me up in my own playground. I've seen what you do to people who are not prepared."

Connor smiled softly and picked up her laptop and purse. "Oh, by the way, Regina Bailey called. Wanted info on the Solder case. Told her to take a number." Connor teasingly batted her eyes at him as she walked to the door, closing it behind her.

Damn, that's all I need. Regina Bailey. Who is feeding that woman? Maggie walked in and handed Ben his coffee. He looked at his secretary and wondered. When she smiled at him, he was certain she'd never violate his trust. He picked up the phone.

Lucas answered before the first ring had finished. "I'm glad it's you, Ben," he said. "Are you free for lunch? I'll come over."

"That's why I'm calling. I don't mind being kept up all night by a woman, but a dead one..."

Lucas would have responded with humor had he not tossed all night himself. "I tried reaching Dr. Able at the hotel. If he's there, would you ask him to come, too?"

Ben didn't know where Malice was either, but was sure it wasn't Home Town Suites. He turned over his hand, looked into his palm, and mentally pictured the numbers Malice had traced. "I'll get him. Meet us at The Coffee Cup." The owner understood the need for privacy and had designed a room for just that purpose. It was his niche to success in the restaurant wars.

"I haven't had any of Calvin's fried chicken dumplings in too long. Make it 1:15; the lunch crowd should be done by then. I'll set it up." Ben was about to say 'right-oh,' but instead, he said, "I almost forgot. Regina Bailey called.

She's the one asking questions about your lady friend. We can't let her get wind of what we know."

Ben arrived at Brooklyn's office in time to grab the thick slab of wood that was closing behind the detectives.

Connor arrived last. It was cool enough that her rust colored leather skirt was not a fashion mistake. Everything about her said she'd never make such an error. A dragon-fly pendant fastened a multicolored scarf of fall colors against a matching silk turtleneck. All three men stood to greet her. Brooklyn watched, aware that she had not gotten that kind of reception. Nonetheless, she understood it. Still in her twenties, Connor had the look of someone born to the finer life, but had not yet received her inheritance.

The older Dory Martin spoke first. "As usual, you look very nice, Ms. Crawford."

Connor smiled at the detective and thanked him, glancing to Dr. Riley whose apologetic look said that he'd noticed, but had been too distracted earlier to say so. Ethan Wash simply shook her hand, proving he was not fully sophisticated enough to appreciate what was Connor Kingsley Crawford. Or, perhaps he was still brooding from their last encounter.

The proffered refreshments taken, Brooklyn looked at the detectives. "Tell me what you found."

The three men took their seats once Connor had slid gracefully into hers. Without preamble, the young detective began. "We talked to his neighbors. Seems Solder was a busy man. Had a lot of visitors, women mostly. No one knew them by name. About a week before the murder, one neighbor found a car parked in her space. She wrote down the tags. The car was registered to a man in Winston -

Salem: a Jessie Matthews. Seems Mr. Matthews likes women enough to try and be one."

Brooklyn looked at Connor and Ben. Had they been right about Solder's lifestyle? Could it have been a man dressed as a woman who killed Solder?

Detective Wash continued. "Mr. Matthews said that he and Solder had been lovers. He came to Greenville 'for old time sake'. Not a bad looking drag. Fooled me."

Saving his partner from politically insensitive territory, Detective Martin took over. "Matthews said that Solder didn't have a dating preference. She was very cooperative; gave Ethan a picture from her show." Martin motioned to Wash to show the photograph.

Starting with Brooklyn, each looked upon the glossy with appreciation at how Jessie Matthews transformed into the femme diva whose look even Connor envied.

Detective Martin continued. "Ms. Matthews performs at underground clubs in Winston and Greensboro. High clientele, so he said. His alibi holds."

Detective Wash resumed. "Matthews said Solder moved here for an old friend. Someone he knew as a teenager who had introduced him to the lifestyle. Matthews said this person was a local big shot."

Although she hoped it was coming, Brooklyn couldn't wait. "Did you find this person?"

Detective Martin responded. "Not yet. It could have been a woman, or a man masquerading as a woman."

"That's my cue," Ben chimed. "We found strands of hair on Solder's body and in the bedding from his apartment. Some were synthetic, some human. The samples suggest the person was wearing a wig."

Connor took over. "I checked local wig shops and learned that some manufacturers use a mixture of human and synthetic hair. You can't find this blend at your forty-dollar shop. There's only one store in the area that carries it. Unfortunately, because management has been lax for several years, we got nothing."

Ben spoke. "We found two strands of European male human hair entangled with the synthetic."

"So, the killer is white?" The young detective asked with noticeable concern.

"That's not what I heard, Detective," Brooklyn interjected. "I heard that another man, wearing a wig or toupee, came in contact with the victim. None of this excuses Mr. Purdue. What I also heard," she added, looking at the young man, "is that you need to find this secret lover."

☙

Do not walk in darkness
While there is light abound.
Set your steps towards goodness.
Let your hands speak of it gratefully.

Chapter 31.

"Do I have a problem I don't know about?" Malice's voice was not unexpected; Fawks Belnais knew this call would come.

"Standard procedure, Malice, you know that. That's what SCRUB is about." Fawks had lied, perhaps out of habit.

"What have you done, Fawks?"

A skilled liar knows to infuse truth with deception when necessary. This answer required truth. "Your access to the lab has been terminated; your home searched."

"Searching my home is not standard protocol. Neither is terminating my privileges this soon. So what's going on?"

"You tell me. What're you doing in North Carolina?"

"Helping a friend. Didn't Charlene tell you?"

"I take it this *friend* is the medical examiner, or the police. That explains the tests you ran."

"But it doesn't explain why the agency is up my ass," Malice snapped.

Fawks wouldn't say it, but he agreed. All the surveillance said Malice was on a simple fact finding case for a small town. He, too, wondered what that had to do with Chris, Charlene, and the call he'd gotten to lock Malice out of the lab. "Mal, is there anything you want to tell me?"

"Gee, Fawks, I'm waiting for you to answer that very question. Look. I've never asked for anything; but I'm asking for this. Find out whose hand is up my skirt."

Fawks had been concerned days ago when Chris showed up. "When did you first leave for that little town?"

"Why?"

"Just trying to draw some lines."

"October twenty-second. Aside from three days back home that you know about, I've been here."

"I'll get back to you." Fawks clicked off, and went to his personal log. Chris had come on November second at 11:13AM. Beside the entry were several question marks indicating the irregularity of the visit. Why hadn't Charlene followed Malice to Greenville when Mistletoe was issued? The lab visit was the spark. So, the biggest question of all was: who cared? The strategic mind of Fawks Belnais brought him to the same conclusion as Malice. His friend had a problem.

Malice looked at his watch. He had two hours before meeting Lucas at the Coffee Cup. He looked at the photograph that would dominate their assembly. Who are you darling, and who did this to you? Why were you buried in a black cemetery? Unnoticed.

Malice opened his laptop and found the file named King. He made a copy and enclosed it in a polyethylene bag. While the computer burned a second CD, Malice addressed a mailing envelope and slid a note inside that said, "In the Event..." It was addressed to Christian Dingo.

Ben arrived at the hotel as Malice turned the corner to the lobby. Charlene was there with the morning paper and hot chocolate. Malice walked over to her and whispered: "You're more beautiful than I was told." He then met Ben at the front desk and reached out his hand formally. Ben did likewise. As they walked out, Malice said, "Keep an eye out for a green SUV and that woman I just spoke to."

"Malice, I don't know what's going on. I'm not sure I want to know, but are we in danger?"

"I'd never put you, or anyone here in harm's way."

"Harm's way! What's happening here?"

Malice couldn't answer Ben, nor assure him. "I suspect Lucas wants to keep going otherwise a phone call would have sufficed. He wants to know what to do next."

"Yeah. I don't think Lucas has handled but one murder case since he's been sheriff. And that fool killed over a game of checkers with four people watching."

"Are you prepared for this?"

The burden settled in Ben's face as he pondered the question. "Ever since the storm, Lucas has relied on me to help make things right. First, I was just Dr. Riley identifying local bodies, then Iyanla Vanzant, spiritual advisor; now it looks like I'm fucking Sherlock Holmes. Excuse me for saying, but there ain't a damn thing elementary about any of this shit. I don't work for Princeville. Lucas and I go back to childhood, but there's no more I can do unless I clone my ass three different ways, and become bullet proof."

Malice knew he had added to Ben's anxiety the last twenty-four hours. He tried to lighten the conversation. "I suggest you decide before we get there, Sybil."

Ben's frustration broke. "Well, cousin, I suggest you do the same. I suspect it's your balls he'll be stroking."

Malice shifted against the cloth seat of the unmarked county car. "I'm just here as a favor, remember? I can't stay. There are other matters that need my attention."

"You mean like the SUV that isn't back there?" Ben motioned to the rear of the car with his head.

Chapter 32.

Lucas pulled into The Coffee Cup parking lot seconds after Ben and Malice arrived. The three made their way into what used to be an old country store. Farm artifacts decorated the thick, planked walls. Old metal signs hung on the walls dominated by a fat, shiny-faced Aunt Jamima, and the Coca-Cola bottle cap.

Calvin slapped Ben on the back and extended his huge hand. "Been a long time, Doc. Good to have you back."

"Thanks, Calvin. Took me this long to work off the calories from the last time, Ben joked. "I brought you two more victims for the heart attack specials."

Calvin pushed Ben on the arm in retaliation. "Now, who was on your table because of my cooking?"

"That's because bullets are faster," Ben laughed, and introduced Lucas to Calvin.

Calvin gave Lucas a firm shake. "You've been around here before."

Ben continued. "This is Dr. Malice Able from DC."

Calvin let go of Lucas and greeted Malice with the same exuberance. "Pleasure to have you both. Let me show you to the back. You'll be alone as dirt-daubers. If you need anything, press the buzzer over there." He nodded to it over his shoulder. "We still have all of today's specials, and if it ain't on the menu, just ask. I can whip it up real quick."

A young waitress breezed in moments after Calvin had shut the reinforced door. Ben settled on the fried chicken dumplings he craved, Lucas chose Salisbury steak, and Malice thought the baked trout would be safe.

"By the way," Ben said to Malice, "In case you're wondering, Calvin calls dead people dirt-daubers. The man is sick. But you have to admit, it's a good one. You see, dirt daubers are a solitary species of insect that dig into the ground and—"

"Yeah, I got it Ben," Malice interrupted.

"Disrespectful if you ask me," Lucas added.

"Yeah, but it is funny," Ben said in defense. "Calvin's a good guy."

The young waitress pushed through the door with a serving cart. On it were deep serving bowls of turnip greens, mashed potatoes, creamed corn, rice, gravy, cole-slaw, hush puppies, and biscuits. She placed everything in the center of the table. She then lifted plates from the second shelf of the tray and placed each meat entree in front of its intended.

"Holy smokes!" Malice said. "No wonder these tables are so huge."

The waitress smiled. "Oh, that's just round one. You may have a second helping of anything on the table, including your meats. Later, I'll bring deserts and other goodies to choose from." After surveying the expected look of stupor on their faces, she turned on the word: "Enjoy!"

Ben picked up his spoon and lifted a steaming mound of dumplings from his bowl. Crumbles of bacon and chunks of fried chicken sat in the creamy sauce surrounding the broken strips of cooked dough.

Lucas scooped creamed corn into his side bowl and piled a heaping of mashed potatoes beside his Salisbury steak. He drenched the meat and potatoes in light brown gravy, and reached for a biscuit.

Malice stared at the table full of food; the fabulous aromas forced him to follow suit. He took a sample of the turnips, leaving the hefty chunk of fatback in the bowl. The green tendrils were sweet in his mouth; he couldn't help but go 'hmmm.'

Once everyone had rested their forks and had leaned back from the table, Lucas spoke. "My curiosity got the best of me." His eyes went from Ben to Malice. "I want to know who she is." He waited for them to prepare for his next question. "What do I do?"

Ben rubbed food from the side of his teeth with his thumb. Malice took a swallow of tea for the same purpose. Neither spoke.

"So, what, Ben, you think I should put her back in the ground? And exactly where would I put her? You think I can just dig a hole and toss her in, no name, no nothing, the same way she came out?"

No response.

"What am I suppose to do? We don't even know where she came from."

Silence.

Lucas dropped his fork. It clanged on the side of the plate as he leaned back in desperation.

Malice broke the tension. "Look. I will answer any questions I can. You asked me to identify her, I've done that."

81

Lucas crossed his arms over his chest, his fingers under his armpits. "With all due respect, Dr. Able, that's not entirely true."

Malice was beginning to see he might have underestimated Lucas Belton. "Please, elaborate," he said, seeing if Lucas was prepared to go the distance, and glad that he wanted to keep digging.

"When you came, you said you'd identify all nine bodies."

"I gave you a face and the details of her death, Sheriff. It is not up to me to give her a name nor find out how she ended up in your cemetery; that's your job."

Ben rested an arm on the table. The sound was meant to distract and temper the brewing debate. The problem was, both men were right.

Lucas adjusted his presentation. "Doctor Able, Ben said you are the best in the country. From what I've seen, OJ should have called you."

Malice leaned forward in his chair and drank more tea. Ben was right; the sheriff was stroking his balls. He set his glass on the table, and looked at Lucas. "Who says he didn't?"

Lucas didn't know whether to smile or be struck with awe. He chose deference. "I hear what you're saying. And you're right. It's up to me to solve my problem. All I'm saying is, I need help. This is way beyond hauling old man Jacob in for DUI."

Ben cleared his throat. "Why do you need to do anything, Lucas? It's a thirty-year-old Jane. I recommend you put her bones back in that pretty box, send it to the nearest crematory, and be done with it."

"Yeah. I could do that." The others heard the 'but' that should have followed his statement. They added the ending. Something like 'Yeah, I could make her a dirt dauber.

And while we're at it, let's give somebody the deal of the century'.

Malice lifted a forkful of coleslaw and crunched the raw cabbage, hoping he wouldn't hear what Lucas might say next. Ben simply stared at his friend.

Lucas chose to leave it for now. He followed Malice back to the bowls and took a scoop of turnips. He doused them with peppered vinegar, and bit into a hushpuppy. The sweet cornbread was still warm. The mush in the middle surrounded by the grainy fried particles was comforting. The nerves in his stomach needed more. He went to the buzzer.

"Yes sir, is there something you need?"

"Yes. Another piece of Salisbury steak, please."

Malice spoke with his mouth full. "And trout."

"You might as well bring the chicken dumplings too," Ben added.

"Did you get all that?" Lucas asked into the speaker.

"Yes sir. Will you need any of the side dishes?"

"No, just the meats, and more tea. Thank you."

The three resumed their afternoon repast, only slower.

"Lucas, I understand what you're trying to do. And, brother, I love you for it. That's what makes *you* you. But this is a can of leeches. We have no idea where this will lead, and who's involved. You have to ask yourself if you're ready for the consequences. Somebody did not want that woman found. That somebody could still be very alive."

Stretching his arms across the table, Lucas sat up straight. "I have considered that. But it was murder."

"And what makes you think whoever did it won't do it again? How do you know that somebody hasn't been keeping an eye on you, or me, or Malice for that matter? Whoever buried her probably knows those caskets washed up and has to be wondering if she was one... of.... " Ben's eyes widened. "Holy shit."

"What is it?" Malice asked.

The stare on Ben's face turned to concern. "Regina Bailey. Somebody knows this lady is out of the ground. They've been using her to get information."

Malice turned to Lucas, "If that's true, somebody is waiting to see what you do."

Unable to think of anything else to say, Lucas looked at his table companions and asked the obvious. "Who could it be?"

"The bigger point here, Lucas, is, whoever it is, has access to my office."

Lucas stared past Ben and Malice. He put his hand to his face, resting his fingers across his mouth. "That means it's somebody in law enforcement."

"It means more than that, Lucas." Ben leaned back in his chair. "It means we already have a problem."

"Perhaps you're right, Ben. I'd never forgive myself if anything happened to either of you." He pushed an empty bowl aside. "Pack her up; I'll call the crematory."

"I'm not sure that's going to solve your problem, Lucas," Malice said. "If he knows about her, and Ben is saying he does, he also knows that I took her to Washington. And if he knows that, he can speculate that we already know more than we should."

"Then, what do we do?" Lucas asked.

Ben took the question. "Looks like we keep going."

Chapter 33.

Only the fine-tuned sounds of the Taurus wagon passed between Ben and Malice on the drive back to town. The ringing of Ben's cell phone interrupted the swishing of air against the windows.

"Ben, it's Brooklyn. Can you stop by?"

"Anything wrong?"

"It's the Solder case. Best if you see it. I told your secretary she could reach you at my office."

"I'll be there shortly." He turned to Malice. "Gotta make a stop. I can drop you at your car if you need to get back. If not, I'd like you to meet someone. Assistant DA. Since Lucas is moving forward, she'll be helpful. Good a time as any to meet her."

Taking a side-glance at Ben, he said, "Seems the lady has your attention."

"I've accompanied her to a few things. She's smart. Ambitious. I don't mind telling you she fills out a dress. She's five-feet-nine inches of tough stuff. Yeah, I'd like to be more than an armrest..."

Malice didn't interrupt.

"...But she's coasting with the park brakes on."

Malice hesitated and then said, "I don't date a lot, so I'm the last person to tell you about women. But I see a lot of relationships. The two ingredients that seem to make them work are patience and respect."

"Perhaps you're right." Ben breathed deeply. "And sometimes you have to cut your losses."

He whirled the car into a reserved space at the judicial complex. Malice followed him down the brightly painted corridors leading to the Office of the Assistant District Attorney.

Michelle greeted them and instructed Ben to go in." She hesitated for a second. "May I offer you and ..."

Malice smiled at the ADA's first line of contact. "Dr. Able," he said, extending his hand. "Just along for the ride, but thank you for asking."

"My pleasure, Dr. Able. Are you sure?"

Malice patted his stomach. "No, nothing... well, perhaps a private room to make some calls."

"Certainly. There's a small conference room two doors down. I'll show you."

"After you meet Ms. Beaudeau," Ben said.

"Of course." Malice pushed Ben towards the closed door just as it opened.

"Brooklyn," Ben said. "I'd like you to meet Dr. Malice Able. He's helping with the Princeville matter."

"It's a pleasure to meet you, Dr. Able. I've heard of your work."

"You know my work?"

"Only as much as Ben has told me—which wasn't much, and what I've heard around the hallways, which was a lot. Of course, I make it my business to know the best minds in fields that impact my profession. Over the last few days I've researched but can't find a thing on you. Not even a photograph. Whatever I expected to find, you're not it." She caught the ambiguity. "Oh...that didn't come out—"

Malice smiled. "Not to worry. What I do won't find its way to the Internet. Ben's told me great things about you. I understand you're going to the bench. Congratulations."

Brooklyn blushed. "It's not official. I'm simply one candidate."

"I doubt you're a *simple* candidate Ms. Beaudeau." The words were meant to be charming, but sounded like something else to everyone in the room. In an effort to change course, Malice looked at the wall directly ahead. A framed

needlepoint quote drew his attention long enough to collect himself. *'To understand, you must surrender everything
you think you understand'.* Based on what Ben had said
about her, the sentiment didn't fit. "Interesting quote."

"My mother made it for me. It's one of her philosophical
enlightenments."

"And you don't prescribe to it?"

Ben intervened. "Brooklyn is too analytical for such.
There's usually a right answer, and a wrong one in her
book. And *surrender* is not in her vocabulary. Speaking of
which..." Ben looked at Malice's hand.

Malice let go of Brooklyn. "Your secretary has offered
me a room... to make phone calls while I wait."

To Brooklyn's ear, Malice's voice was forged at the center of the earth from silver and brass, tempered in the
depth of his mysterious sea and came forth clear as crystal.
It rode on the crest of a blue-green mist that was both allur-
ing and dangerous.

His voice matched his face. A curly crop of hair framed
stoic eyes brimmed with knowledge, and truth, and uncertainty. Whereas Ben stood with her eye to eye, this man
she looked up to.

"Michelle will get whatever you need," she said. Brooklyn touched her hair with the hand Malice had held, unaware. "I'd love to hear about your work. I hope you'll do
me the plesure of lunch while you're in Greenville."

Safely behind closed doors, Malice allowed himself to feel
the tightness in his chest. To question why Brooklyn had
affected him. Her five-foot-nine body could stand against
any model. It was clear that she thought adding little more
than lipstick would downplay her beauty. And that wearing her hair straight, with just a bend of curl would mini-
mize her glamour. She was wrong. But what he felt had

nothing to do with appearance—an unsettling fact that he hoped Ben hadn't noticed.

Chapter 34.

Malice reached into his pocket for the phone and pressed one of three codes he'd consigned to its memory. Fawks picked up immediately. "What have you learned?"

"It's only been a few hours, Mal. I'm no psychic." "You're the best at what you do, Fawks; and what you do is figure things out."

Fawks marinated in the compliment for a second and exhaled. "A senator has taken an interest in your life. Seems he's from the town where you are now."

"What?"

"Could be he's just concerned about the flood."

"Then why Charlene? Why not send a delegate, or for that matter, come himself for the press?"

"The questions go deeper given he knows about the tests you ran at the lab."

"This is bizarre." Malice thought for a second. "What's this guy's name?"

"Vincent Haiger."

"Thanks, Fawks. Keep me posted. About anything." Malice assumed Fawks had nodded. He'd seen him do it countless times after a phone call had ended, silent confirmation intended only for himself. Malice sat for a few minutes staring at the painting on the wall. A grove of trees on somebody's farm. In the background, broken corn stalks with ragged brown leaves butchered by the groping suction of picking machines. He repeated the name Fawks had produced. Vincent Haiger.

The next call was to his mother. He'd told her that under the circumstances, it was too risky to share his identity. Still, he needed to see the look of love reclaiming its bond that he'd imagined in his grandmother's eyes.

He was ending a cryptic voice message to Chris Dingo when Ben stuck his head inside. "Perfect timing," he said. On the walk to the car, Malice talked, in part hoping to avoid any words having to do with Brooklyn. "Just talked to Mom. Told her I've decided to meet my grandmother."

"That's great. It took you long enough, but are you sure?"

"Yeah. Everything's under control. Can you arrange it for me? I don't think I should just show up at the woman's door."

"Are you kidding? That's the southern way. We don't make appointments to say hello, and a surprise visit any day is like Christmas. Leave it to me," Ben smiled. "You know what; Lucas is going to her house this evening. He's meeting Ms. Mava Pelta. She has dreams."

"Dreams?"

"I'm sure Lucas didn't tell you because you'd think he was consorting with root doctors. Now that you're staying on, and the case is really yours, you should be there."

"Interesting," is all Malice could say. He wouldn't tell Ben that his own mother believed in *the gift*, as she called it. He'd grown up with stories about potions and shamans. He'd met one or two psychics who left him with questions, but none with the powers her stories had described. "Do you think we should call Lucas; make sure it's all right?"

"Oh no," Ben laughed. "Remember; the element of surprise. I want to see Lucas' face when he tries to tell you about Ms. Mava."

Malice laughed, too. "Okay. I'm in. I haven't had a good tease in a while."

Hours later, Malice piddled in the hotel room on the city's tab while he waited for Ben's return. He propped the pillows against the headboard and stretched out across the bed. The weather was still a lead topic on the local News; specifically, the possibility of more rain. A thoughtless scare tactic to attract viewers. The jet stream the man pointed to on the map would dissipate long before it reached the Carolinas. He turned to Breaking News.

...

"Another body has been found in what federal authorities, which are now involved, are calling a serial killing. Police have no clues as to the identity of the bodies, the killer, or his motive."

...

Malice sat up in bed. He knew, just as he did the first time he'd heard the story, that another one had tripped. That's what they'd called it when a deviant crossed the line into murder. He felt the perspiration roll down the center of his back. He looked into the mirror on the dresser. His face glistened with guilt. He felt an urgent need to the shower. Shortly, he could think again and the thought that came was of Lester McAdoo.

Chapter 35.

"I didn't ask for this!" The man chained to the metal desk in the small detention room pounded the desk. His eyes wide, pained confusion permanently embedded on his face. "What did they do to me?!"

Malice looked at the man and then his yellow pad of notes. A manila file of medical reports, criminal background, childhood history, and psychological profiles lay to his left. He knew more about Lester McAdoo than the thirty-one year old knew about himself.

"According to this, your mother had syphilis. She left you in a trash container. You spent the first three years of your life in a state ward until you were transferred to a private facility as part of a study on brain cell restoration. Seems you did not respond well to the treatment. They were unable to help you. Fast forward twenty years; you say a voice calling itself Ezekiel chose you for a special mission that ended in the unmerciful deaths of a Pennsylvania family," Malice offered.

When he returned to his car, he wrote in his pad. Subject confirmed. And based on the Breaking News report, another one like Lester McAdoo was out there.

Out of the shower, Malice sipped a drinkas he finished dressing. He made a call to the airport from his car; Charlene had no need to know that. There was a flight to DC at ten-forty-five. The next call was to his old colleague, Baru Fugama.

Fugama's voice was spent, like a man who had gone on a 'can't lose' gambling trip and came home empty-handed.

"We must talk. Yes, yes. Come."

Malice walked into Ben's office and announced he'd drive to Ray Lee's. For most of the drive, the two were silent. Ben, thinking about Brooklyn and the look he'd seen pass between her and Malice. Malice: the News story.

Ben spoke first. "I hope we can wrap this thing up pretty soon. I didn't mean to keep you from your life this long." As he said it, he couldn't tell if he meant that, or if it came from some place else.

"Then you'll be pleased to know something's come up. I'm leaving for DC tonight. You'll have to drop me at the airport, if you don't mind."

"What?" He stopped himself from asking why. "Look, I know Lucas can't pay you anywhere near what you're worth, but..."

"This is not about money, Ben. In fact, it's a helluva case.

"Look, What I just said, I didn't mean to suggest—"

"No, we're cool." Malice assured him. "It's like I said, something's come up."

"Oh my god. The serial killer. I heard the News. You've been called back on that, right?"

Malice had to direct Ben's attention elsewhere. "Tell me what you know about Senator Vincent Haiger."

"Where'd that come from?"

"Just getting the lay of the land. I understand he represents this district."

It sounded like the lie that it was but Ben didn't challenge him. "Native son. Typical black child from meager beginnings. He has a sister in Baltimore who's also a lawyer. He graduated from UNC at Chapel Hill; she went to North Carolina Central. He established himself in Greenville before making a run into politics. Became Attorney General, and eventually made a play for a US senate seat. Story has it, someone pulled some strings."

"Who?" Malice asked.

"Don't know. But they knew how to funnel money."

Malice knew all about the shell game. The government had money pretzeled in places they'd never connect to the source. "So Haiger has at least one puppeteer."

"Like all politicians. But in his case, no one has seen behind the curtain. Two reporters tried and found themselves writing about tea parties. Despite how he got there, he's done a lot for the state over the past twelve years."

"Do you know him?"

"Met him a few times. Seems like a decent man. But who the hell knows; he's a politician. I assume he must be half decent, he's Brooklyn's uncle."

"What?"

"Yeah. He's the reason she went into law even though her mom's a lawyer, too. She worships the man. Haiger helped Brooklyn with her career, Harvard, and all that. Brooklyn was born in Baltimore, but wanted to follow his footsteps, so started her career where he did —right here in Greenville. I'm sure being his niece set her up, but she's proven she belongs."

"And her promotion?" Malice asked. "I mean, going to the bench after three years is unusual; that often takes years."

"Like I said, she's a damn good ADA. I'm sure this is where skill meets opportunity."

"You say she was hand-picked?"

"Yeah, well, a local judge has taken an interest in her career. Connor, Brooklyn's paralegal, told me he nominated her. I think his interest is professional. Connor thinks it might be something, but I just don't get that vibe from the man. Besides, not that it means anything, but he's old enough to be her father."

"This man have a name?"

"William... Henry... Pascal."

Chapter 36.

Malice listened to the sloshing water as he slowly steered the car through remnants of mud. Through the darkness that settled around them, he could see that the town was no closer to salvation than the weeks before all the Samaritans had come and gone.

The car found better traction as it climbed a small slope and wound through a thin grove of trees. Faded light shone up ahead like a beacon to a sailor.

"Well, here we are," Ben said. "Lucas and Ms. Mava are here. That other car looks like Davis'. He's Ms. Mava's younger brother. Their mom, Ms. Carrie Agnes, has been your grandmother's best friend since your mama was two years old. Ms. Carrie Agnes lived a few houses down. Hers was swept into the creek and stopped a half mile away."

Malice turned off the engine. The curtain on the door got pulled aside and a face peered out. It was Lucas.

"Are you ready?" Ben asked.

Malice pulled the handle on his door. The little bell, warning that the headlights were still on, dinged.

Lucas stepped onto the wrap-around porch. Davis stood behind him.

Malice straddled a small puddle on his way to the porch. "Evening Lucas." In the dim light, he could see the uneasiness in Lucas' eyes, and the question on Davis' face.

Ben spoke from behind. "I told Malice you were meeting with Ms. Mava tonight. Since he's on the case, thought it would be good for him to hear what she has to say, since she's on it too."

Uneasiness turned to embarrassment. "Come on in."

When Lucas turned his back, Ben punched Malice in the side with his elbow.

Inside, Rae Lee and Carrie Agnes were setting the table. "Hey, Auntie Rae." Ben called, "Set two more places."

"Who is that?" Rae Lee questioned, looking up from laying flatware.

Carrie Agnes poked her head into the living room. "Oh, it's Ben Riley. Look, Rae Lee, it's that handsome young Dr. Ben," she yelled back. "Who is that with you?"

"Now don't go questioning our guest, Carrie Agnes," Rae Lee admonished. She smiled in Ben's direction. "Good manners make good company."

Ben hugged Ms. Carrie, then kissed Rae Lee on the cheek. Rae Lee smiled and patted Ben's chest. "You should have told me you were coming. I would have baked a cake."

"That's a lie and you know it, Rae Lee," Carrie Agnes scoffed. "Now who is this good looking man with you, Ben?"

Mava offered the introduction. "That's Dr. Able, Mama. He's helping with the bodies that washed up. I told you about him."

"Bless you, baby," Rae Lee said, taking Malice's hand in both of hers. "Come on in and sit down to dinner. We got plenty."

Malice took the tiny wrinkled hand in his. He felt her lukewarm essence and immediately loved her all over again. She favored him with the smile that had always put him at ease. He saw his mother in her eyes.

Ben interrupted. "I told Dr. Able about your gift, Ms. Mava. Since he's helping out, whatever you could share might speed us along." Ben looked over to see Lucas burning a hole into the floor; sure that Lucas hoped it would swallow him whole.

"I wish I'd known about your dreams earlier, Ms. Mava. My mother is a strong believer. I'm eager to hear what you can tell us about this woman." Malice looked over to see Lucas' head spring up.

"None of that talk right now," Rae Lee chirped. "Dinner's getting cold. Mava, show our guest to their places. Davis, you say grace."

Dinner progressed with small talk. How school was going. When the church would resume services. About help coming from all over the country. Carrie Agnes couldn't hold it. She turned to Dr. Riley. "I'm glad you're here, Ben. I was gonna ask Davis but you're a better one to say. Tell us about that man you got over there that done messed with his privates. Is it true how they say he messed with his privates? Why would a man do such a thing?"

Ben and Malice stopped chewing. Rae Lee dropped her fork. "Ben, don't you talk about that nonsense at my table."

"All I wanna know is did he do it, that's all," Carrie said, cutting her eyes at Rae Lee.

"Ms. Carrie, I can't talk about that. Until it goes to trial, all information is confidential."

"Humph," Carrie Agnes said back. Rae Lee sighed relief.

To everyone's relief, Lucas changed the subject. "Aunt Mava, do you remember any more about your dream?"

Mava began by repeating. "The woman reached a baby out to me, wearing a sundress and a JFK button. And there was that sweet flower smell."

"We didn't find a campaign button in the coffin, Aunt Mava. So maybe you dreamed about somebody else."

"Well, Lucas, that's what I saw."

Malice said, "The button might tell us the time period in which she lived, Lucas. Dreams are not always literal."

Ben added a thought. "It could be telling us something about who killed her. Maybe she worked in the local democratic campaign office or she's pointing us in that direction. Or maybe to someone in DC or Massachusetts, the Kennedy stomping grounds."

Before they could finish all the speculations, Carrie Agnes moaned. "Lord, lord. Shame they kilt that poor man. He was the best president this country ever had. Such a waste. And then Dr. King. And if that wasn't enough, they took that nice little Bobby, too."

Malice knew by now not to let Carrie Agnes have too much rope. She'd divert the mystery back to the dead man Rae Lee didn't want at her table.

"That's a good point, Ben. About the politics, I mean." He turned to Mava. "The smell. If Lucas took you to a flower shop, could you pick it out?"

"Baby, I don't know. All I can tell you is it smelled sweet, like jasmine or gardenia. Besides, there ain't no flower shops around here, and those flowers don't bloom this time of year," Mava answered.

"Then maybe the smell was a clue about the time of year she died. When do those flowers bloom?" Malice looked from one to the other for an answer. As he settled on Rae Lee's face, he met her puzzled stare, like she was trying to place him but couldn't. He was pleased that something in him was familiar, made her search her memory.

"Mid-spring, early summer," Carrie Agnes offered, not to be dismissed from the conversation.

Setting aside her failed recall, Rae Lee chimed in. "Maybe it wasn't gardenia, Mava. Every year, in the spring, there's that plant that grows wild everywhere. It smells so sweet you can't stand it for long. Some people call it Carolina Jasmine, but around here, it's Yellow Jasmine. There was a story about the plant we use to tell a long time ago."

Carrie Agnes, not allowed to talk about the dead man, jumped in. "Rae Lee, don't nobody—" when Malice interceded.

"Please, I'd love to hear the story. Please continue."

97

Rae Lee smiled at Carrie as if the two were wallflowers and she'd been asked to dance. "Well, the story goes that a beautiful woman named Tanjene was so in love with a man that she followed him here from the islands. She was a voodoo priestess who ate the petals of this flower every day. The fragrance came through her very skin."

Malice smiled to himself. It was the same story his mother had told. He leaned back in his chair and listened as if hearing it the first time:

Chapter 37.

It was summertime in Freedom Hill in 1875. A man named Levi Athan came from Jamaica and made his home on the hillside of this small southern town. He felt right at home because just like Jamaica, Freedom Hill was a land where black people ruled and owned their homes and businesses. The one schoolhouse educated all its children.

Levi Athan was a schoolteacher. He taught math and science, English and geography. He also taught the children their true history as he knew it to be. What they could not learn from their mothers and fathers, Levi Athan taught them at the Freedom Hill School for Boys and Girls.

The children loved his stories of great African men and women. "Africa is home to all mankind. The first language, community, art and buildings ever designed were in Africa," he told them. Some of the elders said he was a Keeper of Knowledge because he knew so much. The kids took to calling him Keeper. He inspired them with tales of the ancestors' strength, intellect and perseverance, and made them believe.

Shortly after Levi Athan left his homeland, a beautiful woman followed him to Freedom Hill. Tanjene loved him; she wanted only to be his wife. Tanjene was so beautiful that butterflies circled her head and play in her long dark hair. Her eyes were like black pearls that had fallen in fresh snow. Her ebony skin glowed. And when she moved, a delicate fragrance trailed from her like midst.

She made no secret about loving Levi Athan. Every day, she cooked a delicious meal and carried it on her head to his house where she left it on the porch for him to find. She always appeared in public impeccably dressed. And if ever someone visited her unannounced, she was properly dressed then, too.

While Mr. Athan educated the boys and girls, Tanjene taught mothers the art of Vodun, the world's oldest religion. For thousands of years, African Queen mothers had kept the temples and religious history. Tanjene taught these new daughters to speak to the spirits. They prayed to the gods for health and prosperity and called upon the ancestral spirits for guidance and protection. Vodun was a good and powerful force in everyone's life. It taught that everything in the universe is connected, that nothing has life apart from everything else. Because many of the people were aware of Vodun, they were happy to have Tanjene teach them.

Tanjene was as good a teacher to the mothers as Levi Athan was to the children. With Tanjene's help, the town became more beautiful. Women talked to the Earth Mother and the goddess of rain. "Be merciful and kind," they asked. Their prayers were answered. Crops were plentiful, flowers of all kinds bloomed throughout the year.

Soon, the town began to whisper. "Why won't the schoolteacher marry her," they asked each other. Everyone in town knew how much Tanjene loved Levi Athan. But Levi Athan did not think he could support Tanjene, this beautiful woman whose scent was so sweet that she attracted butterflies. "Too much pride to marry," someone answered.

Tanjene could not stand to have the town think poorly of Levi Athan or pity her love for him. So, Tanjene decided to help the man she loved. She would remove all obstacles in his way. She went to her garden and sat beside her favorite flower, whose white petals she ate, whose delicate fragrance flowed from her every pore. She dug around the plant until a hole circled the root. She prayed to the mother of prosperity. As she prayed, she'd eat a portion of the flower. She'd swallow, pray, and eat some more. For a day and a night she prayed and swallowed until every leaf was gone. Nothing remained except the very root. She then spoke a prayer no priestess of Vodun is permitted to say.

When the prayer was done, all of the plant she had eaten came spewing from her stomach. It flowed into the hole, back onto the flower's root. She covered the root with warm dark earth and fell into a deep sleep for days. While she slept, the flower grew back as if nothing had happened. Except when it bloomed, instead of white, the petals had turned yellow—and so had Tanjene's eyes. Butterflies did not follow her anymore.

Levi Athan did not know what Tanjene had done. He was an eloquent speaker and devoted to the cause of justice. He traveled the state uniting Black people to demand their rights and was away while Tanjene slept. Upon his return, he knocked on her door to tell her of his success.

"My beautiful Tanjene, what has happened to you?" he asked as he stepped away.

"I did it for you," she said. She closed her door, sank to the floor and cried.

A few months later, the people asked him to represent Freedom Hill in a great political conference. He was so impressive in his remarks that the following year, they voted him to the United States Senate. Levi Athan was now able to marry Tanjene. He still loved her but she had changed. She was no longer the beautiful woman that butterflies wanted to follow. And whenever the flower she had eaten was in bloom, the fragrance that came from her was so sweet it made people sick. And every year, in the fall, on the same night that she swallowed the flower and spat it out again, she fell into a deep, paralyzing sleep. When anyone asked about his lady, Levi Athan lied. "She is not feeling well today."

Tanjene wanted to meet his new friends but he was ashamed of her and made up one excuse after another. The final straw was when she could not attend a big celebration she had worked so hard to help him achieve. "Only wives are permitted to come," he told her.

"I will marry you today," she replied. But Levi Athan lowered his eyes and said nothing.

At that moment, Tanjene realized he would never marry her. She ran back to the garden and fell on her knees. She tore away the plant's petals and let them fall to the ground. She spoke dark Vodun words and cursed the flower for eternity. She vowed:

"Poison the lips of any
Whose kiss upon you play.
Bring death to any
In whose stomach you lay."

The petals mingled with her grief and spilled from her eyes until there was nothing left of her.

Levi Athan cried for Tanjene. He blamed himself and became more obsessed with work. He went on to serve two terms as state senator, and eventually became a prosperous man. But Levi Athan never married. Any woman who fell in love with him became ill. They said a sweet smell came over them, making them sick. And so he died a lonely man.

But for all the years of his life, he never forgot Tanjene; the flower whose petals she ate was everywhere. It spread all over the landscape in the spring like a vine, spilling its sweet fragrance through summer. Some have fallen *into a heavy sleep from smelling the flower too deeply. Doctors were fascinated and found ways to use the plant in surgery and created medicines to relieve particular pains. But they abandoned Tanjene's plant when animals swallowed it and died.*

After all this time, that flower still grows wild in the countryside of Freedom Hill. And people still tell the tale of beautiful Tanjene, whose eyes were once like black pearls in fresh fallen snow. Some talked about Levi Athan and how pride caused his misery.

Others glorified Tanjene's love. They claimed she was the reason the town prospered and could elect a state senator. All the good Levi Athan was able to do was because of her. They created a festival to honor Tanjene. On the day of her death, the women wore the yellow jasmine; its fragrance fill the air. On that day, Tanjene lived again. It is the day most couples married and butterflies came to play.

℧

Done telling the story, Rae Lee smiled at Malice. "The smell is so pretty but it's cursed."

"A cow ate it once and died," Carrie added.

Lucas and Ben looked at Malice. The woman had been poisoned. "Could it have been that simple?" Lucas asked. "Doctor Able, you can test the plant, right?"

Unable to follow along, Davis asked, "What's this about?"

As Ben told Davis what he could, the break gave Malice time to think about Lucas' question given his lab use in DC was over. When Ben finished, they all looked at Malice. "I

103

can reschedule my flight. If you can gather some of this plant, including the root, I'll take it with me."

"Lucas, that plant grows up the trellis in my back yard," Davis said. "It's dormant now but I can dig up a piece of the root and drop it off for Dr. Able in the morning on my way to work."

"Well, that's all worked out," Rae Lee said, signaling the end of talk about dead people and poisons. "Mava, help me with that wonderful peach cobbler you brought over? Since Dr. Able now knows all our family secrets, he can share some of his. Seems only fair."

Ben laughed. Malice smiled broadly, too. She hadn't found what she was looking for in memory, and was too polite to ask him directly.

With a bowl of cobbler and coffee in front of each person, all eyes went to Dr. Able.

"Where do I begin," he said, clearing his throat. "I'm an only child. My father died before I was born. Being here with Ben has been great. He's become the brother I never had. And Lucas is one of the finest men I've ever met. My work takes me around the world, but I've never seen anything that feels better to me than being around this table." He hoped that was enough. He wasn't ready to take her back thirty years.

Ben knew Rae Lee would not reclaim her grandson tonight. Everyone smiled at Malice except Mava, who pasted an unsettling stare on the side of his face.

Like Mava, Rae Lee looked at Malice, unsure why, but feeling unsatisfied. She was about to question him, but Carrie Agnes stole her chance when she said, "Did you hear about that serial killer? My goodness, somebody's chopping off people's hands and feet, mixing them up and nailing 'em to a cross."

Chapter 38.

Malice awoke in his hotel suite in Greenville feeling anxious. He hadn't slept here for several days. He thought again about Lester McAdoo, who had awakened one morning and needed to kill.

At the front desk, Malice picked up a stapled brown paper bag. Inside were quart-size Ziploc bags with samples Davis had labeled as instructed. The same clerk who checked him in was there. He asked about the woman in Suite 451.

Learning she'd checked out, he feigned disappointment and picked up a complimentary newspaper at the corner of the registration desk. It repeated what he'd heard on Breaking News. The Mechisedec Murders. Because the hands and feet of victims were nailed to a cross, news groups had called in religious experts for speculations. He'd listened closely to one doctor of religious studies from Cornell University.

"The cleaning of the hands and feet is interesting," the professor had said. "It suggests two things for me. One, the killer sees himself as a servant. It is an act of humility. This person must know something about the Bible. The inferences to the Books of John, Matthew and Luke—the New Testament prophets—are not a coincidence. Jesus, at the last supper, as described by John, washed the feet of his disciples, telling them, 'If I, your Lord and Master, have washed your feet; you also ought to wash one another's feet.... The servant is not greater than his lord; neither he that is sent greater than he that sent him. If you know these things, happy are you if you do them.' The professor paused for effect. "The killer may see what he's doing as an act of kindness. As if he is serving these victims in the same way Jesus served His disciples."

The professor got so caught up the anchor had to remind him there were two things. "And the other?"

"Oh, yes, yes," the professor chuckled. "The second thing is, he could be telling us something about his heritage. From the first century BC to around 70 AD, it was a Jewish custom to bury the dead by leaving them in a cave for a year, then placing the bones in an ossuary. This would be the equivalent of an urn today except it contained the actual bones of the deceased. Based on archeological finds, in these ossuaries, sometimes the feet were missing, other times not."

On another News channel a panel approached the killings psychologically. A profiler suggested, "The killer is exceptionally intelligent, but detached. Perhaps an orphan, someone abandoned or neglected by his parents very early in life. A fair amount of strength is needed to separate body parts, dig holes, and erect the five-foot crosses. The killer is a male between 30 and 40 years old. His profession allows him mobility; he travels in a vehicle that can accommodate his materials—the beams and such—and move about unnoticed." He thought the FBI, for whom he consulted from time to time, should look for a refrigerated truck, something that would keep the parts from decomposing too quickly, and could be concealed among other items.

Malice had drawn some of the same conclusions: orphaned, young, intelligent, but stopped short of the killer being a truck driver. A good twelve-pack cooler and a couple of ice packs would do. In fact, Malice was certain the killer would use something just that simple, just that portable and readily available. He could purchase lumber anywhere without attracting attention.

On another channel, a State Bureau of Investigation agent described where and how they came across the two mutilated bodies in Florida. "A poem-like note was left on the first victim that said 'King of Peace'.

The anchor turned quickly to another guest who sat in a side chair sipping from a cup with the station's logo prominently in view. "Why do you think he signed that one note, 'The King of Peace' and not the others?"

The expert offered his learned opinion. "The King of Peace is also called King of Salem. It is, according to Hebrews: Chapter 5, a priest chosen from among men, ordained for men in those things pertaining to God that he may offer both gifts and sacrifices for sins."

Anchor: Called by whom?

Expert: By God. Kings were once thought to be angels sent by God. Monarchies, like England, were based on this belief system.

Anchor: For what purpose? Who was this Mechisedec?

Expert: Kings are suppose to do what is best for the people, to establish rules of community and pass judgment on wrong-doers. Not a lot is known about Mechisedec. What we do know is he negotiated peace between Abraham and King Sodom. We only get a glimpse of him in Hebrews. But, this was a king to whom Abraham gave the first recorded tithe of ten percent; so this King was highly revered.

Anchor: And this is what the killer is doing?

Expert: That is hard to say. In this case, I can only speculate given what we know about the victims. If the killer is using Mechisedec as a model, the scripture gives a clue about him. Hebrews 5 asks, 'Who can have compassion on the ignorant, and on them that are out of the way; for that he, himself also is compassed with infirmity'.

107

I think in this case, the killer was seeking to make them 'perfect' in the eyes of God. The murders are labors of love. The washing of the hands and feet, the offering of praise in their crucifixion—all these suggest the killer considers himself a servant to his victims.

Anchor: The offering of praise?

Expert: Yes. Prayers.

Anchor: Agent Billings, did the victims have any physical or mental defects – infirmities? And what are these prayers?

The agent pursed his lips tightly and tapped his feet, wishing he could arrest the professor for interfering in a police investigation. His annoyance was tempered by knowledge of critical evidence that this asshole didn't know. Even the medical experts were scratching their heads.

Agent: None that we've determined just yet. As you know, we are not releasing the names of the victims. We're trying to make connections between them before we give their names to the public.

Expert: [Attempting to smooth over his blunder:] Their infirmity may not be physical but spiritual, or even moral.

Anchor: [To the Agent] The doctor is suggesting this may be about sacrifices for sin, especially since prayers are involved. Did the victims have criminal records?

Agent: As I said, the prayers are verses that we are not at liberty to discuss. We've determined that, in the past, yes, the victims had been involved in criminal activity and had been released from prison in the last eighteen months.

Anchor: So these victims could have been gift offerings for the families they hurt as easily as they could have been atonements, Doctor?

Expert: Yes. The killer may have been trying to save, or punish these victims. Ordained Priests of the Mechisedec

Order had the power of retribution and salvation. The Scripture says, 'For it is impossible for those who were once enlightened and have tasted of the heavenly gift, and were made partakers of the Holy Ghost, And have tasted the Good word of God... if they shall fall away, to renew them again unto repentance; seeing they crucify to themselves the Son of God afresh, and put to him an open shame'.

So yes, it is very likely these men had professed to have tasted the good word of God, then defiled that by coming out and committing more sin, or used the word of God in a vain, self-serving fashion. The killer may have seen this as an infirmity in character or faith.

Anchor: And these Priests. They were after the Order of Mechisedec, is that right Doctor?

Expert: Yes. Mechisedec means King of Righteousness, King of Peace. Without father or mother, having no descent, having no beginning of his days or ending of his life, but made like the Son of God. These Priests abide continually.

Anchor: Meaning the killer sees himself as Mechisedec and these murders are just the beginning?

Expert: Unless he is caught.

With that, the anchor pasted a solemn look across his face and announced a station break. Earlier on this station was the first time Malice had heard the moniker 'Mechisedec'. The prayers left with the bodies were a vague clue, but however they arrived at the name, later in the day, every station, every expert would make it fit.

109

Chapter 39.

Malice stepped into the concourse at Dulles airport and was greeted with a spectacular display of Christmas, and it wasn't yet Thanksgiving. Evergreen wreaths and candy canes hung in mid air from the ceiling. Standstill Santas waved to travelers throughout the airport. He had forgotten about such in Greenville. Because of the storm, everything was off schedule. In Princeville, it was likely Christmas wouldn't be announced at all. But here, almost embarrassed because he felt it, the herald warmed him.

Malice considered going to his condo and brewing a pot of his special coffee. He suspected everything would be left in perfect order just as Charlene had done in Greenville, but he'd know. Instead, he took the beltway and made the appropriate turns that took him to Baru's front door. He parked the rental car out of the way and went in, finding the key where Baru said it would be.

Malice settled into the guest room quietly, taking in the man's sparse surroundings. He'd been here last a year ago, for a Thanksgiving dinner Baru had catered. It looked different now. No decorations. No food aromas, no music. Baru never married so there were no photographs of family vacations, or evidence of the extra touches that women brought to a home. Malice felt its emptiness.

Baru broke Malice's reflection. "My friend, I am so glad you are here. We have much to talk about. Come." Baru held his finger to his mouth to signal silence. He ushered Malice outside, and said, "Drive the rental. We can't be too careful. One never knows what we are capable of doing," he laughed. "Go to Fisherman's Wharf; I have a taste for the best crab cakes in three states. Then we talk."

Malice wasn't waiting. He started the conversation as soon as the car was out of Baru's driveway. "Another one has tripped, hasn't he?"

There was a slight lift of Baru's eyebrow. "Oh," is all he said.

Malice imagined the question that must have looped in his colleague's head. "Yes, I know, Baru. Zeus II. Babies injected. You were on that team. All those serial killers I studied in the field. I was out there doing research, wasn't I? Being used. So tell me. Is this one of them?"

Baru breathed heavily. He was ready to talk about the thirty-year old corpse, an unborn baby with sickle cell anemia, and their death by some unidentified poison. He was ready to tell that Christian Dingo had paid him a visit and the content of their discussion. He had rehearsed it all, but he wasn't ready for this.

Guilt settled in the lines on his sixty-three year old face and etched the furrows deeper. "Yes, I worked with Zeus II; was twenty-nine years old at the time. My mother and father were members of the original team. Can you imagine the reputation and expectations I had to live up to?"

Malice looked at Baru, affirming he had some idea. Truth was, he didn't care. "The question, Baru."

Baru looked tired. Malice considered he might be glad to share what he'd done with someone who would understand. Who knew the gravity of his sin.

"Only one in eighty ever killed. If it is, this one has exceeded the changes in all the others." Baru looked at Malice with a question of his own. "How did you learn of them; what do you know?"

"The field research. My team, Prometheus, used the chemical Zeus had found to try and recreate the physical features of people long since dead. The Re-imaging Process was successful; we tested it on the dead whose images we had on file. Naturally, we wondered if we could age the image to show what a person might look like now if they had died years before. We could. We could recreate and age, backwards and forwards, any person whose code dust we collected. I guess about that time, you all must have known your subjects were evolving into something you hadn't expected. Or maybe you knew all along.

"Anyway, Fawks called me in nine months ago and asked what I thought about studying the chemical composition in serial killers' brains. Before I knew it, I was on my way to correctional institutions all over the place, poking into the minds of people on a list given to me by Fawks."

"Obviously, you found something disturbing that led you to me," Baru added.

"It wasn't disturbing as much as it was strangely coincidental," Malice replied. "It wasn't until Berkowitz that I began to see the parallels. Each claimed to have heard some Spirit telling them what to do. Berkowitz said a 6000 year-old incubus invaded the neighbor's Labrador and commanded him to do evil. While in prison, he finds God and begins referring to himself, no longer as the Son of Sam, but the Son of Hope."

Malice kept going. "Each killer went after people he judged to be unclean. Berkowitz killed people who engaged in premarital sex. Another asshole killed college students because their GPAs were below 2.0: The Lethal Ivy Leaguer. Said the world had enough dumb-asses, no need to graduate them with permission to be stupid. Interestingly, all of our killers had sexual identity problems.

"In each case, there was a note describing who the killer thought himself to be. And now, we have the King of Peace."

Baru's fascination was obvious. "I still don't see how the empirical research led you to me."

Malice laughed a little out loud, as unexpected to him as it was to Baru. "You think I'm speculating?" His laugh went back to the place from which it had come, equally unexpected. Like a Jack-in-the-Box. "There was nothing empirical about it. It was the scientific data. I haven't figured out which ones we made, but I know we did." On that statement, Malice guided the car into one of several empty parking spaces at Fisherman's Wharf.

Inside, an older waitress, who looked like she'd served one plate more than her share today, showed Malice and Baru to a corner table near a window away from the main dining room. Neither spoke while waiting for their orders to arrive. Both looked at each other as if the features on the other's face marked the squares in a game of chess, each thinking the same question. 'How much does he know, and how much do I tell him'?

Their appetizers delivered, Baru dipped the oversized spoon into his clam chowder hurriedly. One would have thought he hadn't eaten in days, but fast was always his speed. Another quirk of his un-fulfilled genius. Baru reserved his time for analysis and contemplation. Eating was a wasteful necessity. Malice, on the other hand, stirred his seafood gumbo, releasing the aroma, savoring the rich tomato and basil broth on his senses.

Baru pushed the bowl aside and wiped his mouth. "Delicious," he professed with a half smile of satisfaction.

Malice wondered how he could tell, and went about spooning the bits of shrimp, clams, Italian sausage, rice, and okra into his mouth deliberately.

Baru rested his elbows on the table, leaned in, and stared one last time for a sign that Malice was bluffing. He didn't get it. Mechanically, he leaned back and the words came slowly from his lips. Shortly after, he fell into a rhythm of comfort and relief.

113

"It was 1968, fifteen years after the first discovery. Zeus had begun around 1952. Farming the re-imaging code in living people had not been perfected but they were close. They'd used brain damaged or paralyzed patients because there was less chance of pain or harm to the subject. Results were good.

Needless to say, there were curious whispers about whether they could harvest these genetic codes in living people and switch them. Whether the foreign code would override the native code, if they would blend to form something other than nature intended. They tested animals with no success whatsoever. Over time, studies suggested the younger the subject, the better results. No one dared speak such a thing, but it was too intriguing not to ponder.

"Fast forward twenty years. Zeus II worked under the theory that the code, at the right point of introduction, could reconfigure a person's physical structure.

"We experimented with adults. Like with the animals used in Zeus I, results were disastrous. In some patients, lips changed, the contour of the eye, the shape of the ears. But the changes were no more than might be achieved under cosmetic surgery but with less predictability. The team concluded the body had already received genetic instruction and held the blueprint in cellular memory."

Baru stopped to see Malice's reaction. There was nothing—not a glint nor a glaze. While grateful for the non-judgment, he was equally intimidated by Malice's calm. Baru pushed himself further into his chair and braced himself on its wooden arms. He was about to speak the unspeakable. His body stiffened as he rubbed the handle of his spoon between his fingers.

"Zeus II decided to test younger subjects, where the body's code might not be fixed. Like with older subjects, children were gotten from places they would not be

114

missed, not likely to live and no one to care if they didn't. Sadly, we had our pick of the poor things. The team conjectured that the optimum age for reassignment was eight years old.

As in most discoveries, we happened upon something we had not intended to find, and had no way of predicting. Mind you, the chemical caused death in older subjects. But it cured birth defects in young children and reversed any damage from premature delivery. Not only were the results phenomenal, they were permanent. They named the discovery Reju-8, it's code name: Solomon."

The biblical reference was not lost on Malice. King Solomon, thought the wisest man in the Bible, was said to have ordered a child cut in half when two women both claimed the child was hers. The real mother, rather than see the child killed, begged that he be given to the other woman. The sacrifice exposed the rightful mother and the child was returned to her.

Most people make that reference to King Solomon. But Zeus II was being more obscure. They were applying the proverb that said: "Train up a child in the way he should go; and when he is old, he will not depart from it." Malice searched his knowledge of King Solomon's proverbs and found another, more appropriate for Baru: "He that walks in integrity walks surely: but he that follows crooked ways shall be found out."

Fugama didn't stop to see if Malice understood. His words were like puke; they couldn't be stopped. "But even that wasn't far enough. Zeus II took the reassignment theory further still: to the womb."

Malice could no longer hide his disdain. This was why he was leaving the agency. But hearing it out loud made his skin crawl. He was sure Baru saw that reaction. There were limits to man's meddling into the mysteries of God.

At that moment, he wished his drink were something stronger. He cupped the glass of lemonade to his mouth and drank anyway.

"It had a disastrous side effect; something we discovered too late, or paid too little attention when it first observed. As the subjects aged, they demonstrated a greater propensity for violence. This was especially true when we introduced the female code into male subjects. Oddly, female babies could absorb the male code without difficulty.

Conversely, male babies with female code grew up to have sexual orientation conflict and tended to show more aggression towards girls. If adaptability is the criteria, the old debate about which gender is superior would be answered in a nanobyte if our findings were made public. We abandoned that testing after a few years."

Malice slid his empty glass and bowl to the end of the table for the waitress to collect. He wiped his mouth and laid his napkin over the bowl. "But, what you have out there now is different; isn't it?"

"Yes. We were able to keep tabs on most to study their progression. Unfortunately, some slipped through our system. Most of the boys showed early signs of deviant criminal behavior, some advanced to serial killer. That is how we recovered many of them, from incarceration. When I saw the clip on CNN a few weeks back, I knew this was one of ours, and whoever it is never showed up on our radar. This one skipped all the dysfunctional stages that put most in the legal system and went straight to the Mechisedec syndrome. We only know of three who came close to this level."

"Mechisedec?" Malice said, inflection in his voice for the first time, signaling a puzzle piece falling into place.

"Yes, Mechisedec." Baru confirmed. "That fool on CNN was someone we used to help us understand all the possible implications. We brought in top psychologists, physicians, and theologians under the guise that we were improving our profiling systems. A little preventive intelligence; apparently, the same thing you were told.

Interestingly, the work of the theologians eerily fit what was manifesting in our subjects. We attached the name Mechisedec to describe the behaviors. I guess the professor thought he'd use it to raise his stock. Guess it worked; he's now introduced as an expert on the influence of religion in serial killers."

Malice remembered the expert on CNN saying he had consulted with the FBI. He also knew that any future work with the Bureau was falling like a rock off Mount Everest.

Baru Fugama ended his story. "This one is different, Malice. He is advanced beyond anything we ever thought possible."

Chapter 40.

Yield to nothing earthly
Except in reverence to our Creator.
Fix your hands to pray on this.
And your feet to dance thanksgiving.

❧

Malice returned Baru to the empty Virginia mansion. The failed, unheralded god looked at Malice for some encouragement that their creation would be caught. He searched his own soul for assurance. There was nothing.

Malice studied Baru's face. He saw the question he'd been asking himself, saw on his own face since learning about Zeus. 'What will you do'? Having no answer, Malice reached for his satchel and handed Baru a plastic bag instead. "Do me a favor. Since I'm persona non-gratis, break this down to its chemical components for me." He heard the dictation in his voice and tempered it with his next statement. "Can you bring it home with you tonight?"

It was still a weakly veiled demand, but Baru could not refuse. He took the sample of root and stem and nodded with a quiet smile.

"There's no danger, Baru. This is not about Zeus," Malice said.

"No. It has to do with a long-dead corpse, possibly poisoned, and a fetus with sickle cell anemia," Baru admitted. "If that is so, I wouldn't say there's no danger." Baru glimpsed the split second of the unexpected on the younger man's face.

Baru snorted a quick, anxious laugh. "Truth is, I thought this was why you came in the first place." He read the questions as they flashed across Malice's eyes, and answered as best he could. "Christian paid me a visit. Handed me a report. I knew it was your work the minute I laid eyes on it. You have signatures in your statistical parameters; they are very subtle but I've learned to spot them. You ask the computer to do things in certain ways that many scientists don't even consider. It's the difference between producing a good drawing, and creating art. A simple brush stroke in the right place differentiates what hangs in a bowling alley and what graces the Musee du Louvre." Baru nodded approvingly. "Not many see that distinction. Just like few scientists know that even in science there is art. But you my boy…"

Malice let the corner of his lips turn up on one side of his face. Subconsciously, his head lowered. This was a compliment he hadn't seen coming. He acknowledged that he might be putting Baru in danger after all, a danger his colleague knowingly accepted.

"What is it you want to know?" Baru asked, easing Malice's concern.

"Compare the toxin in that report against the composition of the toxins in this plant. If they match, I want to know how much is lethal to humans, specifically a female her size. Here's a copy of the toxicology for comparison. While you're doing that, I've got some research to do of my own."

"I understand." Baru took the report, and as he turned to exit the car, looked back across his shoulder. "By the way, Chris said he was meeting with someone early the next morning who wanted this information. Whoever it was twisted Chris sideways. Only a few can do that. Watch yourself."

"Thanks, Baru." Malice was glad for the confirmation, but knew if Chris was involved, whomever he'd met that morning had juice. He'd already proven that.

Baru added, "One more thing. If it's any consolation, I still hear those babies cry."

Chapter 41.

"Doctor Benjamin Riley, please; Dr. Oran Mansell calling." The man's voice was soothing in Maggie's ear, like a flow of water over rocks worn smooth with time and patience. Hearing Dr. Riley was unavailable he asked the woman her name.

"I'm Margaret; but please, call me Maggie."

Maggie. In his head, little white worms squirmed in clusters and spilled. "Well, Margaret, I saw Dr. Riley's plea on the American Council of Counseling Psychology website; I'm calling to volunteer. Mansell is spelled like it sounds."

Throughout the conversation, to Maggie, Mansell's voice felt like an invitation to sleep in a meadow.

While he awaited Ben's call, Oran Mansell looked at the diplomas on the wall that greeted everyone who walked into the room. The afternoon dust-soaked rays of sunshine were like spotlights on the framed glass announcing the doctor's authority. BS: Biology, Yale. MS: Neuro-Psychology, MIT. PhD: Psychiatry, Boston University. There was one more but he bored of reading. Were it not for the cherub sconces spraying trailing plants that softened the space, these four great trumpets would have intimidated the meek.

While rummaging through the desk, he let the phone ring five times before he picked up. It was Ben Riley.

Hearing what he expected, Oran Mansell ended the call saying, "I can't promise any kind of schedule, but I want to be of service."

Ben processed the conversation after hanging up, and couldn't shake the feeling of a spider crawling down his spine. Despite the inviting quality in his tone, something in Mansell's voice reminded him of the day the storm had come.

Chapter 42.

Connor didn't like it and everyone within ultrasound range knew it. She had no power to do anything but curse. "Son-of-a-bitch!"

Ben pushed open the door to his office and found Connor clenching her teeth, crossing and uncrossing her arms. She gripped a sheet of paper in her left hand as if it had cursed her mother. She pushed the letter at him. "Did you know about this?"

Ben took the crumpled sheet and read across its folds and wrinkles. "No, but it doesn't warrant this reaction. So, another ADA gets the case; makes sense given Brooklyn may go to the bench. The DA's office has a strong case because of you."

"The case is circumstantial and you know it. But that's not the point. Not only will Brooklyn not try the case, she'll not even hear it."

"Connor, I don't get it. She's taking you with her so what's the attitude?"

Connor couldn't tell him that the letter meant she no longer had a reason to be near him. She palmed the back of her skirt and plopped into the chair.

"I guess I've gotten too close. Frankly, I think Purdue was just an angry husband in the right place at the wrong time." Connor stood, reached onto the desk and handed Ben an envelope. "This arrived a few minutes ago. All we need now is a suspect to go with the results."

When she had reached the door, Ben spoke. "This might be a bad time to ask, given your attitude right now, but I was hoping you'd go with me to Brooklyn's swearing-in party. Unless you have a date?"

Connor turned and stared at him blankly. "Excuse me?"

"It's not a date or anything. Just colleagues supporting a friend."

Connor knew he was asking because Brooklyn invited Dr. Able to escort her to the event. She had said Ben might ask her. 'Don't make me regret going against my policy'.

Connor let the surprise slide off her expertly made-up face. "Why on earth would I think it's a date? I can find my own way to Brooklyn's shindig; thank you."

"That's not the point, Connor. I just thought it'd be nice to hang out under different circumstances. Sorry if I offended you."

Connor leaned back on her high heels and shifted her weight. "I'm acting like a child, aren't I? I guess losing this case has me rattled.

"Rattle-snaked, I'd say," Ben replied.

Connor laughed. "Okay, to show there're no hard feelings, I'll pick you up. How's that?" In her heart, Connor was happy to have Ben by her side even if Brooklyn was the woman at the center of his offer.

"Okay, young lady. You're on." The grin still broad on his face, he fastened his eyes on Connor and chuckled.

"What's funny?"

Ben shook his head. "Girl, you are a wagon load of surprises. Hearing you curse was a major turn on."

Connor winked at him and closed the door behind her. On the other side, a smile of satisfaction filled her eyes and tickled her cheeks. Dr. Riley, you ain't seen nothing yet.

Ben looked at the envelope from the lab in Atlanta. He pulled the DNA analysis from the brown sheath, the first line told him what they already knew. Male. Caucasian. As he scanned further down, something nagged at him. It finally clicked. "I've seen these markers before."

Chapter 43.

The man the Press had dubbed Mechisedec pulled back the drape in his bedroom and looked out into a dark rainy night. He'd heard enough of the so-called experts analyze his actions, speculating what he'd do next. What do they know about me? About what I've done? He touched the window; the dampness cooled his fingertips.

My God,
No man may judge my actions.
As no man may judge You.
For this bold sin
Upon them be your admonition.

The chiseled young man with the deep, searching eyes peered through the dreariness. He allowed himself a memory—something he rarely did after performing what he called his service to God, and to the children he returned to their Father.

He'd begun with ex-convicts. Prison tattoos offered a perfect ruse, but the weather was equally effective. Into the conversation, he'd say, 'It doesn't matter what the sky is doing, it's the freedom to enjoy it that counts'. Freedom. Every convict savored that word as if every letter ha been chipped from diamond.

The real converts were the easiest; shame led them. When promised the mystery of life, the blood of God, each man went eagerly, never to be seen again. That's not entirely true. One's hands were nailed to the cross found in Virginia. Another's feet were in Florida.

Mechisedec listened to the rain drum against the window. Each drop slid slowly downward, joining all the drops that had come before it. He was one of them sent by God to cleanse the world.

My Lord, my God
Your Will is my will
My deed your Deed.
I am the Day Spring of your thoughts
And the Winter's breath of your resolution.
All are saved through surrender.

Mechisedec let the drape fall into place, and returned to his chair. The wind whirled hard, as if fighting the rain. He did not anticipate the darkness that swirled around him nor the visitor who entered his head.

We were friends who have grown distant from one another.

You made me choose.

So now, you cling firmly out of defiance to a cause, which you have seen through—and you call it 'loyalty'.

I have work to do.

Ah, this business of death. Everyone treats death as an important matter: but as of yet, death is not a festival. We do not accuse nature of immorality when it sends us a thunderstorm and makes us wet: why do we call the harmful man immoral?

Because God requires us to choose good over evil. Moral over the immoral.

All 'evil' acts are motivated by the drive to preservation. Is that not God's will for man?

A large branch fell to the ground outside, waking him from his trance. He blinked several times before picking up the newspaper. He read the four-day-old AP story on a woman's body that had washed up from the flood in Princeville. The white woman, possibly murdered over thirty years ago, and buried in a black cemetery, was still unidentified, according to the reporter. It went on to ask if anyone recognized the woman in the photo. Regina Bailey had offered her email address and phone number.

Mechisedec studied the face, and reread the story. Speaking in almost a whisper, he heard himself say, "Yes. Princeville."

Chapter 44.

The drive back to Greenville seemed unusually long. Everything Malice had learned in Virginia occupied his brain. Beginning with Fugam, ending with Carolina Jasmine. The equivalent of one baby aspirin was enough to kill. She'd ingested three times as much. Even if it was suicide, someone had to bury her. Unnoticed, unmarked, unmourned.

Fawks confessed that he had initiated Mistletoe, but 'someone in higher authority took over,' he'd said. A joint investigation with WAM and CIA.

Ways and Means was a clever euphemism for the secret warlords who ran IMIDD, both of which they had (ways and means). The International Medical Investigation and Defense Department had funded the research Fugama's parents had begun. Fawks' inquiry had dug up a name. Vincent Haiger.

Chris was equally revealing. Dressed in his signature jeans and pullover, a black beret covered most of his thick red hair. He rubbed a Q-Tip between his fingers. "Got your mail. Never expected a present from you."

"Well, it is almost Christmas. You'll know when to open it." Malice answered.

"What if I said I have an idea what it is?"

Knowing that Chris had seen his reports, and had intelligence from Charlene, little though it was, Malice smiled and said, "That would not surprise me." The smile waned. "But I doubt you'd be right."

The glide of their steps through the dry grass of the National Zoo marked their journey into secrets and lies. Holiday music swung from the empty branches of oak and cherry trees lining the sidewalks and somersaulted through the air.

"Could you do it, Chris?" Malice asked even as he knew their relationship was an unfortunate circumstance if that became his mission.

Chris looked at the crack in the sidewalk over which he stood. He slipped his hands casually into his leather jacket and retrieved his gloves. With the grace of a southern gentleman, he put them on, turned to the path nearest him and strolled away.

Malice watched Chris' confident stride, almost in rhythm to the instrumental melodies of *What Child is This*.

Chapter 45.

Oran Mansell stepped off the plane and looked around, deciding Greenville was as boring as he'd imagined. Arriving at the hotel within the twenty minutes the agent had promised, Mansell settled in and called Ben Riley's office. He got Maggie. Enthusiastically, she directed him to the restaurant she'd selected for his meeting with Ben.

Their orders placed, Ben began. "I got your vitae, Dr. Mansell. You're much younger than I expected."

"Good genes. But try getting a date when you're thirty-three and look twelve."

Ben laughed. "I have to admit I didn't know much about you until recently. I discussed your visit with the psychology professor at Greenville University, who has also volunteered. He looked at me like I'd blasphemed when I asked who you were. Reached in his bookshelf and handed me your book: *Phenomenal Character: the Link between Love and Crime*; demanded I read it before sitting in your presence. Fascinating stuff."

Dr. Mansell smiled. "I'm told that book is required reading in some psychology departments. I'm not sure I'm due the credit. The course on Intentionality at MIT formed the basis of those theories."

"Intentionality?"

"Yes. The doctrine of Intentionality suggests that what is characteristic of mental phenomena is the 'non-existence' of a peculiarity. Things like beliefs, desires, regrets. These peculiarities, when directed towards an object—like a person, place or thing—causes the individual to act upon that object in a particular way."

"I see."

Mansell continued. "These actions form our experiences. The essence of any experience is the feeling it generates, its phenomenal character. This phenomenal character is what I've spent years trying to understand and measure for its predictability."

"I'm not sure I see the connection."

"How a person feels about something and then acts upon it is at the heart of criminal behavior just as it is for love or hate."

"So you're saying a person in love is likely to act in the same way a criminal acts?"

"No, not necessarily in the same way, but acts from the same place. Therefore, the results can be exactly the same."

"I see," Ben said again. "Love has caused many people to kill or do serious bodily harm."

"Conversely, the criminal kills from some other passion, not love, and certainly not from love gone bad. The parallel is that a person does loving deeds because of the feelings that arise for the doer, or the positive effect it is expected to have on the recipient."

"So it is this feeling that the person in love shares with the serial criminal?"

127

"Exactly. A serial criminal does what he does because of the way it makes him feel."

"And that's why they have what we call signatures," Ben said, making connections. "They have to do the same thing, the same way, trying to get the same result."

"Nothing we know about the brain, external conditions, or theology, explain this mysterious capacity of the conscious mind to act upon nonexistent, non-materialistic characteristics. If we can understand that!"

Ben was hooked. His excitement danced like water in hot oil. He was getting the mental stretch he hadn't had since medical school. "What I took from the book, Doctor, is that crimes are committed based on how a person feels about a certain person or event happening to him or her. Even if the event happened years before, the feeling of the experience lingers always just below the surface. That feeling develops into a belief that causes the person to act upon it at some point in their lives. Is that right?"

"Congratulations, Dr. Riley. You have distilled 300 pages into the only few sentences worth reading. But while psychiatrists may not say much in practice, we can wrap ninety thousand words around a sentence, and a *great* work is born."

Ben grinned. "But that doesn't explain why the crime, itself, is committed. Everyone has belief systems. Everyone has feelings. They're what make us human. But not everyone kills or rapes or robs because of them."

"You're absolutely right. There is a single characteristic difference between the criminal and everyone else. Some say it's a cellular distinction found in the genes. Personally, I think any person can commit a crime. Biblically speaking, Cain killed Abel out of jealousy. He believed God favored his brother's offerings over his. If murder were in the genes, from where did it come? Adam and Eve were perfect beings from God's imagination."

Mansell watched Ben lean back in his chair. He had hit a nerve. "Understand, a crime can be anything society says it is. But some acts defy definition. One death, one rape, we can rationalize away. But those who do it repeatedly confound us. It raises fear of our primal nature. The book speaks to those repeated acts that exceed understanding.

"I know this is frightening stuff, Dr. Riley, but society wants to believe that these people are anomalies. How would we function otherwise? If the man next door, watering his yard at seven in the morning, becomes a psychopathic killer at night, what, then, about the person in bed next to us? About ourselves?"

"So, what is that characteristic that makes one a serial criminal, and the other the man next door?" Ben asked.

"Ah, now *that* is the question! In rare cases, it might be a chemical imbalance. But of the majority of subjects I've studied, the serial killer is the one who *likes* the way killing or raping *feels*. That feeling is generally triggered by a perceived violation of the person's belief system."

Mansell kept going. "The man who kills a parent because he's been abused begins his road to crime out of revenge, a protection mechanism. But then, something happens. He finds he likes the feeling of power it gives him. That act opens a door to the person that he always knew was there, but was afraid to name.

"In other cases, the trigger is a perception that the crime will enhance the person's ego in some way. The rapist, for example. In both cases, the crime is about power. More often, criminals start out protecting some deep vulnerability. But ultimately, all crime is about power. Power replaces vulnerability. Thereby, you have Intentionality. Acting in some way based on character qualities that exist only in the mind."

The conversation went on like that through dessert. It ended when Ben asked, "Doctor, have you followed the Mechisedec murders?"

Oran Mansell looked quizzically at Benjamin Riley. "I am familiar with them."

"What do you think triggered him?"

Oran Mansell sat back in his chair. After a very pregnant pause, he said, "Mechisedec, as he is called, is something else all together."

Chapter 46.

Vincent Haiger didn't bother to look at Christian Dingo. "I'm going to North Carolina. My niece is taking the bench. You'll come as a member of my staff."

"Meaning no disrespect, but I don't type."

"I understand you work for the Census Bureau, is that right?"

Dingo smirked. "That's what they tell me." Curiosity made him ask: "Is this a continuation of our previous conversation?"

"No. Doctor Able proved a complication but was never the issue. You'll be informed once I assess the situation. I'll expect resolution within twenty-four hours of your instructions."

When Dingo left, Haiger called William Pascal and spoke without introduction. "Tell me again what I'm walking into."

Pascal took a small breath. "Brooklyn is sworn in at eleven o'clock tomorrow morning. The Solder case has been passed off to a junior DA. He'll take his instructions from a supervisor with political ambition. He tends to bend the rules and doesn't let truth get in the way of justice. I'm sure I can direct him with the promise of funding his campaign. Since Brooklyn's familiar with the case, it's been reassigned to me."

Haiger smirked at the irony.

Pascal continued. "The trial begins next month. We have nothing to worry about." He didn't tell Haiger that he was looking at the latest newspaper story featuring an old drawing of Joy Marie with the headline "Who Is She?" It reminded him of the missing children on milk cartons, except no one had reported her missing. Now, thirty-three years later, she was on the front page, staring back at him. He heard his own breathing.

Since Pascal had stopped talking, Haiger assumed he was done and filled the empty space. "That's all good, William, but I'll decide if I have nothing to worry about." He finished the next sentence in his head. If I'm not satisfied, Christian Dingo needn't worry about typing.

Chapter 47.

Malice had called Ben, who called Lucas. The three met at the Coffee Cup. With the sketch filling half the front page, the need for secrecy was gone, but Malice preferred the privacy anyway. So did Ben.

"Maybe it's better this way," Lucas said. "If she was murdered, the killer will know she's back from the dead, and likely tip his hand."

Ben and Malice knew there was some truth in Lucas' rationale. No one ordered lunch, just coffee and apple pie. While they waited, Malice asked, "How are things going?"

"The mayor's a frog's hair from losing his mind," Lucas laughed. "Lord knows we need the help and supplies coming from everywhere, but every deed has its price."

Ben grunted in amusement. "Yep, the bitter with the sweet, huh, my man. They're killing you with kindness."

"I guess it wouldn't be so bad except they think they know what we need better than we do. Those are the ones spiking Lemley's ass. He cussed somebody out just the other day. Some man from 'I-know-best' city limits with a PhD from 'I'm White University' wearing an 'I love Negroes,' tee shirt got his ass kicked all the way back to good-god-damn."

Laughter burst across the room. "Speaking of 'good-god-damn,'" Ben said through catching his breath, "I think we're ready to move on the counseling program. Three of the eight who responded are white. I've talked with them, and they know they might have a little more difficulty getting people to open up. That aside, I have to tell you I'm surprised at the response. In fact, the last one to sign up is already in town. A heavyweight. Heads up the counseling program for the federal prison system, eastern region."

Malice reacted. "Prison system? Who is he?"

"Dr. Oran Mansell. We had dinner last night. I haven't been that impressed with anyone since meeting you."

"I know him." The reply, true to his habit, offered no clue about what Malice thought of the man, or how he knew Mansell.

"Yeah?" Ben inquired.

"We haven't met but we've talked by phone about some inmates I interviewed while doing research. You're right;

he's brilliant. His theory on criminal behavior is controversial, but provocative. I'm surprised he has time."

"Me too. But he said he needs to be here. I got no problem with a man getting what he needs."

"Yeah," Malice said, recognizing his own need to be in Princeville. He shifted the conversation by laying out data on the investigation. "We know how," he offered. "We also know the most likely reason why. Once you know why, the who becomes a matter of deduction."

Ben followed his cousin down Logos Avenue. "A white woman, pregnant by a black man thirty years ago, that's the most obvious why," he suggested.

"The most critical piece is no one reported her missing," Malice added. "Why not?" he asked, looking at Lucas.

"What if she didn't live around here?" Ben offered. "She could have been from another city, or another state for that matter."

"That's possible," Malice said. "But whoever buried her knew that cemetery. She was buried in a plot that someone knew wouldn't be disturbed."

"Then her lover must have done it," Ben followed. "A black person from around here would likely know that."

"Then I should have found some evidence of that. DNA was not the science it is now; people weren't concerned with what they left behind." Malice reached into his brief case and laid that report on the table. "The person whose hair I found was a close relative—a father, brother, uncle.

Lucas added, "Don't forget that casket didn't come from the economy room like the others."

Ben studied the report. "What I'm seeing doesn't rule out suicide, Malice. She could have arranged all this herself."

"Then why didn't *someone, anyone,* report her missing? Add to that, she was nearly full term. Why would a mother kill herself that close to giving birth?"

Looking from Ben to Malice, Lucas leaned back in his chair. "She knew her killer. But a family member?" All three knew statistics pointed to exactly that. Lucas challenged them further. "But what white person, especially back then, would know the cemetery that well?"

"I don't think one would," Malice replied.

"But we just said she was probably killed by a relative," Ben said. "And that person knew the cemetery."

Lucas, again, offered the most likely conclusion. "Whoever killed her had help; before, or after the fact."

That's my guess, too, Lucas," Malice shared. "I believe she came from a small family, perhaps they didn't get along; she likely held different views from the rest of them. Whether she was in love with the father or not, whether she sneaked around or flaunted it openly, she was having a black child. That news must have created major friction."

"But she was in the last days of the last trimester," Ben reminded. "Why kill her then?"

Lucas offered, "Maybe she thought she was safe and that's when she told them the truth. Maybe they wanted her to leave town, but she wouldn't."

"Yes," Malice agreed. "That's reasonable. They couldn't control her. Ends up a crime of passion."

"Does that tell us anything about the family?" Lucas asked. "Sounds like they were well off, and didn't want the scandal."

A small grunt muffled in Ben's throat. It could have been a chuckle had the words that followed not sounded so weary. "Lucas, you know as well as I do that all it has to say about them is that they're white. When it comes to blacks, hate is the great equalizer between rich white folk and poor ones."

"It may have had nothing to do with hate. In fact, I don't think it did," Malice rebutted. "At least not in the historical sense. You said yourself that a black person probably helped bury her. The killer's attitudes about blacks would be irrelevant."

"You're right," Ben agreed. "Besides, like Lucas said, the casket suggests wealth. We have to find out who she is. Once we know that, we'll likely find who killed her. And it now seems that he, or she, had an accomplice."

The three men silently agreed. Each pondered the implications of a black person being involved—someone who could still live in Princeville. Malice saw Lucas' discomfort that such a person could have shaken his hand and smiled in his face all these years. "There is no evidence that a black person participated in the murder. And it's only speculation that he participated after the fact," he offered.

Lucas appreciated Malice's effort but had to agree they were looking for two people, and one was from Princeville. "There weren't that many grave diggers back then. Maybe one of them will remember something. I'll check into that and call Regina Bailey. See if she's had any response from her story."

"Speaking of Regina Bailey, I thought we agreed to wait until Malice got back before releasing information," Ben admonished. "That may not have been the best move."

All eyes went to Lucas. "Wait a minute; don't look at me. Besides, the picture in the paper is not the one the artist did, or didn't you notice?"

Ben glanced through Malice's reports, ignoring Lucas' defense. He leaned in closer to the sheet with the symbols like Morse code, describing someone's code of life. He still didn't look up as he mumbled to himself, "Oh, my god."

"What is it," Malice asked.

"I got a DNA report on one of my cases. Raymond Solder was a black bisexual found murdered just after the storm. They have a suspect in custody whose wife was involved with Solder. The two men fought.

"Neither Connor nor I think the man they arrested is guilty, but there's nothing concrete linking anyone else. Anyway, we found strands of hair that suggest a white male was with Solder around the time of his death."

"So what does that report have to do with this one?" Malice inquired. He was glad for Ben's Reader's Digest version, but would have preferred a CNN brief.

"Unless my memory is blown to hell by all this, they're the same. Look at the fourteenth codon, the Glutamine protein. It caught my attention in the report."

Malice took the the report. "Yes, I noticed the high concentration of that amino acid. The lucky bastard probably never had an ulcer, heals quickly, sports a lush head of hair, and is mentally sharp. It's unusual, but not rare."

"But what are the odds of you finding it on a woman dead for over thirty years, and me finding it on a man killed a few months ago?"

"Are you saying Solder and this woman might have been killed by the same person?"

ᘓ

My Lord. I am in a place of great tribulation.
All are righteously grieved, save one.
To this one, I bring your salvation.
To all others, I bring your grace.

Chapter 48.

Connor arrived at Ben's house for their date to Brooklyn's affair. Night was already saying goodbye to a cool twelfth day of December. She carried a garment bag and small tote. Responding to the curious look on Ben's face, she said, "Don't worry; I'm not moving in. I ran out of time. You don't mind, right?"

"Only if I can watch," he teased.

"Ya know, men have never disappointed when it comes to a comment like that," she replied, and proceeded to fill his hands with her things. "Which way?"

Unsure how to interpret her statement, Ben thought it best to show Connor the bedroom, and put flirting back in the box.

Judge Pascal reserved the entire Magnolia Room and had it transformed for a black tie affair. A stiff, white linen table-cloth dressed each table. Tea-light candles sat inside crystal goblets surrounded by magnolias. Winter evergreen and red berries sprayed from the centerpieces. Huge Christmas wreaths, spilling silk magnolias and winterberries hung throughout, completed the majesty.

Malice had arrived promptly at six o'clock to escort Brooklyn to the Magnolia Room where she greeted the very first and last guest personally. The majority of them were her friends and colleagues: lawyers, prosecutors, judges, local politicians. High-profile business executives, politicians, and leading citizens shook her hand, kissed her cheek, and smiled approvingly at her appointment.

Brooklyn introduced Malice to people with whom she thought he'd enjoy conversing, her uncle being the first. Although the two men had never met, she felt reticence pass between them. Malice joked, "I have to be careful what I say; the Senator approves my salary." Both men laughed, each aware of the whole truth that hid within the half. She was relieved when Connor and Ben arrived. Her assistant looked like an Egyptian goddess in the sapphire blue silk dress. Every man's eyes followed her into the room. Brooklyn tried to place the man with them, but could not find him in memory.

Oran Mansell kissed Brooklyn's hand. You bring elegance to the bench," he said.

Brooklyn blushed, unsure why, and politely withdrew her hand.

The pleasantries done, Ben ushered Mansell and Malice to a quiet spot near the balcony. "Doctor Mansell, Doctor Able and I are working on an unsolved murder in Princeville. The body washed up with the storm, literally. Perhaps you can help us profile the killer."

"I'm intrigued. But I don't think I can be of much use."

Malice spoke. "Doctor, we have reason to believe the killer is still in the area. We found a hair on the body with the same DNA as a hair found in a case Dr. Riley is working on now. That means whoever killed the Princeville Princess may have killed Ben's victim. It seems fate has bought the best criminal psychiatrist in the country to Greenville. Perhaps for this very reason."

Ben's skin tingled. It was the first time a moniker had been used in any local case that he could remember. 'Princeville Princess'. He liked it. He had never been in the midst of forensic intelligence to match what was standing beside him, and would never be again. A surge of blood coursed though his body and settled in his pants. No one noticed him shift. He'd always thought a hard-on for work was a figure of speech. He rationalized his arousal being caused by secretly watching Connor undress, and redress for this evening. Maybe it was from watching Brooklyn, and imagining the possibilities if he were taking her home tonight. He glanced in her direction.

The skin on Oran Mansell's forehead slid upward. "It seems we are at an inimitable intersection of time and fate. Intriguing. Let's meet tomorrow morning."

Malice kept an eye on Senator Haiger, whose combination of down-home boy and sophisticated politician was masterful. He first excused himself from this conversation, but, remembering Fawks' revelation, he said to Mansell, "On second thought, let me introduce you to the senator."

While the men shared murder and mystery, Connor and Brooklyn shared news of their own. Aside from her mother, Connor was the only person in the room to whom Brooklyn could show her excitement. Everyone else saw the paragon that made her appointment a foregone conclusion. She said, to her clerk, "Something about Dr. Mansell bothers me."

"Yes, I had the same reaction," Connnor replied. "According to Ben, the man's a mahatma."

"Yes, I've heard of him; speaking of which, how are things going with Ben?"

Connor smiled. "Thanks for making this possible. Working with him was great. This evening I made sure he got a glimpse of what he's missing."

"What did you do?"

"I changed at his place." Her smile broadened. "I arranged to pick him up. Took this dress and a travel bag of makeup and stuff. Made sure he saw me in the shower."

"Oh, my god!"

"I left the towel he gave me in the spare bedroom so he'd have to bring it to me. I knew he'd hang around to watch. He is a man, after all. Hag Ragnell could walk by, and a man would wonder what she looked like underneath her warts. I glimpsed him down the hall in the kitchen. So, when I entered the bedroom, I left the door cracked, and dipped the towel low in the back like I was dropping it, before I moved out of view."

"Oh, you hussy!"

"Nothing happened. I got dressed, and so did he. When I met him in the living room, the look in his eyes had changed."

"Was it the look you wanted?"

Connor smiled. "What do you think?"

"Girl, I am scared of you." Brooklyn fanned at Connor's arm.

"By tomorrow morning, he will be too, but in a real gooood way." Connor looked to where Ben stood laughing with Malice, Mansell, and Haiger. She stared at Ben until he looked her way and smiled at him when he did. After a five-second stare, which she mentally counted, she lowered her head, and returned her attention to Brooklyn, who was shaking her head. "Just tilling the soil, sister, tilling the soil. But enough about me. Tell me about that gorgeous Doctor Able. He's smart, mysterious, and sexy as hell."

Brooklyn looked at Malice with reserved appreciation. His skin was the color of Carolina clay, rich with iron and warmed by a copper glaze. She liked the way it glowed in the candlelight, the playful, slow curl of his hair. "Yes, he is, isn't he?"

"The man should rule a country," Connor added.

All attention was diverted when Judge Pascal clicked his glass at the dais. He began by stretching open hands in Brooklyn's direction. The room responded in applause. Before the accolades faded, he began a short speech filled with pride. When done, he walked down and escorted Brooklyn to the podium. There, Senator Haiger met them, draped his niece in a flowing black robe, and led her to face more rousing applause.

Brooklyn looked confidently at the audience of friends, family, colleagues, and honored guests. She opened her mouth and said, "Starting tomorrow, unless you're a lawyer, don't let me see any of you before me when I'm dressed liked this."

The room erupted in laughter. Brooklyn hugged one of the men who had orchestrated her position to the bench, and shook hands with the other. She smiled warmly at the look of satisfaction on both their faces.

Chapter 49.

Connor dropped Doctor Mansell off at his hotel. As she steered the car onto Ben's street, she felt him watching her. With the car in the driveway, and the motor off, she said, "I'll just be a minute collecting my things."

"No, stay for coffee. I'll feel better knowing you're driving fully awake."

Connor hesitated before accepting. "Thanks, that's very sweet. You make the coffee, and I'll pack my stuff."

While the coffee brewed, Ben took off his jacket, and put a CD on the stereo that played low in the background.

Connor ambled into the living room with her overnight bag about the same time as Ben entered with the tray. She put the bag by the door and joined him on the sofa.

The aroma filled the room and mingled with the wounded songbird. Iambic sips of the hot liquid pooled on their tongues and warmed a path downward. The combination of masculine piano notes and feminine vocals telling a story of love lost gave them both a moment of pause, made them notice each other. Connor knew she had to let

Ben take the lead. To be the aggressor at this moment would ruin everything she'd built between them.

Ben set his cup on the table. "The reception was great, wasn't it?"

"Perfect."

Once he'd begun, comfort rested Ben's shoulders, and left again as he confessed he wished his life had been different. "I'm doing exactly what I want to do; I just never expected boredom. Lately, I wish some of them had died under some bizarre circumstance. Anything but a knife or a gun... Sounds morbid, huh?"

"Not at all," she answered. "You need to be challenged. Greenville hasn't provided that; I'm not sure that it can."

Ben picked up his cup and sipped—as if he'd said something he should wash from his mouth. It was the taste of regret. Some of envy. But mostly of acceptance that this was his life and he chose it.

As the melodies played softly around them, Connor reached over and gently squeezed his hand. Ben squeezed back. When the song ended, Connor let go his fingers. In a low voice, she said, "Thanks, I had a wonderful evening. But tomorrow, everything changes."

Ben followed her to the door. As Connor bent to pick up her bag, he took her hand and held it. Connor looked at him and saw what she had hoped one day to see. She heard him speak two simple words that made her heart grow in her chest. 'Don't go'.

Ben gently pulled Connor to him. When she was near, he stepped towards her, his mouth slightly open. He leaned down the six-inch distance between them, and kissed her. When she opened her eyes, and looked again into his for a clue, something to tell her what to do, she didn't see sadness, but want. Was it for her or something else—someone else—he couldn't have?

142

Ben put his arm around her back, and pressed the flat of his palm against the midnight blue chiffon until he could feel its softness through his shirt. He kissed her deeply. When he let her go, all her questions had vanished. Ben led her to the guest room where she had dressed hours before. A small nightlight cast a soft glow upon everything, creating more shadow than form. The music from the living room trailed throughout the house in search of them. Found them, in each other's arms.

Ben filled his mouth with her lips, as her perfume filled his nostrils, as her soft flesh filled his hands. When he stopped, Connor could not open her eyes, would not for fear the sensation inside her would escape. Or, that there would be something different in him she prayed not to see. She felt the smooth zipper of her dress quietly separate, releasing her body from its hold, and fall softly to the floor. A black bustier pushed the mounds of her breasts up, forming a deep cleavage into which Ben laid his kisses.

The breath Connor had held escaped in a gasp. Her hands cupped the head of this man who went in search of the hardening bump pushing against her bra—as much in need of his mouth as he was in search of it. With expert hands, he unhooked the spandex that separated his mouth from her hardened nipples. The warmth of his tongue, the firmness of his lips upon her breast softened her knees. Ben gathered her in his arms and laid her on the bed behind him.

Connor opened her eyes to see him joining her nakedness. The nightlight illuminated Ben's strong body and, yet, made him appear gentle, unsure. The room filled with the scent of passion; heat absorbed her.

Ben knelt at Connor's feet and kissed them, letting his tongue play on her ankles. His hands went upward, smoothing a path, clearing the way for his kisses. The soft flesh of her thighs made him speak, forced him to acknowledge her beauty. Made him go forth eagerly to the nest that held a single beaded jewel as its treasure.

The giant shadows of their mingled bodies moved when they moved, emulated every touch, repeated every grip of fingers upon flesh. As if possessed by the unspoken pain in the music, of a woman in search of something to fill her, Ben let his body rest on top of Connor, allowed her to feel his weight, then introduced himself as man to woman.

Connor held her breath beneath him. The weight of all his fears covered her. She let go her care of who or what Ben might need, and gave permission to every touch, voice to every sensation. Allowed herself to be the vale in which he sought solace.

Ben tilted himself, inviting her to take, to give. To search, to kiss, fondle, to find. And was excited by Connor's quest to know him. She touched him, loved him, found his weakness. When he could take no more, he called her name as if it freed him.

Chapter 50.

The day started with a cup of coffee for four people in different parts of the city. Each pondered today and how to control its events: Judge William Pascal and the trial. Senator Vincent Haiger and his past. Brooklyn Beaudeau and her new responsibility. Malice Able and the man called Mechisedec. Each about to permanently impact the other.

Malice called Lucas and invited him to sit in on the meeting with Dr. Mansell. "Can you get a hold of Ms. Mava? It's time we revisit her dream."

"Looks like Aunt Mava already knew; she called me last night. Wants to see us this evening. Does that work for you?"

"Perfect."

ਙ

Vincent Haiger made a similar call. To Christian Dingo. When he hung up the phone, he replayed the conversation he'd had with Pascal before going to Brooklyn's party last evening.

"Talk to me," Haiger had said in Pascal's chamber.

Pascal had gone to the window. Looked out onto a bleak December evening. The dampness from the hurricane lingered. "That storm set so many things in motion: Able's arrival in town, Brooklyn's appointment, this meeting... so much dread." He sighed heavily, and spoke just audibly enough for Haiger to hear him, as if speaking to the clouds that rolled slowly toward goodnight.

"Have you ever wondered what your life would have been had that day never happened, Vincent?" It was a rhetorical question. "I don't think I would have gone into law. It's possible I did so that I could mete out the justice Joy Marie never got. If anyone ever looked at my record, I wonder what they'd find?" Pascal half laughed, "I might get someone to do that; I'd be interested in seeing how this whole thing might have affected my judgments."

Pascal faced his co-conspirator. "I've never been able to talk to anyone. Not like this." He looked hard at Haiger. "I'm not losing it, Vincent. Just remembering my sister. Wondering what her life would have been like, too, wondering about the child she never got to see—your child."

The weight of his words must have been more than he could stand. Pascal took a side chair across from Haiger. He continued talking, his words losing themselves in the

145

deep Persian rug. "You were a good lawyer, Vincent; who became a good senator. If any good came from what I did, I guess your life is the best result." William Pascal spent a few moments tapping the side of the chair with his palm.

"Times were different then. Had I confessed, I probably wouldn't have seen a jail cell, much less prison. Joy Marie was an embarrassment. No one would have blamed me for what I did. But it would have been different for you, wouldn't it? You could have been charged with her murder, and become as much a victim as Joy Marie, especially after you beat my ass senseless when you learned what I'd done."

Pascal stopped talking. The look on his face was a question forming for the first time. Why hadn't he blamed Vincent? As quickly as it came, he dismissed the thought to youthful arrogance and fear.

Pascal filled the lungs that lay flat against his ribcage. A memory made him smile. "Did she tell you about the time she tied me up and left me in a kudzu patch? She was my kid sister, but had ten years more nerve." His smile widened. "I was no bigger than a canker worm. Cried my eyes dry and no one heard me." The smile left him. "When mother and daddy died, I sold that patch of kudzu."

William Pascal returned to the window with one more memory he didn't share. Outside, streetlights ad begun their first warm radiance, not yet fully aglow.

Haiger's reflection ended with a knock at his suite. His assistant announced Christian Dingo. Only after the door had closed did Haiger speak. "I hope you were not too disappointed being left behind last night."

Dingo didn't respond. Just as well. Haiger couldn't care less how he'd spent the evening.

146

"Looks like you get to do what you do," Haiger said. "Discretion is crucial."

Dingo replied, "It always is, Senator."

The remark did not faze the man who was about to order murder as if it were on the breakfast menu. He slid a copy of the morning paper to Dingo and tapped the face of the man holding his niece's hand. "Self-infliction. Tonight."

Chris studied the photograph. The caption underneath identified the man as Judge William Henry Pascal. "Tonight doesn't give me enough time for research. Is there any reason he'd commit suicide?"

"Don't worry about that. An envelope will arrive at your suite this afternoon."

With Christian gone, Haiger recalled the last of his evening with Pascal. The part where William repeated murdering his own nephew in the womb. My son, Haiger thought to himself. The first time Haiger heard the story, William Pascal explained it as a misfortunate natural event. This time, the words came out differently.

"She loved the smell of gardenia," Pascal had recited, "I placed one on her plate. She'd always cut a bloom for her room. The day before, I shaved the root of the yellow jasmine into slivers, dried them in the oven. I ground it with fresh peppermint and mixed it in her salad. I watched her turn into potter's clay, then propped her on the settee like she was sleeping. I sat on the hassock she kept there to elevate her feet so they wouldn't swell. I rocked that settee until the rooster's evening crow."

Haiger breathed deeply, in part to clear his head, but more to stop the emotions stirred by his part in the death of his only child and the first love he had known. His efforts were futile. His own memory of that day came like an

147

echo from a deep, deep well. How, in exhilaration, he had confided to Raymond Solder that he would be a father, and on the same day learned that Joy Marie loving him had nothing to do with her death. How he hated William Pascal from that day to this. Now, after thirty years, that secret had claimed Raymond's life too. And in a few hours, it would claim another.

Chapter 51.

Calvin delivered a cart full of breakfast foods and scattered them across the large vinyl-covered table. Eggs, toast, bacon, dollar pancakes, jelly, butter, hash browns, orange juice, and coffee. Oran Mansell's expression was the same as everyone who sat at the Coffee Cup for the first time. Succumbing to the aromatic assault, Mansell heaped his plate as he listened to Ben, Malice, and Lucas recite data on the Princeville Princess. While one talked the others buried the blades of their knives into perfectly browned link sausage, or swirled white mushroom gravy into grits.

At the right time, Malice spread out a set of index cards. "Here's what we believe about the suspect: He's a relative. They share genetic markers. He's still alive and has possibly killed again." He went through the cards until he'd laid out seven yellow 3x5s.

Mansell pushed his plate aside and studied the cards. "I agree that he was acquainted with the victim. She trusted him. It's interesting that he chose poison. It's not a method that comes from passion but forethought. Killing her was not personal for him, but a necessary evil. The pregnancy did not affect his decision. Poison is generally a woman's method of death. I'd venture to say he has sexual identity issues. He's particular about his appearance, well-groomed, very neat and works in a profession that affords him a display of power."

Ben condensed Mansell's profile. "So, we're looking for a white, middle-aged, G-Q, closet homosexual who can thump his Armani covered chest and back it up?"

"You have a knack for summations, doctor," Mansell said. "What I find interesting is that he has killed again, after thirty years. Or he's killed before and more carefully covered his tracks. Tell me about the case with the matching DNA."

When Ben was done, Mansell confirmed. "Your guy is definitely homosexual, a cross-dresser, I suspect. This killing was personal, and passionate. He used a knife. Not at all the same motivation as with the woman. He knew this victim intimately."

Lucas asked Mansell one last question. "How could he kill an unborn child? Those little bones..."

Mansell's whole body shook. "Are you telling me the child died with her?"

Ben answered. "I guess we didn't make that clear."

Each at the table thought he understood Mansell's reaction. Each had had an emotional response to learning a child was killed in its mother's womb.

&#x0G8;

While Ben, Lucas, and Malice laid out the two cases to Mansell, Connor sat alone in Brooklyn's new office. It was a lot like the old one, only larger, with tasteful wallpaper and matching paint. The sofa and recliners from her old place fit beautifully with the decor. Connor tried but couldn't concentrate on the file that lay on her lap. She stood and looked at her reflection in the full-length mirror. An angel pin sat quietly in prayer above her heart. She'd hesitated when picking it out, but decided it was appropriate—a symbol of her gratitude for last night. In the quiet space, she relived everything, including waking up beside Ben this morning. She could feel her skin glow beneath the leather skirt. Connor returned to the sofa and laid her head on its arm, wrapping herself in angora and afterglow. The door opened.

"Sleeping your first day on the job?"

Blushing, Connor found herself deciding between telling the truth and a lie of omission. She settled on a little of both. "Good morning. Just holding onto the memory of last night, your Honor. It was magical," she smiled.

Brooklyn studied her new law clerk. "What is it? Something's changed."

"You bet your ass," she teased. "I now work for a judge!" Connor could not speak of her evening with Ben for fear what was happening between them would crumble once it passed her lips.

"That's right, Miss Thang, so a little decorum, please."

"I'm sorry. Won't happen again." Connor walked over to Brooklyn, and hugged her tightly. "This is so wonderful. You're gonna be a great judge; I'll see to it."

ʘ

Outside the Coffee Cup, Ben couldn't help himself. "How'd things go last night?"

Malice heard Ben's real question. "I was just an escort, man."

"She looked great, didn't she?" Ben said.

"Yes, she did." Malice searched for more reassurance he could offer. "We had a nightcap, talked about her giving up the Solder case. She's worried about her performance as a judge. I listened, encouraged her, went home."

Malice held onto the car door before getting in. "Connor's a beautiful woman. Brooklyn speaks highly of her." Malice noticed a change in Ben's demeanor. "What happened with you two?"

"I'm not sure, man."

Malice waited for Ben to explain the guilt that made his words linger like fog. Finally, Malice patted his cousin's shoulder. "Let's have a drink before seeing Ms. Pelter."

"Can't make it, but I'll take you up on that drink."

Malice paused. "I've decided to tell."

A huge smile took over Ben's face. "Then count me in. I wouldn't miss seeing Aunt Rae's face if Solder's killer walked into my office with a confession tattooed on his ass."

Chapter 52.

Judge Pascal took the bench. In his mind, he heard roaring water. He looked up to see Oran Mansell seated in the back. Something in the man's presence at the party caught his attention long before Ben introduced them. It was more than the odd combination of youthfulness draped in wisdom that comes only with experience. As Ben recited Mansell's credentials the night before, and why he was in town, Pascal had had a brief moment of recognition, not of the man himself, but of something unknown, un-named. It was why he'd invited him to coffee.

As Judge Pascal expected, the attorney for Thalamus Purdue argued against a continuance. "The State has failed to produce any substantial evidence and is unfairly keeping my client incarcerated while it tries to meet its burden," she stressed.

The new prosecutor argued that he had just gotten the case and needed more time to prepare.

The Defense rebounded. "My client has been a prisoner of the state for three months. He's been treated like a tin of fruitcake."

The prosecutor reacted. "The State has accused Mr. Purdue of a brutal murder. If my colleague wants 'A Christmas Carol' ending, she should catch the afternoon matinee."

The court ruled. "The State will not hold Mr. Purdue hostage while it looks for evidence against him." He ordered bail; the trial would stay on scheduled.

In chamber, Pascal removed his robe and thanked Oran Mansell for coming. "I didn't expect to see you in my courtroom. What did you think?"

"Lively repartee. Those two will make for an entertaining trial."

"The State's evidence is circumstantial, I will not keep a man from his family through the holiday because we think he did it."

"Are you defending your decision?" Mansell took the cup of coffee Pascal handed him, and sat in the side chair near the window. "As the prosecutor pointed out, the Grand Jury found enough evidence to bind the defendant. Less evidence than I heard in this case has convicted people of far lesser crimes, and the accused don't usually get a holiday pass."

Pascal reconsidered this exploration. He could not offer innocence as explanation for his decision. "Tell me about your work, your role in the System. By the way, offering to counsel the people of Princeville is laudable."

"Thank you. But I'm being selfish. My work has forced me to Princeville. The short of it—like you—my judgments change lives. I've studied criminal behavior. Talked with them, profiled them, helped some, and been shaken to my very soul by others. I've seen things in the criminal mind that, if people knew existed, parole would cease to exist. In fact, we'd institute mandatory execution immediately after sentencing." Mansell let that comment sink in. "So, you see, helping Princeville is my therapy."

"What have you learned about criminals, Doctor? Tell me about the ones you've redeemed."

So, we get to the heart of the matter, Mansell thought. He sipped his coffee while considering the question. He looked at Pascal, whose personal appearance matched the room. Everything in place, hair meticulously combed, manicured nails. One thing stood out. His tie. It announced a man who skirted the edges hiding behind stoic conservatism. It had color, lots of it, splashes of chaos that attracted rather than repelled.

Mansell set the cup heavily onto the saucer to alter the desperation in the room. He went to the window and looked out on a bright December morning. He studied the view, and pulled the vertical blinds until he shifted the light, changing the feel of the room from morning bright to subdued. As the blinds danced and swayed, finding a resting place, Mansell leaned against the wall and put his hands into the pockets of his Brooks Brothers suit. He repeated Pascal's question. "The ones I've redeemed?"

"Yes. Redemption? Is there such a thing?" Pascal asked,

Mansell paused. "Every criminal I've ever met had a moment in their lives that, if they could, they'd live in that moment forever. They remember it with profound clarity. In every set of eyes, I see a longing to have that moment once more."

Mansell studied Pascal's eyes. He had not connected yet with Pascal's sin as he had with Ben's.

"Oddly enough, they don't envision tomorrow. There is only today and yesterday. So they go back in search of what many of us hope for in our future. Happiness... good fortune... love. That moment never involves material things or even satisfaction with their crimes. It's something a parent did or said that made him feel like he was the only thing in the world that mattered. If it wasn't a parent, it was someone whose attention and approval mattered. Every one of them can recite every word, recall every smell, every sensation attached to that moment."

Pascal shifted in his chair. It was the signal Mansell needed. "Just imagine. For one moment, you felt like you belonged, that you mattered. That someone had seen into your heart and loved what was there. At that moment, it's as if you felt the kiss of God, Himself."

Mansell had disturbed Pascal's soul as much as the darkened room disturbed his mood. He wasn't sure which caused him to go to the window. Absently, Pascal took the corded string in his hand and pulled it harshly, letting the light flood back in. He stared into the park.

Mansell finished. "*That moment* is redemption. I believe it is why so many turn to God in prison: the promise of unconditional love."

Deep in thought, Pascal did not hear Mansell leave. He thought to himself, if I could take it all back, would I be happy again? He tried to find that moment he'd return to if he could. His mind searched through time like a bee through a meadow, buzzing the tops of several moments, and brushing the boundaries of others. But it never landed.

Pascal sat at his desk and clicked on the word processor of his computer. His fingers tapped lightly on the keyboard for less than a minute. He stared at the lines on the screen far longer than it took him to type them. He clicked the mouse and the printer quietly slid forth a sheet of paper.

Pascal opened his desk drawer and withdrew a sheet of five labels he'd produced some time ago. Only two were left. He affixed one to an envelope with no return address. He inserted the printed page then sealed it. On his way to the courtroom, he stopped at the postal slot. He looked at the name on the label one last time and dropped it into the same slot as the three he had mailed before. It would reach Regina Bailey tomorrow morning.

Chapter 53.

Chris Dingo picked up an envelope that had been slid underneath his hotel door. There was nothing descriptive about it; his name did not even appear. He tossed the manila onto the oversized coffee table while he finished preparations that would end a man's life. He'd already checked locations and done surveillance on traffic flow to ensure, as best he could, that there would be no surprises.

Shortly, he reached for the envelope that would tell him why. From that, he'd decide how. Before handling the contents of the envelope, Dingo put on a pair of gloves made to his specifications. He wasn't hiding fingerprints; his would not show up in a database anywhere. They offered the protection of latex, the comfort and the flexibility of lambskin, and wouldn't disturb anything already there. Only two other pair existed in the world, and he owned them, too.

Chapter 54.

Oran Mansell charmed Vanessa to regain entry into the judge's chamber. He sat at Pascal's desk and touched things, trying to intuit an energy that would reveal what he wanted to know. He looked at the computer but decided it wouldn't yield much. He opened the desk drawers, all of them, and looked from one to the other at what lay on top. In the center drawer were newspaper articles, all of them about Princeville's flood. The photograph with the caskets, like unborn children in the fluid of a troubled womb, was on top. In another drawer was a strip of labels with one left addressed to Regina Bailey at *The Rocky Mount Tribune.*

He studied the newspaper articles. The casket photograph, compelling though it was, was not the latest story, and yet it was on top. Most were written by Regina Bailey, who focused on the personal impact of the storm. The most recent story included a picture of a woman with the caption "Who Is She?" He stared at the beautiful young woman with the wide grin that made him smile for just a second.

Mansell put everything back in place and went to the window where Pascal had spent most of their earlier visit. He looked out upon a small park where many of the court employees likely had their lunch. No doubt to air the stench of depravity from their clothes. The trees were brown and empty except for a spruce that had been decorated for Christmas. Several dozen Poinsettias circled the park's boundaries and peeked from the spaces between green shrubs. A life-size electronic angel opened and closed her arms in Mansell's direction. Its head would bow in prayer.

Mansell did not turn around when the door behind him creaked open, and closed. "I'm sure his Honor is not surprised to see me." When Pascal had hung his robe and gone to his desk, Mansell turned. "We have more to discuss. Yes?"

Pascal pressed the intercom button on his telephone. "Vanessa, you can go now, it's been a long day." He listened as his secretary made the appropriate resistance and reluctantly acquiesce. "Good night, Vanessa." He waited until he heard the deadbolt fall into place before releasing the button.

"Anything you say will remain in this room," Mansell assured him.

When Pascal had sat down, with no response, the doctor pushed further. "Interesting view." Mansell resumed the stance he'd had earlier in the day, his back pressed against the wall, legs crossed at the ankle, hands in his pockets. His body language said I am no threat to you. Trust me. His melodic voice, the one that made people tell him their deepest secrets, said, "Tell me about Joy Marie."

Heavy-hearted relief showed on Pascal's face; a tear fell across his cheek.

In your darkest hour, cry.
I am the arms that cradle your pain.
The keeper of your fear.
Your servant, your Lord.

Chapter 55.

Dingo followed Pascal from his office. He'd waited outside the judicial complex in his borrowed car for hours. The owner wouldn't find it missing until she left work hours from now. If all went well, she'd not miss it at all. Dingo did not know the dark haired man who emerged with Pascal and patted his shoulder as they parted company.

Earlier in the day, he'd driven in another borrowed car to Pascal's homestead to study the house while waiting for the brown envelope. The wraparound had been restored to the period in which it was built, but with modern luxuries that did not interfere with the art and pride of craftsmanship that had been forsaken for contemporary idealism in too many southern structures since then. For a moment, it felt like home.

Bypassing the standard security, once inside, Dingo had found Pascal's method of suicide. A drawer full of every sleep prescription available made it obvious. Haiger's note provided clear motive. As he combed the house, he found a set of house keys that didn't fit any door on the premises. He made impressions of each one for reproduction.

Dingo parked the stolen car in a cluster of trees off the main road. Within minutes, Pascal was out again and got into an SUV. Dingo quickly assessed whether he should wait for Pascal to return, or keep him in sight. He decided to follow. Pascal traveled down a rental district of neatly kept houses and eventually stopped. Dingo passed by and parked in a grove of darkness. The house Pascal entered was similar to all the ones they'd just passed, only nicer. Dingo put on a pair of night shades that washed everything in green. He quietly approached the house and thought of picking the lock, but tried the set of keys he'd made instead. One of them fit.

Dingo crept through the house until he found Pascal in a bedroom, undressing. Various articles of underwear lay on the bed. An attractive dress hung on the door. Dingo expected to see a woman wearing nothing come from the bathroom any minute. He cursed, thinking Pascal could be here all night. The man was slumming, getting ghetto popped –and–obviously had it on lockdown since he could come and go as he pleased. The idea had not fully formed in Dingo's brain when he saw Pascal pick up the panties and put them on. *Oh fuck* echoed in Dingo's brain. He crept outside to think.

Minutes passed as Dingo played scenarios of how Pascal should die now since he could not predict what might happen next. Within those minutes he cursed Haiger. Still, an aging, cross-dressing federal judge made for a good suicide. Ultimately, he went with the original plan—death by overdose—distraught over killing his sister all those years ago, pretending to be her, and killing her all over again. Given the pharmacy of drugs at the primary house, Dingo was certain there was a bottle of something here. Now the question was, did he do it here, or wait for Pascal to return home? Who would look for him here? Was he meeting someone? Surely, the SUV had a tracking device. When Pascal didn't show up for work, his secretary would alert the police. It was settled. Pascal would meet his Maker in this backwoods tenement.

Dingo went back to the house. From what he could tell in the low light, Pascal had made tea and was watching an old home movie of a birthday party. The phone rang; he heard Pascal give directions. Dingo had to rethink his plan once more. *Dammit, Haiger. This is why I do it my way in my time.* He decided it was too risky to kill him now. Besides, Pascal meeting someone dressed as a woman tweaked his curiosity. He settled in to wait.

A knock on the door came ten minutes later. From his view, Dingo only glimpsed the visitor when he, or she, crossed the room. It first appeared to be a woman in a hooded floor-length coat. He changed his mind when the visitor said, "Hello, William." He guessed the man was a priest of some Order he did not recognize. The priest entered with a tote-size container in each hand. *Maybe he's come with sacrament to relieve Pascal's guilt.*

"You don't seem surprised," Pascal said, as he clicked the pause button on the remote.

"This is why she died. To protect my secret," Pascal continued. "What do I do? Please help me sort this out. Seeing her, that box—floating in the photograph… She wants justice."

Pascal went on to tell an intricate story of sex and murder. At some point, Dingo took a Q-Tip from his pocket and swabbed the outside of his ear. He had just heard Pascal's latest secret: that he had killed Raymond Solder, and why. Dingo imagined the look on Pascal's face. Contorted in pain and confusion. But Pascal's words came from a place devoid of passion, empty of life. Remorse should have floated through his story like ghosts, but it didn't. He just sounded tired.

The priest spoke. "You want salvation. To know that God forgives?"

Dingo heard no reply, the lustrous brown wig did not move. But he imagined the woman Pascal had become was weeping. He did hear the priest open a container and invite the man in the beautiful dress to drink.

"This is the Blood of God."

Pascal must have done as he was told. He breathed heavily, like the sound of moss caught in an aged cypress tree. Next, the cleric laid Pascal on the floor. Absolution had begun.

> My God, I am your Servant
> Gatekeeper to your Mercy
> By my Hand, Your Will
> By My Deed, Your Grace.

William Pascal felt himself floating like a cloud. Not like the rain-soaked one that had returned Joy Marie, but one that formed and reformed itself into shapes brought alive by imagination. Past today, past last year until fifty years had gone by. He knew exactly the moment—his twelfth birthday, the one he was watching on the screen. His father had rented a carnival, with horses and carousels. The high-light had been the hot air balloon that whisked him across the entirety of his inheritance until his father and two field hands brought out a giant box wrapped in festive paper. It was the bicycle he'd wanted since he was nine years old but his mother had said he was too young to have. He remembered grabbing his father's neck, and hearing words meant only for him. This was his moment.

The cloud that had brought Pascal to redemption re-formed, changed itself into mist, and moved from spar-kling light to a soaking darkness that squeezed him like his father had done that day.

Dingo was not prepared for what he saw next. Something silver sliced the air. Its gleam fell across the room four times. The priest mumbled another prayer. He stared at the image on the screen then pressed play. He picked up his containers, and went out into the night. Since Ding had not heard the priest drive up, he did not expect to hear him drive away, but he listened anyway.

Nothing stirred outside the house, or in. Dingo moved stealthily into the living room. He could see the woman, beautifully made, with her eyes closed, her head tilted in his direction. He did not know what to expect, but did not expect what he saw. He was certain Pascal was dead, but there was no blood anywhere. Neither were there hands or feet.

Curiosity leapt like a frog strutting across water. *How in hell did he do that? No blood? An instant coagulate?* As he squatted by the body to ponder the questions, he rested the Q-Tip in the cavity of his ear. Immediately, as it registered that he'd just witnessed Mechisedec, and was admiring the man's precision, his sixth sense reset and alerted that he was not alone. As quickly as the danger registered, a searing pain, inflicted by a stampeding red horse, trampled his brain. All the blood in his body surge upward. His eyes rolled. As if a switch had been flipped, everything went black, even the pain.

Chapter 56.

Mava peeked out before opening the door. Ben and Malice were greeted with the same delight as the last time, except Rae Lee was gregarious and Carrie Agnes reserved. In the midst of pleasantries, Mava waved Malice into the room where Carrie Agnes and Rae Lee had first heard about Mechisedec. With the help of a small lamp, darkness shadowed everything, producing an eerie feeling among all the old things Rae Lee cherished. Mava hurriedly shut the door and began patting the skirt of her polyester uniform as if something was there that shouldn't be.

"The bad thing you're chasing is chasing you," Mava blurted.

"Excuse me?"

"I can never judge the time of these things, but I didn't think it'd be this soon. That feeling I get has been getting stronger all day 'til now, it's like I can't sit down. You know that feeling, Dr. Able?"

"Yes, ma'am I do, but you'll have to tell me what you're talking about."

"Yes, ma'am."

"Last night, I saw a young man in trouble, a white boy. He looks up to you. A few minutes ago, I dozed off, and there he was, except he's in real trouble, and you have to find him."

"Who am I looking for?"

"Don't know his name sweetie; he plays with his ear. And he's someplace he shouldn't be."

"Chris!" Malice said, both asking and confirming. "What kind of trouble?"

"The kind you put in God's hands," Mava replied.

Malice pulled open the door and walked quickly into the kitchen where Ben was telling Carrie Agnes and Rae Lee about Brooklyn's party.

"Ben, I have to go. Lucas will be here shortly; ask him to take you back to town," Malice instructed. Seeing the look on Ben's face, he added, "I have to check on a friend."

Malice turned to his grandmother. He studied her for a moment, and put his arms around her neck in a warm embrace. "My mother asked me to give you this." He brushed Ben's shoulder on the way out the door. By the time he reached the car, he had dialed the emergency code that rang Chris' phone. Every agent must answer immediately by entering a three-digit response.

The phone vibrated in Chris' pocket for the programmed length of time and instantly began emitting his location when Chris did not answer.

Malice grabbed his satchel, and withdrew the reader that would give him the location within seconds. As he sped from the driveway, Malice said out loud, "He's here."

Malice turned his car onto a street of row houses and slowed where the machine said he should turn. Police cars, an ambulance, and a coroner's van crowded the driveway. Malice sat for a second, considering his options. He grabbed the NSA badge that identified him as IMIDD and half ran up the street to one of the officers who stopped him. Malice showed his badge.

The middle-aged patrolman looked at it, back to Malice, and pressed the button on the small walkie-talkie sitting like a parrot on his shoulder. When the static hushed, he said, "You should come out here." When the officer in charge got to the street, the patrolman handed him Malice's badge.

The detective studied the credential. "What are you doing here, Doctor?"

"I'm in town on another matter. I saw the lights and thought I'd offer assistance."

The detective looked at Malice, trying to discern how much to believe. "And did that other matter bring you to this street?"

In a split second, Malice knew not to assume this man was a corn-fed high school graduate playing cops and robbers. The edge in the detective's eyes said that would be a mistake. "I'm a forensic specialist with a branch of the government. I thought I could be of service, if not, I'll be on my way," and reached for his badge.

The detective handed back the badge. "Which branch would that be?" When Malice did not answer, the officer tempered his position. "I'm Detective Van Every, State Police."

"Thank you, detective. What have you got?" Malice walked one step behind Van Every, respecting the man's territory. Under other circumstances, he would have taken over, period.

"A judge is dead. From the looks of things, I hope his pappy ain't alive to see this."

"Excuse me?" Malice asked.

"He's in drag. He could have dressed himself, or was forced, we can't say just yet. The Judge is a big deal around

164

these parts. Another body was found with him. Not sure he'll make it. We're trying to decide if he's the perp, or one of the judge's closet pals who happened in the wrong place at the wrong time."

"What makes you think he's not the doer?"

"Damndest crime scene I've ever seen. If he killed the judge, he must have tripped over his dead body on the way out."

Malice reached into his pocket and withdrew a set of gloves he'd gotten from his satchel the same time as his badge. "Why couldn't the judge have hurt him in the struggle?"

"Well, he could have..." the detective answered, as they neared the bodies "...but I'm just not sure how he could have with no hands or feet."

"Mechisedec!"

"Looks like," the detective replied. "I'm guessing that's why you're here, Doctor. Whatever you can add will be helpful before this hits the national fan. If the other man is Mechisedec, we don't know what he did with the parts. We're searching every vehicle in the area. From the looks of things, he killed the judge someplace else and brought him here. Fell, and jammed his brain."

"From the looks of things?" Malice questioned.

"Yeah, no blood on the scene."

"Even if he was moved here, there should be blood transfer, Detective."

"Uh, huh. So tell me, Doc; why isn't there?"

Malice bent to look at the covered body and did not answer. When he lifted the sheet, he was taken aback. "It's Judge Pascal."

"You know him?"

"Met him at a big event last night."

"The swearing in for Ms. Beaudeau?"

Malice looked at the chalk lines indicating another person had been close by. "Where is the other man?" The detective pointed to the kitchen where two medics continued efforts to stabilize the body for transport. "What are his injuries?" Malice asked.

"From the looks of things, a Q-Tip is lodged in his brain."

Malice felt the air in his lungs go cold. He walked over to the gurney and looked at the body strapped to the cot. "What makes you think this man is not a victim?"

"No identification. Only a phone like I've never seen, and I've seen a lot of things. Radio Shack didn't make this. It vibrated a while ago. There is no recall button, no voice mail, and no way to determine who he called, or who called him. He was also wearing a set of gloves you won't find at JC Penny."

As Malice processed Van Every's briefing, the detective added, "There's something else." Van Every handed Malice the plastic-wrapped suicide note. "This was in Q-Tip's pocket. Add it all up, special gloves, no ID, phony letter. All the markings of a hit man."

Malice read the letter through the plastic sheath. He studied it, the paper, the corners, the folds, before focusing on the handwritten words.

"My whole life is a lie. I killed my sister to protect that lie. Death is both justice and mercy. I pray she forgives me and can now rest in peace." -- *William*

Questions raced through his brain and piled into each other like a Jeopardy marathon on speed. Malice felt the need to say something so he echoed Van Every's mantra: "From the looks of things..."

Malice went back to the living room and knelt by the judge. He studied the amputations expecting to find laser marks which would instantly cauterize the cut and explain the lack of blood. Looking closer, he saw the blood was coagulated into a hard gel. He stared so intently, that he didn't hear Van Every until he'd repeated his name.

"Doctor, do you have an opinion? This is why you're here?"

Getting back to his feet, Malice hoped he had erased the bewilderment from his face. He had just seen a medical phenomenon that even he could not comprehend. "Detective, may we talk first thing in the morning? Right now, I'd like to go with the suspect to the hospital and speak with the doctors. I'd also like to have someone from my agency present for the autopsy, if you don't mind. He'll be here first thing in the morning."

Van Every searched Malice's face again with eyes that had seen firsthand the minuscule workings of obscure government departments with alphabet names. That marginal acquaintance was enough to garner his cooperation, reserved though it might be. Finally, he said, "Be in my office at seven o'clock, Doctor. I can't keep the Judge's murder a secret, but if this is the work of Mechisedec, and he's in Pitt County..."

"I understand, Detective." As Malice got to the door, he turned to Van Every. "By the way, whose house is this? It's nice enough, but I can't see the Judge living here."

"Don't know yet. The judge lives twenty some miles away."

Malice followed the ambulance as it rocked and wheeled to Pitt Memorial Hospital. He called Fawks and told him what he knew. Chris was in critical condition, his phone and other evidence were headed to the State Police Department lock-up, that Chris might be charged with murder, and by morning, linked to Mechisedec.

"What!"

He wished Fawks would prove him wrong just once. Malice listened as Fawks got all his questions on the table. "I don't have any answers, but I strongly advise that someone get here before seven o'clock tomorrow morning." Malice instructed his director in one more thing. "I'd rather have Fugama, but send whoever is involved with the Mechisedec autopsies."

Fawks did not hesitate, didn't question Malice's request. He simply said, "Good, they're the same."

Chapter 57.

Judge Pascal's death led the morning News. No matter how early TV sets were turned on, a photograph of Judge William Henry Pascal filled a corner of the screen, and a talking head told a shocking story of murder.

Malice picked up Fugama and drove directly to Detective Van Every's office. The drive was long enough for Fugama to bring Malice in the loop.

"We told the local teams that the victims had been given a chemical that powdered their blood. That's not entirely false."

"What part is true," Malice asked.

"That something powdered the blood is true. We did not tell them the blood was mutated, contained DNA that could not belong to the victims."

"Are you saying they all had transfusions?"

"I'm saying the blood composition was different." Fugama breathed deeply, from the fatigue of his early morning flight as much as the burden of secrets. His words were as flat as the pavement that raced towards them and vanished beneath the car. Daylight was just an hour old but did not herald the hope promised in each new day.

Fugama's sigh said only the truth was left. "Mechisedec is one of ours. He is the most genetically advanced specimen we've discovered to date. We believe the victims are drinking his blood."

"So, what? Vampirism is one of the oldest myths going, whether it's gore on a movie screen or sanitized little shot glasses passed around on Sunday."

"You don't understand, Malice. Most humans average twenty codons in a strand of DNA. We've seen a few who have developed, or turned on twenty-four. These people heal faster, are less susceptible to disease; are actually attuned to esoteric vibrations. We call it the X-Effect.

"Naturally, when this Mechisedec came on the scene, we had to determine if he was our creation. Your interviews with serial killers proved helpful. With it, we were able to distinguish, on the surface, your pablum-produced psycho from a Zeusian. Regrettably, the more heinous the crime, the more likely he was ours. One of the most telling characteristics is that a Zeusian is more inclined to associate himself with God. Most would leave a note or make a comment to that effect. Mechisedec left only one note—the first time he killed—announcing himself the King of Peace. After that, his actions spoke for him."

Malice interrupted, "Get to the point, Baru!"

"Mechisedec's blood is the closest thing to the actual blood of God that we might ever see. Scientifically speaking, he *is* God. He has activated all sixty-four codons. That makes him a Supreme Being. We believe he is offering them sacrament with his own blood. It is so rich in amino acids, of varieties the average human body will never develop, that it actually forces other DNA into some kind of mutation that turns the blood into a jelly bean."

Malice parked the car with a jerk. Unfortunately, there was no time to hear more. Van Every pulled into the parking lot at the same time. Malice introduced the two men, by saying, "Doctor Fugama will be assisting with the Judge's autopsy."

Van Every gave Fugama the same suspicious look he'd heaped on Malice. "That's not how I heard it." Neither contested the remark.

Ben met Malice and Fugama at the door as soon as Maggie announced them. "I couldn't believe it. I rush here and get a call saying do nothing until Dr. Fugama arrives. That would be you?" Ben asked, looking past Malice, and extending his hand to the man who looked like he had stumbled into the morgue for a reservation. "I can see why you guys are involved. I've never seen anything like this."

Malice didn't tell Ben he hadn't either. "Sorry I didn't call you last night. I had to orchestrate a few things."

Ben looked from under his eyelids. This was the closest Malice had come to talking about his profession. Ben waited for more, but that was all he got.

"Dr. Fugama will fill the gap," Malice added. "I'm meeting Detective Van Every at the scene." Before leaving, he asked reluctantly, "Is Brooklyn all right?"

Chapter 58

"I made a few calls. The Judge did have a sister," Van Every said. "Rumor says she left for Europe about thirty years ago. Never came back. Bad family blood. Q-Tip did his homework."

170

Although the name was not what he would have preferred, Malice was grateful Van Every called Chris something other than John Doe. "Have you found her? With a name and DOB, I can do an international canvass."

"That's the odd thing, The crew at the Judge's house hasn't been able to locate anything—no letters, old pictures—not even a family Bible. One of my men is looking for family members who might remember her. You and I are going to Pascal's office, interview his secretary, get a feel for what happened last evening."

℮ℴ

Vanessa must have begun crying the moment she turned on her TV and gotten ambushed out of her routine. She had been told to wait at home, but she couldn't. She had gone to the office, opened the door to the judge's chamber, stared at his chair, and wept.

By the time Van Every and Malice arrived, Vanessa looked like a puffer fish with streaked pink lips and swollen red eyes. Van Every chose not to reprimand her for invading a potential source of evidence. He also didn't bother to pull out his pad to find her name—he read it from the engraved brass strip on her desk. "Ms. Allmon?"

All she could say was, "No, no."

Van Every knew the words were a chant designed to turn back time. She'd be in denial for at least another day. "Have you touched or moved anything in the judge's chamber, Ms. Allmon?"

"Noo." This mantra was directed at him.

Malice tried to listen. He'd been in the South for weeks and the drawling accents hadn't bothered him until now. Vanessa made a little word like 'no' sound like two syllables through a nosebleed. He imagined her being stranded here from another time, when nostalgia came of age and gave birth to gentility. Where melancholy was a ruse to conceal a Southern woman's strength.

"I'd like you to retrace the judge's steps from yesterday. What did he do, who did he see? Did he seem distracted, was there anything unusual?"

Vanessa blew her nose in the wad of wet tissue she'd smothered in her palm. She gingerly lifted two more sheets to add to the collection. She stared at the white ball as if it held the answer to all the detective's questions.

"It was a regular day. He had gone to Ms. Beaudeau's swearing-in party the night before; he didn't have an early case so he came in around ten to rule on a continuation in the Purdue case. He had a visitor after that, Dr. Mansell. They talked for about forty-five minutes, until the judge had to take the bench."

"Dr. Mansell?" the detective questioned.

Malice answered. "He's a psychiatrist. In town to help in Princeville. The judge met him last night."

"Uh-huh. Why was he here?"

"Dr. Mansell is the prison system's eastern region director for behavioral programs. It's his signature on recommendations to the Parole Review Board. Maybe it was a meeting of professional camaraderie."

Vanessa continued as if that exchange had not happened. "Dr. Mansell returned later that afternoon. He waited in the judge's chamber. He was only there a few minutes before Judge Pascal returned. It was still early but the judge suggested I leave for the day. I resisted, of course, but he insisted."

"How did the judge seem?"

Vanessa slumped a little, as if her head was too heavy for her shoulders. She looked into her tissue for the answer. "He seemed tired, withdrawn. He's been that way the last month or so. Heavy-hearted."

"Do you know what that was about?" Van Every prodded.

"No. He never shared his personal life with me. But it started right after the hurricane. I think what happened to Princeville bothered him deeply. I'd see him staring at newspapers. Then there were the calls on his private line; more than usual. I never answer that phone, so I can't speak to that."

Vanessa looked up from her paper ball anticipating Van Every's thought. "When it was installed, the company said calls can't be traced. I really don't understand such things. Today's technology and all."

Malice tired from listening to Vanessa. Her voice made him anxious. He wandered into the judge's chamber. "Has anyone else been in the judge's chamber in the last few days?"

Vanessa's eyes had followed Malice, bearing a look of recrimination. She directed her answer to Van Every. "Yes." She thought for a minute and began to chant names. "Ms. Beaudeau, Senator Haiger, his wife, a few others. I'd have to check my log."

Malice had put on a pair of gloves and, as Mansell had done, took inventory of the judge's desk. Vanessa wadded her fingers tighter around the saturated tissue as Malice pulled the newspaper articles from the middle drawer. He studied everything and put each item in a protective sheath with a pair of tweezers, then picked up the sheet with the one address label to Regina Bailey. Malice stared at it briefly then put it in a plastic bag. He returned to see Vanessa swabbing her nose.

"Did you mail anything to Regina Bailey for the judge?"

Having no idea what he was talking about, Vanessa nodded no.

173

"Did you type this sheet of labels addressed to Regina Bailey?"

Again, a befuddled head-bob. "The judge has a laptop and a printer. Sometimes he writes his own correspondence. He's a very capable man." A faint glint of pride attached itself to her reply.

Malice let her live in that moment before he'd asked another question that sent her eyes deep into her head again. "Were the Judge and Senator Haiger friends?"

"I'm not sure. He's never mentioned him before. When the Senator dropped by, I assumed it was about Ms. Beaudeau. He's her uncle, you know. I figure he wanted to thank the judge for recommending her to the bench. They all went out to lunch: Ms. Beaudeau, her mother and father, the Senator and his wife."

When Vanessa began repeating herself, the two men knew they'd gotten all she could give for now. "A crew will come by to process the judge's chamber. You'll have to stay away a few days, Ms. Allmon. So, please, go home."

"Is it true?" she asked.

Malice and Van Every looked at each other.

"Was he dressed like...like..." Vanessa couldn't make herself say it.

Van Every stepped in. "From the looks of things—"

Malice saw the woman's need to believe something other than what she was thinking, or maybe deep in her heart, already knew. He finished Van Every's sentence. "—the killer wanted to humiliate Judge Pascal."

Vanessa Allmon looked at Malice with thankful eyes that swelled again with tears. She quickly gathered her purse. At the door, she turned and stared into the vacant office. She almost smiled, but it was swept away when a sob tightened the muscles in her face.

Van Every cursed under his breath as he watched anguish drag itself away. "We'd better get a move on. Before the press rolls up my ass, and squeezes me from the inside."

Chapter 59.

Regina Bailey was eager to come in for questioning. She was already in Greenville hunting the story when she got the call.

"No, I don't know the Judge... We've never talked... Oh, he clipped my stories on the hurricane?"

"He had all these stories by you in his desk. And you're saying you never met?" Van Every asked.

Regina Bailey reveled in satisfaction that a man of his position saved what she wrote. "People cut articles for all kinds of reason."

"How did you get the picture of the woman in this story?" Malice slid the protected article under her face and tapped the corner twice with his finger.

She read the banner, appreciating her work, then looked up. "Sweet baby Jesus!" She mumbled something and raced out of the room. "I have to go back to the office. I'll call you."

Regina Bailey's exit put a breeze in the room. Van Every looked at Malice. "You think the judge sent her those leads?"

Malice couldn't resist. "From the look of things." When Van Every seemed not to notice the mock, Malice continued. "Dr. Riley and Sheriff Belton couldn't figure how she'd gotten her information, which was always on point. Dr. Riley thought there was a spy in his office. The judge had labels addressed to Regina Bailey. When you add that to a missing sister and a suicide letter, an unidentified body found after thirty years, what do you get?"

"You get holy shit."

"Yeah."

"Sweet baby Jesus."

ೞ

Van Every's handpicked team met at 1:00 PM. The small conference room looked like an entrant in a 'Ripley's Believe It or Not.' Malice, Fugama, Ben, and two other players piled in. Ben recommended Martin and Wash because their notes on the Solder case might save time. The summations:

The house where the judge was found belonged to the Pascal family, which meant it belonged to the judge. The only questionable thing found in the house was women's clothing. Nothing out of the ordinary in his primary residence—except the slew of prescription drugs.

Phone records showed consistent calls from the number at the main house. An unlisted call came into the drag house at 7:13PM. The silent car alarm had been activated at 8:18PM, most likely by the killer so his work would be found. Getting no response, the operator alerted the fire department, who called the police.

The unknown person at the scene was in a coma. Surgery had removed the cotton swab that shattered his eardrum and disrupted synaptic impulses to the brain. Doctors found his fingerprints had been altered and the skin reconfigured into an elaborate pattern resembling a bar code. There were no other distinguishing marks.

"Q-Tip is the only thing out of place here," Van Every said. "He's either Mechisedec or a copycat. Either way, he's a person of interest."

Malice looked at Baru. They had to lead the team away from Chris. "The judge's suicide letter is genuine, and the Princeville Princess could be his sister" he offered. "We'll know by the end of the day." Malice ended by suggesting the judge could not have buried her alone.

Van Every countered, "Q-Tip could have been that accomplice."

"Not unless he did it from his crib," Malice replied. "The man in the hospital was a baby when the woman was killed."

"If he altered his fingerprints, he could have altered anything else," Van Every answered back. "He could be fifty years old for all we know. That would make him old enough, now wouldn't it?" Malice was never surer than now that this man had been places, done things. He didn't, however, know whether they changed Van Every or affirmed him.

Fugama interrupted Van Every at the end of his speech. "Excuse me, Detective. You are right. The man in the hospital is not Mechisedec..."

Van Every looked at Malice with validation that lingered until Fugama finished his statement.

"Even so, Mechisedec is here."

Chapter 60.

Regina Bailey had the story that made careers. The front page of *The Rocky Mount Tribune* immortalized William Henry Pascal as a baby killer with one question: 'Did He Do It?' Associated Press picked up the story and flashed it across the country.

Oran Mansell folded the paper across his lap. He sat quietly in the DC office, remembering the man Regina Bailey wrote about humanely. He reached for the phone and made a call to Vincent Haiger's Connecticut Avenue office. When asked the nature of his call, he answered, "Joy Marie."

Waiting for the transfer, he peered out the double pane of glass that separated him from the dismal chill that trembled the trees outside. Empty branches surrendered their jutting stance and bent to a mightier force.

"You have my attention."

"Senator," Mansell said softly, "Now that William is dead, you are the only one who knows what happened thirty years ago. You must want someone to know what you've lost. And I promise you this: when you've relieved yourself of that burden, only God may speak of it. Who better than me?"

Haiger accepted Mansell's invitation. If nothing more, he'd learn how much Pascal had told him and if this man was, in fact, no threat. Oddly, he heard the sound of water -- forceful, violent -- in the distance.

At 8:45AM, Brooklyn found herself at Ben Riley's office and pushed through the door without knocking. She expected to see Malice Able but not the frumpy man with them. "I have to know."

The three men heard the anguish in her plea, and felt for her. Each looked at the other, Fugama—uncertain what to make of her request.

Ben spoke first, preventing the others from denying her what she needed. "Pull up a chair."

Not yet in agreement, Malice put the papers on the table face down. He pulled Ben aside. "This is not a good idea."

"She'll never believe the truth any other way, Malice. This is probably the greatest personal journey she will ever make. We can't stand in the way of that."

Malice reluctantly accepted Ben's argument but set the parameters. "Judge Beaudeau, there are details of this case we can't share with you. The nature of the judge's death is one of them. We suspect Raymond Solder and the judge's death are connected. With your background on that case, perhaps you can help sort out what that is."

Ben took over. "There is evidence linking Judge Pascal to the Princeville Princess."

Brooklyn took a deep breath, and sat down, unaware of the forthcoming seismic shake on her reality, shifting, and repositioning her polarities of right and wrong.

"She was the judge's sister, " Malice said.

The first tremor.

"We think a third person was involved, and helped bury her. That person would have known Princeville." Ben carefully explained the connection, ending with, "There is strong evidence suggesting that Judge Pascal was the lover Solder came to town to pursue."

The second tremor.

Malice watched the woman's face transform into something he'd witnessed before in others who had lived every day with clear delineations of right and wrong, true and false, black and white. He watched her begin the brutal cascade into massive gray even as the mind tried desperately to hold onto innocence. He recalled the quote he'd noticed in her office the first day they met: *To understand, you must surrender everything you think you understand.* Surely, it had more meaning at this moment than it ever would.

Brooklyn looked around for her rocker only to find this was not her office, so she pressed her elbows deep into the cushioned arm of the chair in which she sat. When she spoke, her voice was like penlight being devoured in a long dark night. "Solder was the judge's lover. He knew Judge Pascal had killed his sister. That knowledge got him killed. Then he must have been the accomplice."

Malice moved her closer to the most damning truth. "The calls he made, and got on his private line could have been to and from Solder. But the secret calls continued after Solder was dead. That means someone else out there knows."

Brooklyn let intellect support her. "The man in the coma?"

"We don't believe he's the third man," Malice offered.

"Wait a second. You're saying the young man in the coma was not another lover? Then how is he connected to this madness? If not him, who?"

"The simplest answer is the third man knew Pascal, his sister and Solder some thirty years ago. He's probably the baby's father."

"A third man..." she said.

Ben reminded them he was present. "The man at the hospital was excluded. The baby's father has sickle cell anemia."

"A black man?" She gasped. "I can't believe a black man from here would help kill a child." Brooklyn protested.

"Maybe he didn't." Ben suggested.

Malice saw that Brooklyn was close to the same conclusion he'd been careful not to voice since he had no definitive proof. Only a gut instinct sharpened by experience, and polished by intellect.

"So, it's someone important enough, either then or now, who could intimidate, or threaten Judge Pascal. A black man that important from this area?" The question left her mouth, and began a jagged ascent from a deep dark place to the crest called Truth.

Chapter 61.

A nurse checked the instruments attached to the man everyone knew as Q-Tip. He had no awareness of her. He existed in a different realm, in a time and place that gave him purpose. He dreamt the dream again.

The time came when a young boy faced an enemy that would not be dismissed by mere beating of the chest or flexing of muscle. A den of angry wolves surrounded his town and fed upon it in the nighttime. Throats were ripped from livestock and the carcasses left where they fell. Chickens were mutilated. Those spared were so frightened that they could not lay eggs. Random rows of vegetables were torn up on every farm; the roots flung wildly wherever the violent force took them. Everyone feared they had offended some unknown god. Prayer circles held hands all over the town. Urgent, fearful pleas from the lips of the saved and un-saved trembled in blood-stank air. Shotguns crossed the laps and shoulders of every man who could afford one. Rock piles weighed the porches of those who could not. Children were kept inside, even during the day. Who knew when the enemy would move to invade their homes and feed on the hearts of their future? Fear became a presence in the town that awoke for breakfast one day, and did not sleep even when the moon shut its eyes for the seconds before daybreak. It went on like this for months.

The boy watched his town change from fever green to decay. One day, he stood from the hiding spot and hugged his mother like a son going off to war. She saw in his eyes what made her fall in love with his father. Others would say those eyes revealed the miracle of love, and the deepest depravity of man. "What will you do," she asked him.

"Become the enemy of my enemy."

The boy went into the forest and secretly studied the wolf. He learned to change his color to white to gray to red. By the next full moon, he had become the largest wolf ever to roam a forest anywhere in the world. He became the shadow of his prey, never revealing his presence until the moment just before victory gripped the throat of fear. He soon rid his people of their threat.

When life was back to normal, his mother searched the trees and left pleas for him to be human again upon every leaf she touched. When Canis Diros did not answer, she returned home and grieved the loss of her son. But, at the next full moon, a red dog appeared scratching at her door. When she opened it, the wolf walked in, went to the fireplace, and lay down. The mother followed him, looked into his eyes, and smiled. Thereafter, she called him Dingo.

Chapter 62.

Ben, Malice, and Fugama broke for lunch to meet with Detective Van Every. Fewer people huddled in the tiny space than before.

Van Every capped off his lukewarm coffee before moving to the board of 'All Else,' the dry erase wall where he displayed ideas, photographs, and facts. A red question mark represented the unknown. There were lots of red marks.

With his eyes on the board, leaning back in his chair, he sipped his coffee, and said aloud, to no one in particular: "My granddaddy ran a liquor still from the time he was sixteen till two days before he died. Never sold a drop. Always gave it away. But everybody he gave it to always showed up with something for him. A cupla chickens, a few dollars they claimed they owed, wood they'd chopped from clearing a piece of land. Everybody knew the arrangement but me. Until I was a grown man, I thought my granddaddy was a generous man, and everybody around him was neighborly."

Everyone understood except Fugama, who looked at the other faces either bobbed in affirmation, or bowed as if the words were holy.

Van Every got up, tapped the double question marks under the column labeled 'Q-Tip.' He then picked up a marker and drew a circle. "So, if it ain't supposed to *appear* to be what it is, how do you disguise it so it looks like something else?"

Malice looked at Ben and Fugama. A faint hint of admiration mixed with contemplation formed around his eyes. Van Every was figuring it out. Or he already had and was waiting for them to confirm it.

Ben listened with curiosity, and ventured to find out what Van Every actually knew. "What are you suggesting, Detective?"

"I'm suggesting exactly what you already know, Doctor Riley. That we have a fucking trifecta here. If Dr. Fugama is right, Mechisedec killed the judge. Since we never found the judge's hands and feet, let's say the man paid our little town a visit.

"We know Mechisedec considers himself some kind of judge sent by God, according to Dr. Fugama. Everyone he's killed before was a criminal. If that follows through, then he knew the judge killed his own sister, and that's why he killed the judge. But then why was Q-Tip at the judge's house?"

"He was at the wrong place at the wrong time," Ben offered.

"I think he was at the right place at the wrong time. But why?" He tapped the board again where he'd drawn the circle. "Because it is what it appears to be." Van Every glanced the room and stared in each face. He strolled to his chair and sat down again. "Q-Tip was there to kill the judge not knowing Mechisedec beat him to it."

Ben studied Van Every's words one at a time. "So you're saying Q-Tip is a hit man, and not the judge's lover?"

Van Every looked at Malice. "Well, what's your guess?"

"Interesting theory, Detective."

"Let's say that I'm right. If Mechisedec works alone, and everything in Dr. Fugama's brief implies that he does, then someone else out there wanted Pascal dead. And if that's true, then we've got a helluva mess."

Ben asked his own question. "How did Mechisedec know about a case we're just putting together? Let's not forget we've solved two homicides in the process."

Van Every rapped the desk with his fingers. "I'm happy for you, Doctor. Right now, my job is to solve the ones that ain't."

"Who else would want to kill the judge?" Malice asked, deflecting Van Every's admonishment.

Van Every did not take his eyes off Ben. "My guess is it has something to do with Solder, one of Dr. Ben's *solved* homicides. For all I know, it might have to do with both Dr. Ben's *solved* homicides." After several seconds, he

184

turned his eyes to Malice. "I've got some of the best paid brainiacs in the country right here in this room. Something tells me we have the answer right here, too. Now who wants to show and tell?"

Malice's curiosity about the man hiding out in the fields of North Carolina turned to admiration. "Detective, we just left a meeting with Judge Beaudeau on this very subject. Stop by Dr. Riley's office at six; I think we'll have a name for your board."

Faguma stopped the group from breaking up. "How did Mechisedec know?"

Chapter 63.

Speculations bounced like pinballs in Brooklyn's head. She made a call. "You are the best at gathering information of anyone I know, Connor. I have a challenge for you. Get me a list of all the boys born with sickle cell syndrome or anemia in Pitt County between 1940 and 1950."

"I thought we had the day off?"

"Sorry, but it's why I pay you the big bucks."

"Right...right...the big bucks...ok...Sickle cell. Did they keep records back then?"

"Only if the child presented with symptoms and was diagnosed. I believe mandatory testing came in the early 70s. That's why it's a challenge."

"Are you looking for someone in particular?"

"Connor, just find what you can, as quickly as you can. In fact, get back to me by five, okay?"

"Is this about the Princeville Princess?"

"Connor, please. Just do it, okay!"

Brooklyn grabbed her coat and walked into the brisk December air, hoping it would clear her head. The smell of hot cider and cinnamon from the coffee shop invited her to cross the street. Christmas bells echoed in the few crannies of her brain that weren't brimmed with murder and mysteries. She chose a table near the window to watch the world go on without her. As she settled in, her phone rang.

"Mom. I was just thinking of you. Yes. Hold on, hold on... You don't have to push. I'm coming home... That's not why you're calling... The paper... Yeah, it's all over the national News... You know one of the men... Excuse me, mom, but you know who... What!"

Chapter 64.

Brooklyn was gone when Ben and Malice returned from saying good-bye to Baru. As the minutes passed Ben's concern turned to worry. Before it turned to panic, his secretary tapped on the door and handed him a large envelope marked urgent. Inside was a list of male children born in Princeville with sickle cell anemia and sickle cell syndrome. When he got to 1944, he stopped. "Oh no."

As the words left his mouth, Brooklyn entered. Malice took the report; glanced each page, and came to the same resting place as Ben.

Seeing heaviness in Brooklyn's eyes, Ben opened his mouth to say something to avert her when Malice interrupted. "You've seen it, haven't you?" he asked.

"Yes."

"But how?" Ben asked. "Maggie just gave it to us."

"Connor faxed a copy to my office forty-five minutes ago. I asked her to send a copy to you."

"Brooklyn, there are pages of names—"

"My mother called."

Ben and Malice looked at each other. Ben's first thought was that he'd been wrong to include her. Malice heard the burden of truth, the painful digesting of something disagreeable.

"She'd read the paper. Regina Bailey's story made it to Maryland." Brooklyn stood at the long window and spoke; each word shaped by her breath on the tinted glass. "Mother remembered Raymond Solder. He was a runaway. A neighbor caught him sleeping in his barn. They let him stay for a while. He and Uncle Vincent became friends. Later, the husband made Solder leave; said he was funny, but couldn't prove it." Brooklyn snickered under her breath. "That's what mom called it. I've never understood that reference. Funny... gay ... homosexual... Mom said she never believed it." Brooklyn's voice trailed off as she pondered that statement.

So, there it was. The connection. Raymond Solder knew Vincent Haiger. And since Brooklyn didn't turn around, there must be more.

"I believe I was given the judgeship to take me off the case. To make sure Purdue was convicted."

Those words weren't what they expected, but each considered its merit. Despite that she had earned the bench, they didn't try to dissuade her.

"I tried to call him. Picked up the phone a dozen times." She turned around to face them, but looked at her hands instead. "I couldn't." She looked up. "I've never been afraid of the truth."

The pain finding home in her eyes, Malice had seen in countless other faces, but had never felt the burn that squeezed his chest right now. He turned away, and laid the report on the table. He stepped aside when Ben moved towards Brooklyn. She put a hand up to stop him.

"We still have work to do."

Malice felt for her. Moved by her determination and strength, the burn in his chest squeezed tighter.

Brooklyn removed her coat and dropped it on the chair. "Since we're running out of time, let's assume Senator Haiger is the child's father. Let's also assume he wanted Pascal and Solder dead. We know Judge Pascal killed Solder. And because it's the only thing that makes sense, the Senator sent a hit man for the judge."

The sting of rejection faded from Ben's face. "Mechisedec," he offered.

"No," Malice contested.

"Why...You think he's—"

"Mechisedec does not take requests. Trust me, no one sends him." Malice ignored Ben's expression. "We wondered how Regina Bailey knew so much about this case. Turns out the judge was purging his conscience."

"So, besides Regina Bailey, you think the judge told someone else, someone he trusted?" Ben asked.

"I think the judge's guilt ate him in little pieces. Over thirty years."

Brooklyn sat down, finally. "What if Ben is right? We don't know how Mechisedec operates, how he chooses his victims. What if they choose him?" The room was silent for several seconds as they contemplated that possibility.

The doorknob turned. Detective Van Every's presence changed the energy in the room. It was more than his Herculean mass; he felt it, too. "Am I interrupting something?"

"Perfect timing," Malice replied. "The list of people who saw the judge over the last few days. Do you have it?"

"What is this about?" Van Every asked.

After Malice brought him up to speed, Van Every searched Brooklyn's face. Satisfied, he dove in. "Let's see who signed in with Ms. Allmon." When he was done writing the names on the board, they studied the list, starting at the top, analyzing and eliminating each person's potential as a confidante. One name remained: Doctor Oran Mansell.

While Ben summarized the doctor's credentials, Malice studied the man in his head; something bothered him. Despite his obvious intelligence and knowledge, the man was too young. Before Ben could finish, Malice turned quickly to Brooklyn, his voice raised higher than any of them recalled ever hearing. "Call your uncle."

She got the cell phone from her coat, and speed-dialed Vincent Haiger.

"Ask if he's spoken with Doctor Mansell."

When Haiger picked up, Brooklyn paused. Clearly, the sound of his voice angered her the instant she heard it. The heavy stare of eyes made her put that aside. "Uncle Vincent, it's me. Look, I don't have time to explain. Have you spoken with Doctor Oran Mansell... When... Look, whatever you do—"

Malice guessed at her next words. "NO. Keep him there!" He grabbed his own phone, and hit a code that went straight to Fawks Belnais. As he gave Fawks instructions, he noticed Van Every's attention to the phone at his ear, exactly like the one that disappeared from Evidence. Finishing the call, he turned to Brooklyn. "Tell the senator help is on the way. And if he wants to live, not to eat or drink anything Mansell offers, not even if he prepared it himself. Nothing!" To Fawks, he said, "He's dangerous Fawks. You are a masterful contender, but this is not the one for making that point. Trust Me."

Brooklyn had hung up, but Haiger kept the phone to his ear to think. He cradled the receiver, put the revolver he kept in the desk in his coat pocket, and went back to his guest.

"So, Doctor Mansell, you were saying..."

"Senator, let's not play games."

Haiger relaxed even as Brooklyn's words played in his head. 'Keep him there'. He concluded killing Mansell would do just that. But, as Mansell talked, the burden of thirty years sat in the middle of his chest. Just as Pascal had purged his soul, Haiger began. He'll be dead soon enough, he concluded.

Chapter 65.

"I met Ray when I was nineteen. By then, he was exploring sex in ways I had never even imagined. When I turned twenty, Ray took me to this dilapidated little house outside of town. But inside, down a flight of stairs, was a room grander than any hotel I'd ever seen. Mirrors and men everywhere. Incense mixed with marijuana so heavy it crawled into your lungs on its own. Private rooms made up a third of the space—for patrons who required a higher degree of discretion.

Raymond spent most of his time in 'discretion'. He'd told me about this rich white boy who paid for his time on a regular basis. He never told me who it was and I never asked.

I was scared to death standing in that lobby. Wasn't sure how to feel about being there. Had every emotion a straight male curious about his sexuality might have. Anger, anxiety, curiosity, excitement, fear, and back to anger. As I look back on it, Ray knew more about me than I knew myself. I didn't know what to do, so I watched.

I went back several times after that, always with Ray. Despite my frequent visits, I was certain I was straight. It's hard to explain, but being there was an experience that I could never recreate with women, as much as I tried.

A year later, I met Joy Marie. She was different from any white woman I'd ever known. We hid our relationship for months. It was the late sixties, and race relations were volatile in the South. It may have been the Age of Aquarius for us but it was a heartbeat from slavery for our parents.

When she told me she was pregnant, I was ecstatic; we made plans to leave town. I worked two jobs and saved every dime. Joy Marie was able to hide her pregnancy for a long time. I don't know how; she was pencil thin.

Anyway, William called me one afternoon; he and I were friends, somewhat. My family worked for his family. Hell, one of my jobs was making deliveries on weekends for Joy's uncle.

William was so cool when I got there. 'I got a job; pays three hundred dollars,' he said. His family was always stepping just a little outside the law. That's how they made their money and acquired all their land. But who was I to judge? It was a lot of money. I couldn't believe the irony and the luck. When I asked him to do what, he said, 'Dig a grave. In the Negro cemetery'.

I'd worked for the funeral home from time to time digging holes. I thought for a minute, unsure how I'd explain if somebody came by. But that amount of money came with lies. He handed me two crisp hundred-dollar bills and said I'd get the rest when it was done.

I couldn't help it. I hadn't seen her, not even a sound that she was in the house; to be that close and not see her— so I asked.

"She's sleeping," he said.

"How about Temper, she around?" Temper was the housekeeper. She was hired mostly to be Joy Marie's play-mate but they became good friends. Joy Marie loved her.

She told Temper about her pregnancy before she told me. Seeing her would be like seeing Joy Marie, but she wasn't there either.

I called Ray. Paid him twenty-five dollars to help me. That was what I would have gotten for digging the hole. We found a secluded spot belonging to a family that didn't live in Princeville anymore. William paid me and asked if I could use another three. By now, I knew I was bargaining with the devil.

I met William back at the estate at ten o'clock. Outof nowhere, he starts ranting."

"That girl has always spit on everything we stand for," he said. "She was daddy's little girl and thought it was cute that she was so cocky. Like him; didn't take gump from nobody—made her own rules. But this time, she went too far," he said.

I knew what he was talking about—she was exactly like that—earth, wind and water, with a hint of fire. But I could only listen. 'Went and got knocked up by a black man,' he said.

My heart stopped. My first thought was that I had just dug my own grave. Sweat formed in the top of my head and eased down the front of my ears. I think I heard it splat on the collar of my denim jacket. I couldn't speak. It didn't ease my stress at all when he said she wouldn't tell her parents who the father was. In my heart, I knew that he knew.

My sanity raced to hell and back when I heard a knock at the kitchen door. He told me to get it. I expected some of his buddies to be there with baseball bats and rope. He had to tell me twice, 'Get the door, Vincent,' when the knock came a little louder. My shoes weighed fifty pounds each, and my legs wouldn't bend, but I finally felt the doorknob on my hand, cold and wet from the sweat in my palm. I tried as best I could to keep composed. If I was about to die, I'd go like a man.

I opened the door so quickly it barely creaked. A gush of air cooled my face. I remember being surprised by how good it felt. Expecting to be shot or punched, I braced myself. But there stood Raymond, surprised as I was.

William waved him in. He handed each of us an envelope. Three hundred dollars plus a hundred-dollar bonus was in mine. I had no idea what he gave Ray.

He led us to the workshop at the back of the house. A shiny black casket with brass handles sat in the middle of the room. Still not convinced the casket wasn't for me, all I could think was it's a mighty fine box.

My mind did somersaults as William talked. "You know what to do," he said. "Take Ray's truck. I'll drive your car inside.' I figured Ray was going to kill me, dump me in the hole he'd helped me dig, and sell my car in the next state. But I could see that Ray was dumbfounded, too.

William was saying. 'I 'preciate you handling this little business for me. Once it's done, I never saw you tonight. Am I clear?'

Ray answered, 'As the glass in the county jail'. Truth was, you couldn't see a damn thing through the glass at the county jail. But Ray had been there, and had no interest in going back.

We all loaded the casket onto Ray's truck. I had driven the road from the Pascal place a hundred times. It never felt the way it felt that night. The engine wheezed as if it didn't want to go. Ray and I had not spoken since we'd left William closing the door to the garage where he'd driven my car, and handed me back the keys. We must have been two miles down the road when Ray broke the silence.

"What the hell's going on, man?"

"What the hell is that suppose to mean?"

193

"It means what the hell is going on? You call me to help you dig a hole. Will calls and offers me two hundred dollars, tells me to borrow a truck. He wouldn't tell me what for, just asked if it mattered. Truth be told, it didn't. I show up, and there you are in his kitchen. Next thing I know, we're on our way to the hole we dug with a casket that clearly didn't get prayed over by no preacher. So, I'm asking you, what the hell is this? Who's in that box?"

I couldn't think anymore. Except for the muffled vibration of the blanketed casket, and the occasional bump from a shift in the load, we continued the trip in silence. Neither of us said it, but we had to know. At the cemetery, we set the box beside the hole and stared at it.

Finally, Ray got up the nerve. He pulled at the lid. It was locked. I had a master on my key ring. The cylinder clicked. I slowly raised the lid. My next memory was Ray wrestling me to the damp mound of dirt, and pinning me between it and him. Dirt filled my mouth and nose. He put his elbow under my neck to keep me from suffocating and to muffle my scream. I held onto his arm and cried like a child. He lifted me over his shoulder and took me to the truck. Dropped me on the bed and wrapped me in the blankets as if I were the baby Jesus.

I don't remember it, but Ray went back and buried Joy Marie. I don't know how he got the box in the hole, but he came back, uncovered me, and put me in the cab. He took me to his row house. The cab rocked as the truck hummed its way down the dirt road and stopped in a grove of trees. On any other occasion, I welcomed Ray's place. It belonged to his friend, the one from the private club. This was their place.

When my mind came back to me, Ray had cleaned me up and set a bottle of vodka in front of me. My fingers were already around a glass that was pressed to my lips.

The heat of it in my throat didn't come close to the knot of anger and pain in my chest, but I was feeling again. I poured another. Pretty soon it didn't scald as before. In fact, it felt warm, like milk fresh from a cow's tit. I rested my head on the kitchen table and cried as the words came wet from my lips. "He killed her."

Raymond was the only person I had told about Joy Marie. When he was sure I could hear him, he spoke. 'I'm going to tell you something, Vincent. Just listen. When I'm done, we can decide what to do'. Those words turned the horror of Joy Marie's death into a nightmare. 'The man from the private room, the owner of this house is William', he said.

Joy Marie told William about the baby, hoping he'd ease the way with their parents. She'd found out about Ray and William and was using that knowledge for leverage. William ranted about being blackmailed but promised to help Joy Marie so that she'd keep his secret. As much as his parents would have hated a black child, they'd equally hate a fag, and disown them both.

Joy Marie reminded him that she could send the child away, but that he would always be gay. He gave in to her demand on one condition: that he know who the father was. Joy Marie saw no reason not to tell.

When they were told, Mr. and Mrs. Pascal put distance between them and Joy Marie. They told her to be gone when they got back from New York. And that bastard saw to it that she was. As fate would have it, they died in a freak car accident a few months later.

I didn't know if it was the story or the vodka, but my head began to spin until I passed out. In the blackness I could absorb the truth. Joy Marie was dead to protect William's secret, and he paid me to bury her, knowing it was my child she carried.

After beating him close to death, I made him write a suicide letter so he'd know his life was in my hands the same way he'd put Joy Marie's life in his."

Oran Mansell opened the small cooler he'd sat on the table in front of him. He withdrew a small thermos and poured a plum red liquid into a sterling silver goblet. He offered it to Vincent Haiger, and prayed:

We share our pain
With Thee Oh Lord
To gain a measure of peace.
And in a single beat of our hearts
Extract a lifetime of wrong.

The goblet fell from Haiger's hands as the shattering of wood echoed in the room. Four men in black rushed through. Fawks Belnais pinpointed the man in the monk's robe. Years of martial arts expertise coursed through every muscle. Two of his companions rushed to move the senator from harm. The third scouted the house.

Fawks went for the monk. He did not anticipate the force that propelled him backwards. The monk's robe whirled, sweeping the air around him. He grabbed the rope secured to his waist and turned the thick thread into a weapon. Fawks sidestepped a snap of the rope, grabbed the cord, pulled forward, and landed a foot into the monk's chest. He sent the same foot in search of the monk's face, but the man crossed his arms and deflected the blow, knocking Fawks off balance. Before Fawks could recover, the monk lunged forward and landed a swift punch into his opponent's ribs.

Fawks sent the monk down with a powerful thrust to the knee. His advantage was short-lived. The battle between equals was brief. Fawks missed a vital strike. In return, the palm of a powerful fist landed on his temple and folded a blanket of darkness over his eyes. Before the other agents could return, the monk was gone.

Chapter 66.

It was after midnight when Detective Van Every and Malice arrived at the Langley Hospital and spoke with the doctor about Fawks Belnais' condition. No one knew the extent of simple contact with Mechisedec. Luckily, he only had a concussion. When all was said, Fawks had saved Vincent Haiger's life. Now the courts would decide what to do with a man well acquainted with murder.

Two agents guarded Oran Mansell's DC office while three more held him in custody at his home. He was apprehended there thirty minutes after the altercation that put Fawks in the hospital, a fact that baffled Malice and Van Every. For Malice, someone beating Fawks was the first disbelief. The suspect going home was the second. The agent at the door directed them to the den where two others, with weapons ready, flanked Dr. Mansell. At the threshold, Malice looked at Van Every who looked at him. They turned again to the man in the bathrobe and Van Every asked, "Who the hell are you?"

Chapter 67.

Malice was satisfied that the captured man was Oran Mansell. He was not, however, the man who had shown up in Greenville and at Vincent Haiger's home. Mechisedec was still loose, and able to steal identities. How he'd chosen

Oran Mansell was a mystery as well as whom else he'd pretended to be.

Brooklyn arrived in Virginia with Malice and Van Every and went to the federal center where her uncle was being held. After an hour, she was permitted to see him. The room was not what she expected. Pictures on the wall, a small cherry stained table, and cushioned chairs gave the impression business was negotiated here rather than confessions. When she asked the single question that haunted her, Vincent Haiger had but one reply. "Live in my pain for thirty years, then ask me why."

Brooklyn's visit was ending as Malice and Van Every arrived. She looked weary. "My department has accommodations. You're both welcome to stay there," Malice offered.

His guests nodded in agreement. The night had been intense; sleep would be difficult, but Malice was sure exhaustion would win. He drove to the complex in which apartments took up one floor of the building, reserved for guests—invited or otherwise. After giving Van Every a key to one suite, he showed Brooklyn to another. She hadn't said much on the drive over. He wondered what her uncle had said, but didn't ask. When he'd opened the door and given her the key, Brooklyn looked at him, her eyes glassy from fighting back tears.

"I can't," she said and backed away from the door. "I don't want to be alone."

The knot in his chest he felt for her returned. He pulled the door shut and softly laid his palm in the middle of her back to guide her. "I don't live far."

198

The quiet swirl of the motor cut the silence in the mid-size car. If she'd been aware, Brooklyn would have noticed how much the city felt like Greenville this time of morning. It imbued the same mystic calm that whispered, 'peace be still'.

Malice showed Brooklyn to the spare bedroom. He drew a bath and laid out towels. While she surrendered to the water's warm dissolve, he brewed a cup of tea. He sat the serving tray with tea biscuits on the table in her room.

The slightest hint of instrumentals, like an angel's lullaby, tiptoed into her space. Wrapping herself in the terry robe she found on the bathroom door, Brooklyn wandered back into the bedroom and sat in the dark velvet chair. The smell of tea led her to its calm. Afterwards, she encased herself between the tightly threaded sheets, and everything else seemed far, far away…

Chapter 68.

"What do you desire, my dear? All the answers between what was, what is, and what will be, are in my care."
The little girl looked around the room. A small boat without sail, drifting across dark water had brought her here. Thick fog pushed back the light, and enclosed her in its quiet arms across the hidden sea.
A hut formed ahead. Its rickety plank swayed gently against a distant moon. A muted beam of light illuminated a pier only wide enough to stand with one foot in front of the other. There were no steps at the hut, only an open doorway too small. Entering seemed impossible, but curiosity called her name.

Once she stepped onto it, the plank turned into the rib-cage of some large animal. Its bones glistened like mother of pearl. Each vertebra was a step, farther apart than her legs would span. As she stretched each leg forward, the bones moved closer together, collapsing the distance between one step and the next. The journey was difficult, but she stretched her little legs until they hurt in order to narrow the gap between where she was, and where she wanted to be.

The doorway widened like a yawning mouth. Inside, the little hut was enormous. Golden light emanated from nowhere, casting a glow on everything, lighting some things, and casting shadow on others.

An overstuffed couch dressed one side of the marble wall, and an old wooden rocker sat peacefully on the other. Trees grew out of the floor, their roots the polished hardwood. Art lined the circular wall, scrolls jutted from large baskets and open books lay everywhere. A scent of spring rain wafted throughout the space and mingled with the smell of roses.

On the far wall was another small doorway, closed. Two larger doors on either side were open.

The figure whose voice she heard stepped from the shadow. The little girl could see the tall, hourglass shape of a woman, with the youthful voice of a child.

"Speak your wish," it said.

"Anything? You will answer?"

"All is answered."

As the girl's eyes focused, she saw that the bottom half of the hourglass was a man. The top of the hourglass was endowed with breasts that artists, across centuries, would paint. The little girl's eyes came to a dead stop when she looked on the face of a hag with flaming eyes. She had gnarled claws, spikes for teeth, and a retched odor when she spoke.

"What are you?" the girl asked.

"Is that your question, my dear?"

"Do I get only one?"

The figure laughed. "I encourage you to think before asking, as the one thing I do not know is when your visit will end. Waste no time on naught."

The room became a kaleidoscope of shapes and colors that swirled like a disco ball. What is this place, why is the room changing, and why am I here were the questions in her head, but the little girl decided to heed the apparition's advice. Her eyes stopped at the small closed door.

"Why is that door smaller than the others, and why is it closed? Is there something valuable in there?" the girl asked.

"Good question, my dear. Behind that door is Truth. It is smaller because Truth does not fluff herself with flattery."

"So, what are the other two doors?"

"Everything else," the specter answered. "I am the keeper of all answers."

"Then you don't always tell the Truth?" the girl asked, somewhat confused.

"Few wish to bother Truth. The door is not only closed, it is locked. Truth requires effort and courage to enter, and does not give of herself easily. Few are willing to give of themselves in order to sit at her feet. It can be a tortuous journey, demanding sacrifice. And even at the end of the journey, some find that Truth is not Beauty, as they'd expected, but can be a hideous crone, like me. They have come running and screaming from her presence. They ignore what they have seen and heard. So many times has it happened that she has locked herself away, and yields only to perseverance."

" Truth is not beautiful?"

"It's a lie she's told."

"Why?" the girl asked, only to see the apparition becoming annoyed.

"I have told you why, and yet you ask why. Denial, my dear, is her dismay."

"What does Truth look like, then? May I see her?"

"She is I, and I am she."

"But you're not locked away; you're here, in front of me."

"So I am."

Chapter 69.

Brooklyn awoke lost in a mist that swirled in her head and put one thing where another had been. Her eyelids opened and closed slowly until the darkened room came into focus and the mist rolled away. The distant smell of coffee lit her senses.

In the spacious kitchen, stained glass windows warmed the morning light, giving life to the daylilies and hummingbirds etched in black. Malice was on the phone to Greenville Memorial. Chris' condition had been upgraded. His next call was to Detective Van Every.

"Good morning," he offered, seeing Brooklyn wander in.

"Not likely," she said as she made her way to the waiting coffee cup. She sat at the cafe table occupied by a bowl of croissants and buttered apple jam. She peered into the cup as if looking for her future, but saw only black. Malice brought over napkins and cream cheese. Brooklyn half-smiled at him, aware of the effort it took to do so.

"What time is Van Every escorting my uncle to Greenville?"

"Not sure. Politics."

"Is he making trouble? Is the media involved?"

"Not yet. They're reporting an attempted break-in. The senator is supposedly in isolation for protection." Malice sat in the seat opposite her and observed. "Van Every and I are going to the hospital to talk with Fawks and then to the lab to meet with Dr. Fugama."

"You're not leaving me out of this."

"Wouldn't try. You have a lot to absorb. There is nothing you can do where we're going but wait."

Brooklyn accepted his logic. She also realized that she had stepped into his world. From what she'd seen so far, he was more than a medical examiner. How much more, she wasn't ready to know, and felt certain he wouldn't tell. Her eyes went back to the pottery that warmed her palms.

"It may be too soon to get into this, but what did your uncle say?"

Brooklyn's back stiffened. "Everything you already knew."

Bits of his confession hurled back at her like the hurricane that had flung rooftops. "How could he have done this?" Her eyes betrayed her again, filling the brim of her lids with tears. She stood to leave.

Malice stepped in front of her. He clutched her shoulders and held her still. Unable to delay her disappointment and shame, Brooklyn surrendered. His neck became the valley into which she cried.

Chapter 70.

Malice awoke with a start. The phone in Fawks' office was ringing. The fatigue that had crept quietly behind him the last few days had caught up and took refuge in his bones. He pushed himself from the leather sofa. The voice was unexpected.

"Fate is unpredictable, is it not, Doctor Able?"

Predictable responses raced to his tongue for export, but he denied them. He pressed the record button, and answered, "So it seems."

"Were it not so, all events would be purely at our whim. Simply the notion of that kind of power and responsibility is too much for most, don't you agree?"

"I'm sure you didn't call for my opinion on metaphysics."

"Actually, yes." Mechisedec continued. "How could you have imagined everything that has happened to your life in the last two months?"

Malice responded. "Are you saying that *you* have that power, planned these events?"

"I do, I did; as did you. Of all the opportunities to go home, you chose this one. You would have gone to Princeville, eventually. Your soul demands it."

Malice felt a tug at his heart. He'd asked himself the same question, why now?

"Home is a holy place, Doctor Able. Don't be troubled by your need to cross its blessed portal; to be embraced in its forgiving bosom."

Malice felt another surge run through him. This man had reached into his soul and found what bothered him most. The thought disturbed him.

"Yes, Doctor Able. I know what is missing in your life."

"Missing?"

"Intimacy. Family. Trust. All the things your mother values, and you don't have. You want to belong; we all do. We all long for something or someone to ease our pain."

"So, you've read some self-help books," Malice replied.

"Now, now, Doctor Able. We all have skeletons and demons. There are things we are running from, and things we are running to. No psychologist need tell us that."

Malice waited for the man to share what had put him in motion. He knew it would come. Every serial killer he'd ever met needed someone to hear the demented logic that informed his choice of victims, his method of crime.

Instead, the monk dug further into Malice's soul. "Fear hides within you, Doctor Able."

"Fear?"

"That you will never love or be loved the way your mother loved your father. The way your grandfather loved. The way your grandmother loves without hesitation."

"And you know this, how, exactly?"

"I felt your hunger."

"Because you are chosen to judge, I suppose."

"Because we are not that different, Doctor Able." Mechisedec paused and breathed deeply. "In time, you will see that. But for now, ask yourself how else can I be fair unless God has entitled me to know the mysteries of the heart, the needs of the soul?"

"Psychosis comes to mind," Malice retorted.

"I'm sure your friend feels differently. I believe he will be thankful for his second chance."

"Chris? You think you *spared* him?"

"Indeed, Doctor Able. Despite your friend's profession, his heart is good. He needs—and wants—a different path. I have given him that opportunity."

"As what, a vegetable?"

"Your friend's destiny was not entrusted to me. He is negotiating that with God as we speak. We were discussing you, Doctor Able. I have sensed *your* sin. Would you like to know what it is?"

"Do tell."

"Detachment."

"It's a gift."

"Perhaps. But people tend to choose what affirms, supports and protects what they already are, or what they fear." Mechisedec waited for Malice to respond. He got nothing. "Tell me about the relationship between your mother and father?"

"So, my father made me do it?"

"Your selection of parent answers that, don't you think? We need our fathers to validate who we are. Our greater Father has asked us to love, to give of ourselves. But you have not done that, Daniel."

Malice couldn't help it. His mind went to the man that he revered because his mother loved him profoundly; and that he resented for his absence in their lives. Immediately after came awareness. "What did you call me?"

206

"Yes, I know who you are. Malec is flattered that his name is resurrected."

"Malec?"

"The angel in hell; its gatekeeper. You think you can retrieve your father from there."

Shaking away the invasion on his soul, Malice said to Mechisedec, "Who are you?"

"I am that which was saved by Temperance."

"Weren't born like the rest of us, huh? No mother, no father?"

"No. But just as you are the product of sacrificial love, so am I."

"Since we have so much in common, we should meet."

"We already have, Doctor Able. And by God's decree, we have further business."

Chapter 71.

Ben Riley knocked on Connor's door. He had promised to talk about what happened the night of Brooklyn's party, but he hadn't been able to put it into perspective. Everything had changed since that night in ways no one could have predicted. Now he stood at Connor's door, unsure what to say, how to feel, what to do.

She invited him in. "How's Brooklyn?"

"Not good." He placed his coat in the hand she held out to receive it.

"She's not going to recover from this, is she?"

"Don't know, Connor. Her world is in pieces. She can't work; she can't sleep. Reporters everywhere. It'll be a while before any of us makes sense of this mess."

Connor escorted Ben to the den where she poured him a drink, then went to the kitchen for the fruit tray she'd made for their talk. When she returned, anguish sat where the man who made love to her should have been. Connor stood for a minute before asking the question she knew would change her, too. "You love her, don't you?"

The question hit him in the gut. He felt unprepared to talk about their night together, but would have crawled through hot coals rather than answer. He stared at the fire's flame in the screened hearth in front of him.

Still holding the tray, Connor took a seat beside him and looked in the same direction. Except for the occasional crackle of fire, silence filled the room.

Ben swallowed his drink. "Maybe this isn't a good time," he said. "I'll call you tomorrow."

Connor watched him walk away. She needed something to consume the distance that instantly grew between them. She picked up an orange slice and sank her teeth into its flesh. The juice trickled towards the growing lump in her throat. Hearing the front door close, she bit again.

Chapter 72.

Two days had passed since the phone call that baffled all six agents. Malice and his team analyzed the recorded conversation with Mechisedec. "The man said nothing about himself," the psychologist pointed out. "This is sure to be the first of several calls we can expect."

"I'm not sure of that, doctor," Malice replied. "This guy is different. The old rules don't apply."

"Are you saying you believe him, that he's chosen by God to judge the quick and the dead?"

"I'm saying this guy makes his own rules and we should be careful about comparing him to a profile... or a movie." Malice faced Fugama. "Have you isolated anything useful in the blood from the goblet retrieved at the senator's house?"

"The blood is so mutated, it will take time."

Malice looked at two others on the team. "How did this guy access Doctor Mansell's records?"

"Mechisedec was in Mansell's office. But we think initially it was by computer link. There's a sophisticated interface on the doctor's computer."

"Have you traced it?"

"Yes."

"And?"

"It begins, and ends in the doctor's office. Somehow, the killer extracts the information as it passes through and loops it back to its point of origin."

"Before you ask, yes, we questioned the company hosting the server through which the data passed. They didn't know what the hell we were talking about. They searched their system, found an encryption code they couldn't break. We assume that was Mechisedec hacking in."

"We know the man is smart," Malice interjected. "He passed himself off as Oran Mansell, speaking the language and participating in criminal forensics as if he was born to it. Makes me wonder."

"What? That he might just be some kind of doctor?" Baru asked.

"Exactly. He seems to have memorized Mansell's book, or knew its contents so well he could have written it himself."

"I wondered that too," Baru added. "The limbs were severed with precision. That requires medical knowledge."

209

"And don't forget he knows something about philosophy and religion," the psychologist reminded them. "Both are required study in some medical professions."

Malice silently agreed. By all evidence, Mechisedec was an intellectual anomaly. He ended the meeting by making new assignments. "We know how he chose the ex-cons. Find out how he chose Pascal. We won't get many chances at this guy. Let's make the next one count. Baru, stay for a moment."

Malice rewound the recording. "The psychologist thinks Mechesidec disclosed nothing about himself. But, this guy says he was an orphan. If he gave us that fact, what other clues might he have given? Listen to this: 'I am that which was saved by Temperance'. Everyone assumed he was being Biblical, but what if he wasn't?"

Chapter 73.

Q-Tip was awake. Despite that he was officially in Van Every's custody, a federal order permitted only Doctor Able to question him. The order said nothing about questioning the physician, which Van Every did.

"Seems aware, but we haven't determined if there's brain damage, or to what degree. We've been restricted from further testing."

"Yeah, I know. The feds coated him with Teflon. Dr. Able called; he's on his way." There was a pause in the conversation while Van Every contemplated his next question. "Did his blood work show anything unusual, doctor?"

"In what way?"

"*Anything* out of the ordinary."

"No, the young man is exceptionally healthy."

"Thanks, doc. Owe you one."

Malice and Van Every arrived simultaneously at Dingo's room. The security guard nodded and shifted the weight around his waist. Malice motioned towards the door, inviting Van Every to enter.

"What's this about? First, I can't question him, now I'm here?"

"Would you rather be someplace else?"

"Not if it were a deserted island with the last ten Playboy Bunnies."

"Ten?" Malice chuckled. "When we're done here, I need you to do something for me." He reached into his shirt pocket and pulled out a folded sheet of paper. "See what you can find about this person. Look locally."

"What, no last name? Make it hard why don't ya." Van Every replied. "Luckily, a name like this can't be attached to that many people around here. And just what would I be looking for?"

"Trust me, you'll know when you find it." Both pushed open the door to Chris' room. It was muted as the doctor had instructed since they didn't know how he'd react to bright light. They found Chris staring at the window. He turned and searched Van Every's face for recognition. It came when he saw the man behind him. "Malice?"

"Welcome back." Malice laid his hand on top of Chris's. "This is Detective Van Every." Malice took a seat beside the bed. Van Every sat across the room out of sight. "Tell me what you remember?"

Chris turned again to the window. His gaze went beyond the blinds, beyond the light, beyond consciousness. He brought back one word. "Nothing."

გვ

My God, I have heard your call.
To you, I pledge my hands and feet
In service to your will,
Mercy shall be your reward,
Judgment shall be my name.

Chapter 74.

"Rae Lee, come look. There's a man coming up the path."
  "Who is it?"
  "Now, don't you think I would have said if I knew
who it was? Some white man."
  Rae Lee flung her dishtowel, waving off Carrie Agne's
remark as if shooing a fly. She peeked out the window. A
well-dressed man wearing a camel coat and Stetson hat
sidestepped drying puddles of mud on his way to their
door.
  "Who is it, Rae Lee? Should we call Lucas?"
  "Lord, no. Anybody coming to harm two old women
in the middle of this tragedy can't have a soul. And if
that's the case, Lucas can't help. Go get the door."
  "Me? This your house," Carrie Agnes reminded her.
"If it's all right by you, I'm gonna get my purse."
  Rae Lee sucked her teeth. She hated that Carrie had
brought a gun into her home, but understood the need to
feel safe. Davis had bought it, getting one with an easy
trigger, so he said. Rae Lee had made Carrie Agnes promise to keep it in her room, locked in the dresser. Carrie
Agnes didn't, of course, fussing that it was too much
trouble to mess with a lock if she ever needed it. So, she'd
put it in a purse and stuck it under her mattress, joking
that she hoped that easy trigger wouldn't go off and
shoot her in the rump. They had laughed at the thought.

Despite her admonition, Rae Lee secured the door with the chain lock and cracked it open as the visitor was about to knock.

"Good morning, ma'am. I hope I didn't frighten you."

Rae Lee could have sworn she heard cool water trickling through tall pond grass. Carrie's heavy steps broke her enchantment. "Is there something I can do for you, sir?"

"No, ma'am. I'm hoping there's something I can do for you. I'm here at the behest of Dr. Riley. As you know, he is convening doctors to counsel the poor people of this community who are grieving so much loss. I thought I'd introduce myself to the residents of this courageous town."

There it was again, the sound of water over rocks. "Oh, yes, Lucas and Ben have made mention."

"I've just had coffee with your neighbor, Mrs. Galebrey. Lovely woman."

From behind Rae Lee, Carrie Agnes asked, "You say you're here at the be-head of Doctor Riley? Just what do you mean by that?"

Rae Lee said, "Carrie Agnes, that is not what the man said." Pretending she had forgotten hospitality, she quickly amended the oversight by removing the metal chain hooked across the door. "Where are my manners?"

The stranger laughed as he entered. "No ma'am, I mean Doctor Riley asked for help. I am here to talk, that's all."

"And just what is it you do that can help us?" Carrie Agnes inquired.

"Lord, lord. Forgive my friend. Please, let me take your coat and hat. Have a seat Mister…"

"Mansell. Reverend, Doctor Oran Mansell."

Chapter 75.

Malice had waved off the medic-copter taking Chris back to Virginia, then called Ben and Lucas for dinner. It would likely be their last encounter for some time. Now, he sat outside Brooklyn's house wondering what to expect and how he would handle whatever he found. Ben had said she wasn't adjusting very well; she was different. Malice could not imagine what it was like to worship someone and have that trust betrayed. His mother had said, 'the lowest rung in hell is reserved for those who betray'. As he headed up the walkway, he hoped it were true.

Brooklyn opened the door. The sunlight forced her to notice the blend of Native American that he'd gotten from his mother, and Caribbean mix from his father.

Malice smiled gingerly as she invited him in. Her home was different, too; felt different from the time he was here not that long ago when Christmas spirit had touched everything with pride. Now, the fir tree, with all its grandeur tried to go un-noticed. The stereo minstrels were silent. Her hair was pulled away from her face and tied with a scarf at the back of her neck. Despite her lack of effort and the stress that resided in her eyes, she was still beautiful.

"What brings you back to town?" she asked.

"The suspect is being taken to Virginia. I stayed to say goodbye to Ben and Lucas, Detective Van Every, a few others. I head back tomorrow."

"Oh. That's nice… That you're saying goodbye…. Oh, I don't mean—"

"I know. Look, it's a stupid question, but how are you?"

"I go back to work tomorrow. Maybe that will help."
She realized she had not shown hospitality and offered to take his coat.

"Actually, why don't you get yours? Come with me to the mall. I could use help choosing a gift for Ben and Lucas." He hadn't considered that idea until this instant. He wanted to hear the elves wish her a Merry Christmas, see the mice wave their hands, and deer bob their heads in her direction. He hoped for the miracle promised in Saint Nick's laughter, and skating teddy bears.

Brooklyn was about to refuse, but Malice said, "Please. I usually drag my mother shopping with me, but she's not here, so I thought of you."

"I remind you of your mother?"

He laughed, "I hadn't considered it, but… yes, you do. Something… about… the eyes." He touched her face lightly with the balls of his fingers. "Ah yes, I see it now; she has the same shaggy plot of grass she calls a brow…"

Brooklyn smiled and touched her hair with both hands. "I'm not—"

It had begun. She smiled. "If you were more ready, I'd have to wear a tux, " he said. "Please; grab your coat."

Shopping had done it; Brooklyn had relaxed, and six gifts lay wrapped on the back seat of his car. One for Ben, Lucas, Ms. Carrie Agnes, Davis, and Ms. Mava. He couldn't decide on the label for gift number six. Should it read Ms. Rae Lee or Grandmother? Since Ben had not told her the night the judge was killed, it was unfair to give her a grandson in one minute, and go in search of a serial killer the next. That would be too cruel.

Chapter 76.

Carrie Agnes poured their visitor more coffee. "I don't believe in such nonsense like 'Get behind me, Satan'. I don't want Satan at my back. I wanna look that devil in the face so I can see what he's up to."

The man posing as Oran Mansell laughed. "Would that matter, Mrs. Carrie Agnes? I suspect Satan is a masterful trickster."

"Ain't that the truth," Rae Lee said. "I've seen a many faces swearing the truth through tears the size of gumdrops and even that was a lie."

"All I'm saying is, when a person is out to harm you, look the bastard in the face." Carrie Agnes followed that with: "Excuse me, Reverend."

"No harm, Mrs. Carrie Agnes. God cares less for the words you use as He does the truth in what you're saying."

"Seems God stopped caring."

"Why would you say such a thing, Carrie Agnes?" Rae Lee questioned.

"I think I understand what sister Carrie Agnes is saying. All one has to do is look outside and see that many have been severely tested to believe in a caring God."

Rae Lee countered Mansell's view. "We are still alive. And God is God. We don't get to question His work."

"If God can question mine, why can't I ask what He's up to?"

"Indeed, sister Carrie Agnes. I suspect the Archangel posed the same question. 'To whom is God accountable?' If He has promised to serve man, why not account for his actions; why add the fear of retribution, why the threat of hell?"

"Which is where Carrie Agnes is going with her blasphemy," Rae Lee said. "Reverend, I can't believe you're defending her."

"I've upset you. Please accept my apology. But I only raise the question sister Carrie is wrestling with to make a point about salvation. God does not take with one hand and judge our loss without also giving something of more value, even as He appears to render condemnation."

"And what would that be?" asked Carrie Agnes.

"Forgiveness, sister. Forgiveness. No matter what you do, what you say, God washes it all in the greatest act of love man will ever know."

Carrie Agnes did not back down. "And what act would that be?"

"The giving of life, sister, in this world, and the next. Renewal. The hope we see in the eyes of a newborn child. The ritual of communion—the celebration of the blood that binds us to each other, and to our Creator. Yes, sister, it is the gift of life."

Both women nodded their heads and said in unison, "Amen. Praise the Lord."

"Have communion with me, sisters. As mother Rae Lee pointed out, even as your world was torn asunder, you have life. That should be celebrated. I have everything we need in my car."

While Mansell was gone, Rae Lee insisted Carrie Agnes take her gun away from what was about to be consecrated space. And she did.

Mansell returned with a small cooler and tote bag. He removed a beautifully embroidered cloth and laid it across the coffee table. He lit three pillar candles: one red, one black, one green. He placed seven shorter white candles around the three and lit them too. Three small silver goblets, gleamed under the candles' glow. From the cooler, he took a decorative thermos and set it in the center of the altar. "Come sisters, let us pray."

The three stood and joined hands around the sanctifying light.

217

Chapter 77.

"Do you know what sin is, Dr. Able?"

"Right now, you top my list."

Mechisedec chuckled. "Christianity would have you believe it is having eaten of the tree of life. But the real sin is not to eat. To always be a spectator rather than an actor in life; to ask for permission rather than forgiveness."

Again, Malice had not expected this voice when he picked up the phone in his hotel room and said hello.

"The point of life is to say 'yes,' Doctor Able, to the good and the bad, the right, the wrong, and all the possibilities in between."

Malice tuned in. "In other words, "It's all good."

"What a lovely phrase. Yes, Doctor Able, it *is* all good. But even as I share this secret with you, you must also know that there is always one forbidden thing."

"Which is what?"

"Ah…"

"So, we're back to you playing dress-up. Before it was psychologist. Now, it's philosopher?"

"Exactly my point, Doctor Able. I am, at least, playing. Speaking of which, I visited two lovely ladies today."

"Are you telling me you've killed again?" Malice went through the list of bodies. All Mechisedec's victims had been men.

"Termination is not always my objective, Doctor Able. Sometimes I restore. The same hand that takes life, gives it; it is a continuous circle. Which is the beginning, and which is the end?"

"So, you're giving me riddles?"

"Hmmm. A riddle wrapped in an enigma. I can't remember where I heard that, but I do like the redundancy."

Malice wondered how Mechisedec knew he was in town, and which hotel, but decided it was a waste to ask.

"Tell me, Doctor Able; did you ask your friend about his experience?"

"You want to know if Chris saw you?"

"What would that matter? You have seen me, and to what benefit?" Mechisedec hesitated briefly to breathe out disappointment "I want to know about his visit with God."

"What is the real purpose of your call, Mr. ...?"

"The name the media has provided is sufficient. And the purpose of my call... I said we would meet again. It is time. Come join me—at the home of a benevolent woman and her dear companion. I am here now."

"And just where might that be."

"I told you home is a holy place, Doctor Able. Where better for us to meet again?"

Malice's brain went into hyper-drive. Was he in Virginia? Could he have found his mother and a friend? "Where the hell are you?"

"Right here, Doctor Able. Princeville is the place you regard as home, is it not?"

Instantly, Malice went from confusion to fear. "Oh my God," escaped from his thoughts.

"Indeed, Doctor Able. "

Malice grabbed his keys and satchel and raced out the door. He made two calls by the time he reached his car. The first was to his team leader. The next was to Van Every.

He wheeled the car around debris and mud puddles towards his grandmother's house. The presents on the back seat flung from side to side. He wished he could call Ben and Lucas, but this was out of their league. Van Every was his most effective ally, and best hope. He instructed Van

Every to bring only one man with him—the best sharp shooter in the squad.

He pressed a code into his phone. When the person answered, he said, "Locate the number and connect me to Rae Lee York in Princeville, North Carolina."

"Hold, Dr. Able. I'll try now." The person was off line for less than ten seconds. "Agent, that line is interrupted. No calls will go through."

Malice hung up the phone and pounded the steering wheel. "Son-of-a-bitch!"

He mentally inventoried the instruments in his satchel. His right hand opened the bag, instinctively retrieved a device, and dropped it in his coat pocket. He withdrew two others and secured them as he'd done on his last assignment in Africa. Rather than speculate that his grandmother and Carrie Agnes were dead, he formulated a strategy for killing Mechisedec on sight.

Chapter 78.

Mava Pelter paced the floor from her kitchen to the bedroom that was a shrine to her husband. She came here when agitation filled her. She'd touch his things, the bowling trophies, photographs of him fishing with friends, scrapbooks of places they'd been. She'd talk to Ferris and remember. Afterwards, she'd be okay; she'd know what to do. But she held the doorknob in her hand as the dream energy coursed through her body and held her still. Fear made her sweat. When she could move, she rushed to the phone and called Lucas.

"Baby, go see about mama."

"What's the matter, Aunt Mava?"

"Something ain't right over there. You gotta go check on her and Mrs. Rae. You gotta go, Lucas."

"But—"

"Now!"

The fear in Mava's voice scared him. Lucas looked at the clock as he dialed. While the phone rang, he took off his uniform and put on his dress slacks and pullover sweater. "Ben, Aunt Mava just called; said something's wrong at Mrs. Rae Lee's... No, she didn't say. I think she had a dream. Probably all this stuff about the judge and the serial killer is messing with her. I'll get to the restaurant as soon as I can. You stay so Dr. Able won't think we abandoned him. I'll call you from the house."

Detective Van Every was not at the specified location when Malice steered his vehicle in place. He screeched to a stop and let the engine run. Only seconds clicked off the clock when he slammed the gearshift into drive.

Pounding the car through caked mud, he jerked to a stop in front of his grandmother's house. Dim lights glowed through the living room curtains. The front door was slightly ajar, music seeped through the crack; the refrain of *Silent Night* passed his ear.

He withdrew one of the weapons he'd secured and slowly pushed open the door. In the living room, a shadow moved. The figure stepped forward. It was Mechisedec.

"Please, come in, Daniel. We have much to discuss before we decide."

Raising his weapon, Malice shouted, "What have you done with them?"

"In due time."

Malice kept his weapon aimed at the intruder's head. "The only decision I have to make is whether to kill you right now, or let them do it slowly in Virginia."

"Well, that is something to ponder. But, before we decide, let's talk. Please, sit, Daniel. I insist." Mechisedec moved to the side chair where he'd spent the afternoon and folded his arms, letting Malice know he posed no immediate threat.

Following suit, Malice rested the weapon in his lap. Mechisedec was not wearing the monk's robe that Chris and Fawks had described. Thoughts of Rae Lee and Carrie Agnes filled his brain, but he forced worry aside and let expertise guide him. "You're quite the anomaly."

"Who better than you would know?" Mechisedec let the statement linger. "But this meeting is not about me."

"Isn't it? Don't you want to tell me all about your mission from God and the victims you chose?"

"Victims? There are no victims, Daniel. Frankly, it is the most offensive word in any civilized society. It should be stricken from every language. There are only choices and consequences that lead to actions and more consequences."

"So, you're back to philosopher. Fine. Then what of those who are hurt or killed by no choice of their own, like my grandmother, you piece of shit?" He was hoping Mechisedec would tell him Rae Lee was fine...

"All have chosen, Daniel. All are part of a fantastic improvisational play."

... but he didn't. "What's your point?"

"Free will, Daniel. That's my point. Isn't that a marvelous idea? To discover and create playgrounds of opportunities where every step requires a choice be made. Therein, the cast is assembled and the play begins."

Malice noticed the calm in the man's voice. It made him listen.

"What is it you want from me?" Malice asked.

"What have you to offer?"

"What did you get from the others?"

222

"The ultimate performance. Their choices ensured your arrival here; they opened the stage for you."

"So now you're a director?" Malice asked.

Mechisedec laughed. "You see how easy it is to slip out of one thing into another? But you have chosen to confine yourself to one meaningless role. So, we are here, Daniel, to discuss that ubiquitous question: 'To be or not to be.' Tonight, we examine your performance and whether you get to participate in this exceptional drama hereafter."

"You seem to be judge and jury. You tell me."

Mechisedec rose from his chair. He watched Malice clutch the weapon on his lap. Instead of showing concern, he went to the window, gently pulled back the drape, and looked out.

"Expecting someone?" Malice asked.

Mechisedec did not reply; he turned and asked a question of his own. "What do you wish the outcome of this scene to be?"

Malice relaxed his grip on the weapon and spoke without hesitation. "You dead suits me."

"Hmmm... I see. How would my death change your life in any consequential way?"

"The rest of the world would feel safe."

"Would they? I'd give that a day. Then what? The question was: how would my death change *your* life?"

"Is this the bullshit you gave everybody else? If so, you bored them to death."

"I see you like playing hide and seek. Fine. Then I shall count. 1... 2... 3..."

Malice jumped from his seat and pointed the weapon at Mechisedec's face. "Where are they!?"

"Out of hiding so quickly?" Mechisedec did not waver except to move his hands towards the pockets of his slacks.

"Where I can see them," Malice shouted. He glanced out the window himself and saw nothing, but hoped Van Every had Mechisedec in scope for a bullet. He moved to give the rifleman a view of his position and to block the shot for now. He needed more time to learn what the maniac had done with his grandmother. "Why don't we sit back down and get this done?"

The sharpshooter positioned herself against a nearby tree. Van Every crouched at the backdoor with a lock pick but it was already open. He slid on his knees and elbows towards the living room within earshot of the two men's conversation. He heard Mechisedec speaking.

"My last question appears to require some thought. So, let us move to Scene Two of this Act. Let's talk about love."

"Let me guess, you didn't get enough as a child?"

"Love, Doctor," he said more sternly. "I'm aware that it's an unfamiliar subject, but try. We are running out of time."

Unsure what that meant, Malice complied. "I don't understand. What am I suppose to tell you about love?"

"Let's get one thing straight, Doctor; we are not playing a game of chess. You have mastered the art of avoidance; your teachers must be proud. But we are deciding your fate, whether you act your part in this realm or the next. As you consider that monumental truth, know this: other lives are affected by what you say and do."

Malice hoped Mechisedec meant his grandmother and Mrs. Carrie Agnes were still alive. But, he looked at the goblets on the coffee table and fear rose in his throat.

"Love..." He paused for several seconds. "You're right. I know nothing about it, except what I've read in books and seen in movies. I don't know if the writers are speaking from experience or wet dreams."

"Uninspired, and not entirely true. You have seen love in action, first hand. So let's try again, shall we. The night of Ms. Beaudeau's party, in her presence, there was a change in you. Tell me about that."

Malice lowered his head for a second. He turned away from Mechisedec to consider the words that formed in his head. He saw a body on the floor at the kitchen door. Since he didn't hear Van Every enter, he hoped Mechisedec had not either. That possibility heightened his curiosity about what the man had been before Greenville, North Carolina claimed him.

"I don't know what I feel for Ms. Beaudeau."

"Insufficient."

Silence stretched like an Indiana highway as Malice considered his feelings. He thought he heard ripples on a pond that echoed in his soul. The words began to flow. "I feel as if I know her. Or, that I want to. When the situation with her uncle and the judge erupted, I wanted to protect her. Making the pain go away was—is—all I think about."

"But you do nothing out of respect for Benjamin Riley."

"Yes."

So, you sacrifice the possibility of love to loyalty."

"If that's what it is, that's what it is."

"That is your pattern, Doctor Able. You sacrifice love. And always to loyalty. Growing up, you denied youthful love for loyalty to your mother. You ignored your heritage, your family out of loyalty to your profession. And now you sacrifice again out of respect."

Mechisedec paused. "What is denied as one thing will always manifest as something else. Anger turns to hate, hate turns to violence. Fear becomes insecurity, insecurity becomes cruelty. That is the balance of creation. What you were handed from the river of love, you poured into the pond of loyalty, over and over again. But love can not be made into anything else—as hard as you've tried."

"What's your point?"

"That *is* my point; and that is your sin, Doctor Able. Abandonment. It is what your father did to you, isn't it?" Mechisedec let the weight of his statement bore into Malice's mind. But he was not finished.

"And what of Ben and Lucas? And remember, Doctor, time is not your friend."

On one side of his brain, Malice was aware Mechisedec no longer called him Daniel and wondered if he knew Van Every was there. This son-of-a-bitch is protecting my identity. Even as he thought it, on the other side of his brain, he heard the water's flow, like a distant babbling brook. The word abandonment echoed with each ripple.

"Ben is the brother I will never have. Lucas is the kindest man I've ever met. His compassion and concern for others exceed anything I've ever known."

"So it does, " Mechisedec replied. "When we spoke on the phone, I told you that all is good, even that which some call evil. And even this truth bears one forbidden thing."

"And you're going to tell me what that is?"

"Just as every seeker must discover Truth for themselves, each has to discover the Forbidden with the same vigor." Mechisedec chuckled. "There it is again, a mystery wrapped in an enigma."

As Malice was about to speak, he heard a car drive up and the car door slam. He looked over to Mechisedec, who did not look the least bit concerned. Malice sprang from his seat and leapt towards Mechisedec. Needing to know about his grandmother kept him from shooting. He yelled for Van Every, "Stop whoever is outside!"

Hearing the commotion, Lucas raced inside before Van Every could get to the door. Malice, and the man he knew as Oran Mansell were in a heated struggle. He saw Van Every coming towards him, but he moved to help Malice. As he did, a rifle shot rang from outside and shattered the glass.

Van Every rushed to the door and shouted to his detective to hold her fire. "Call an ambulance and backup. 11-99. Officer down!"

The officer took off for the cruiser she'd parked off the road. Van Every turned to see Malice and Mechisedec in what would have looked like a dance had they been moving slower. The deftness of each movement made him watch. The whirl of air was their music. They were two instruments of precision performing masterfully. Van Every knelt beside Lucas and felt for a pulse. He stood up and drew his weapon, "Stand down!"

Neither Mechisedec nor Malice interrupted the energy passing between them. Malice yelled to Van Every, "Don't shoot," and moved between the weapon and the prey.

In that second, Mechisedec withdrew a small ice pick from behind his back and jabbed his hand. Blood filled the cavity.

Malice jumped onto the table and lunged a kick at Mechisedec. He saw the ice pick leave Mechisedec's hand and split the air. He knew it was not meant for him when he heard Van Every yelp. His weapon fired. The bullet creased Malice's shoulder. Blood stained his sweater.

Mechisedec folded his body to absorb the kick; there was no time to deflect the force headed for his chest. He stumbled back and interlocked his fingers, letting the blood from his left hand saturate the right. He saw Malice grab something from his sleeve that looked like a small remote control. Mechisedec leapt into the air and flayed his

227

hands towards Malice, sending blood in every direction. Malice ducked. It was enough time for Mechisedec to extend a kick of his own and dislodge the weapon from Malice's hand. He followed the powerful kick with a vigorous blow to Malice's injured shoulder. Malice went down.

Mechisedec grabbed Malice from behind and locked him in a choke-hold, holding his bloody left palm above the bullet wound and whispered. "I have judged you, Daniel. Tonight is the consequence of your choices. What looks like punishment today, becomes evidence of love tomorrow. All is good, even death." As Malice heard those last words, everything went black.

The ambulance and two squad cars arrived on the scene and found three men on the floor. Two were rushed to the hospital. The coroner was called for the other.

Chapter 79.

Rae Lee and Carrie Agnes awoke in a hotel room in Kinston. They called Davis who called Ben. The women could tell them nothing about how they got to the hotel. The last they remembered was taking communion with Reverend Oran Mansell.

When Ben couldn't reach Malice, he left a note with the hostess. He tried ringing Rae Lee's home for Lucas, but the line was down. He called Van Every to report Mansell was in the area, but was told the detective was in the field. Panic grew with the urgent call to come to the morgue. The examiner would not say why.

Nothing prepared Ben for what he found. Lucas' body lay on the table with a bullet wound at the back of his head. A squall of wine and bread churned in Ben's stomach. Nausea wrenched him almost in two. He stumbled.

The only words that formed in his mind, and echoed from his mouth were, "Oh God…"

Ben rushed to his office and found support on the old leather chair. Its comfort did not relieve the pain that welled in him. Throbs of searing red burst in his chest and attacked the air in his lungs. When he could think again, the officer drove him to the hospital for the second assault on his faculties.

Van Every would be okay. The ice pick had punctured an artery in his thigh. The sharpshooter had administered skillful triage that saved his life. Malice's condition was more complicated.

"Doctor Able presented with syncope," the attending physician said. "Given the lack of blood to the cerebrum, surprisingly, there is no obvious brain damage. But there is bradycardia."

"How many beats?" Ben questioned, setting aside his emotions long enough to understand his cousin's condition.

"Fifty-six. Mechanical CPR hasn't raised it. We'd like at least 60 for a comfort zone."

"Doctor Able's in excellent physical condition. That rate may be inconsequential," Ben offered. Based on what he'd learned of his cousin the last few weeks, Ben suspected Malice had slowed his own heart rate at will.

"Doctor," Ben continued. "Did you order an echo-cardiogram?"

"Yes, the results should be available shortly."

Ben thanked the Doctor, and went to Malice's room. He stared out the window into darkness through eyes cloaked in grief. He thanked God that Malice was okay. In the next breath, his lungs burned again with the pain of Lucas' death. He prayed for help to survive the experience. He was certain Sandra would not. He thought of the boys;

they were too young to be fatherless. Their loss became like salt eating away the sinews of his courage. He didn't know if he could handle what would be expected of him this time.

Before he could absorb that magnitude, the door to Malice's room sprang open. Three men came through. Two were strangers; the third went directly to Malice.

"Doctor Fugama," Ben called. It was more a question than a statement.

Fugama understood. "Doctor Able called about an hour ago. He said Mechisedec was back in Princeville. We heard what happened when we radioed the station to report our arrival."

Ben watched Fugama check Malice's chart while one of the men packed Malice's belongings into plastic bags. The other man talked into a phone like the one Malice had given him.

When Fugama was done, the agents wheeled Malice out of the room. Ben started to follow, but Fugama stopped him. "I understand you have an appointment with a widow. Delay does not make it easier." Fugama walked out behind the gurney, and turned towards Van Every's room, leaving Ben unsure what to do.

Breaking News the following day carried a story nowhere close to what had happened, thanks to Van Every's account to the reporters who had surrounded his bed before Fugama's team arrived.

"A man posing as a minister drugged two elderly Princeville women and abducted them. They were safe. Sheriff Lucas Belton came upon the suspect and was shot during pursuit. Sheriff Belton was pronounced dead at the scene." This was the essence of the News.

"What was the assailant's motivation?" one reporter had asked.

"From the looks of things, robbery, most likely. No other reason to bind two old ladies. Looks like he didn't want to hurt them, just wanted them out of the way."

"Why would a criminal go to such trouble?" another inquired.

"Who understands the criminal mind? Ninety percent of what they do makes no sense."

"Why were you there, Detective?" another reporter asked. "Princeville is not your jurisdiction."

"I was meeting a colleague who was visiting the hostages. Told him I'd drop by. He and I happened on the scene and caused the suspect to flee. During pursuit, I was injured. Doctor Able fought with the man and was rendered unconscious. That's when Sheriff Belton arrived, and was shot."

Van Every was grateful everyone assumed Lucas was shot by the perpetrator. He could not tell them about the sharpshooter who thought Lucas was Mechisedec. She explained that only Dr. Able had shown up on her heat sensor scope from inside the house. When Lucas ran towards Malice, she shot.

Van Every's story was plausible. Shortly thereafter, he became unavailable for further comments. No one was told he had been taken with Malice to Virginia for extensive examination. He had been exposed to Mechisedec's blood; the implications where unknown.

Only a few reporters continued the story. Regina Bailey focused on Sheriff Belton's family. She did a commentary on Rae Lee York and Carrie Agne's ordeal, and the evil that could deceive, rob, and ultimately kill in the aftermath of disaster. 'Tragedy, Justice, Fate,' she wrote. 'All three random, all three blind. Yet, all three met in Princeville, to fulfill a purpose only they knew'.

Malice recovered and was fine. So was Van Every. The two were released two days later and returned to Greenville to examine the crime scene. Malice used the time to befriend the man who helped save his life. "What did you do before Greenville, Detective?" He asked.

"Things I don't want to remember, Doc."

Malice looked at the man and quietly accepted his answer. "Where did you do these things?"

"In places I'd rather forget."

Malice was impressed. He moved to another line of questions. "The 'T' on your office door, what's it for?"

Van Every half smiled. "Thelonious." He watched the line at Malice's lips turn into a grin. "My father was a musician, and my mom had a sense of humor. Monk was on the cover of Time magazine the year I was born. My dad was so excited he brought it to the hospital the day my mother gave birth instead of her suitcase. Only three other jazz musicians have had that honor. I still have the magazine."

"Who would have thought?" Malice said.

"Nobody. And I'd like to keep it that way," Van Every replied.

"Done." Malice reached over and laid his fist atop Van Every's. The secret was sealed.

The following morning, Malice met Ben for breakfast. "I'd like to be involved in Lucas's service if you think his wife wouldn't mind. Pallbearer, offer a tribute, something, anything."

"Sandra would appreciate that. The funeral is tomorrow. She's decided on cremation. I think she just needs to keep him nearby. Or maybe she knows those caskets coming out of the ground is what has put him there." Ben looked into his coffee, watching the cream whirl into the blackness and turn it the color of almond skin. Finally, he looked up.

Malice saw the hurt in Ben. It had defaced the glint in his eyes and stolen the glow from his skin. There was nothing he could say. But he tried.

"The body is a miraculous creation, Ben. I've spent my career trying to figure out how it works. You know what I've learned? That life is a singular event that you ought to live the best you can because there are a thousand ways to die. And one day, one of them will knock on your door. Lucas did that."

"What happened that night, Malice?"

He could not lie to Ben. Not now. "Mechisedec happened."

"I figured as much after talking with Aunt Rae. I didn't have time to be scared for them before I found myself looking into a hole in the back of my best friend's skull. And then, finding you in the hospital almost a stick of wood."

Ben was about to ask 'why,' but sucked it back into his jar of stupid-ass questions. Instead, he took a sip of coffee, grabbed his hat, and stood. "We'll talk, later; you free for lunch?"

"Yeah. The Lone Star? For our own private farewell."

Ben stood, rested a hand on Malice's shoulder, and left. Outside, the wind blew on the tear that clung to his lashes and made him brush it away.

Chapter 80.

Malice slipped into the back and sat on the last pew in Courtroom Three. Judge Brooklyn Beaudeau didn't miss a beat presiding over the case before her. Despite her commanding presence, he could see the distance in her eyes.

Malice rested his hand upon the small gift-wrapped box he'd bought into the courtroom. As he turned it in his hand his mind played a distilled loop of the encounter with Mechisedec. Three statements lingered.

You sacrifice love to loyalty.

Love can't be made into anything else, no matter how hard you try.

This is your sin.

The pounding of Brooklyn's gavel broke his trance at the part where he'd been spared. The perplexity of it made him think about his visit with Chris. Mechisedec had wanted to know what he had chosen, but brushed it aside as if the answer were irrelevant. Malice had hesitated in broaching the subject and was surprised when Chris said he'd made a decision.

"What we do is bullshit, Malice. This whole quest for power is bullshit."

Malice looked into the eyes that had eluded everyone, including himself. They were now like windows so clear he imagined blowing on a dandelion and releasing it to the wind.

Chris' next comment wasn't so clear. "What did you see?"

The question worked through Malice, and grabbed at something just below the surface that altered his appearance.

Chris decided to change the subject. "Did I tell you? My language center got a boost!" Chris smiled broadly. "San doute, eh?"

"Yes, no doubt. Who said you can't make a silk purse from a sow's ear?" Malice said.

Chris softened his grin. "I'm taking a year off, Malice. Sort some things. Travel the countryside of places I haven't been. Become a translator for tourists somewhere. Run naked." He laughed. "Epater les burgeois."

Malice laughed, too. "That would do it."

The laughter abated and Chris was serious again. "Speaking of language…I've always wondered how you chose your name. It sounds like Malec, the angel in charge of hell."

"Yeah, I heard that recently."

"Islamic myth says the condemned go to him to intercede with Allah on their behalf. Malec is the silent type. He'll only answer the sinners a thousand years after Judgment Day."

"A thousand years after? What does he say to Allah?"

"Let them suffer."

Malice laughed out loud, "No hope, huh?" even as he thought of his father.

Chris reached for a pen and paper. "I have something for you. You can decide what to do with it when the time comes." He handed the sheet of paper to Malice. "You'll find a key at the first location. It opens a safety deposit box at another. You won't have any problems gaining access."

Malice looked at his friend. "What, your playboy collection?"

"Something like that. In fact, one of the editions is written especially for you. Interesting reading once you get past the pictures." Chris saw the recognition on Malice's face. "The only protection you'll need is from old age and VD."

"Yeah? I hear there's a pill for both." Malice took the paper, memorized the instructions, and went to the restroom where he flushed the commode. Upon return, he listened and contributed occasionally as Chris talked more, and more deeply than he'd thought him capable of doing. He ended their time together with, "Send me a postcard. Often."

Chris' response was: "Dum vivimus vivamus."

Outside, Malice thought on Chris' remark. 'While we live, let us live.'

Brooklyn pounded the gavel, ending his reflection. Malice struggled with decisions of his own over the last few days. He'd made three so far. To help bury Lucas was the first he'd acted upon. As he watched Brooklyn call the next case, the second became crystal as rain and calmed him.

He quietly pushed through the double doors and left the courtroom unnoticed. He found his way to Connor's office. After sharing sympathy for Lucas and concern for Brooklyn, Malice took Connor's hand and placed the gift box there. "Will you see that she gets this?"

She gently pressed the package to her chest. "It's the best assignment I've had in a while."

"May I ask you to do one more thing."

"Anything," Connor replied.

"Reach out to Ben. He needs you."

In his car, before starting the engine, Malice reread the card in his mind that he'd attached to Brooklyn's gift: 'This reminds me of home,' it said. 'Hope it brings you the same comfort'. When Brooklyn opened the box, she'd find a decorative canister of the coffee that made his world seem kind.

It was mid-afternoon. Headed towards decision number three, Malice drove his car along now familiar streets, absorbing the little signs that foretold the power of hope. He'd driven this very path less than a week ago; but it was different somehow. He reluctantly accepted the drive wasn't different, but he. Another Mechisedec message came forth as 'you will thank me later—for killing your friend… For making you fear for an old woman's life... For introducing you to heartbreak'.

The perversity of it thumped his senses like a bongo player free-styling with Miles Davis, from the place where pain took its first breath in the wee hours before day broke the spell of midnight. He vowed, upon his mother's life, that Mechisedec would see him again.

Malice brought the car to a stop and looked up the road to his destination. His mind went to the stories he'd heard from his mother. Tanjene and Levi Athan. The naming of Princeville. He thought of Lucas and his unwavering concern for the people he served. He thought of Ben and his total willingness to help his best friend even beyond death. He saw Brooklyn walking her uncle's footsteps. He could not keep out memories of Judge Pascal and Joy Marie. Even though Pascal had killed his sister, he also gave her justice.

Love was at the heart of each memory. A lump rose in his throat. He forced it back down and rested his head against the window until he could breath again. He put the car in drive and continued up the narrow dirt road. He parked and reached into the back seat for the gifts that lay waiting. He scribbled on the tags and imagined the look of joy he hoped they'd bring.

At the door, he looked into Rae Lee's eyes. Before she could invite him in, Malice reached out a gift to her. "This is for you. It's from my mother."

The tag read: To Ray Lee York. The From said: Denise. "Oh, how wonderful! My daughter's name is Denise, too. Isn't that something?" she smiled. "Come in, baby, come on in. Why would your mother send me a gift? That is so sweet."

Malice smiled. He followed her inside and closed the door as Rae Lee sat on the sofa, about to open her gift when Malice stopped her. "Not yet." He handed her the second box. "This one is from me," he said.

Rae Lee read the words aloud. "It says, 'With Love, your... grandson... Daniel'."

Daniel Malice St.John, II smiled as he witnessed the look of puzzle pieces coming together on his grandmother's face. It was like a stream of water finding a pond. When the last piece was securely in place, she looked up, unable to speak. Tears welled in her eyes. She put a trembling hand to her mouth. He did not fight the mist in his own heart that turned his words into a ragged whisper. "Merry Christmas, Nana."

Chapter 81.

Chris tossed in his sweat. The dream that stalked him grew closer. Bits and pieces of a cataclysmic event were coming, rejoining, brain fluid their liquid fusion. An horrific memory emerged. He was back there, that night in the woods where his ear exploded in pain. Before that a man had confessed to murder.

"I don't know what possessed me," William Henry Pascal had said. "Joy Marie was dead. And as much as I hated her pregnancy, she was happier about that child than anything I'd seen. At the last minute, I couldn't deny her that. I had no idea what to do, but I wrapped her in a blanket and laid her on the kitchen table. I got the sharpest knife I could find and carefully slit her stomach. There was so little blood. When I opened her womb, I laughed. She was carrying twins." Pascal had let out a small laugh laced with pride.

"I took them out and cleaned their little faces. They were so tiny, and I didn't know what I was doing. I got one of them to cry. The other never did. I guess the poison had gotten into his bloodstream first. I tried but couldn't revive him. So I put him back inside the womb and folded Joy Marie's skin over him. I wrapped her belly tightly with the lace runner.

"I combed Joy Marie's hair before putting her in the casket I had hidden in the barn. I washed up, and did what I could for her child. That tiny little boy was perfect. I soaked a rag in sugar water and let him suck on it. I got in my car and drove to Washington. I took him to the first hospital I saw and told them I had found him beside the road. They took him immediately. The nurse asked me to wait but by the time she had gotten him to the neonatal unit, I was back on the Interstate. I never told anyone. When I got home, I called Vincent to bury my sister and his dead son. I realize how cruel that was but I didn't know who else to call.

"Over the years, I've wanted to tell Vincent the truth but I don't know what that is. If the child died, the pain he's lived with all these years is the same. If the child survived, there is no way to find what became of him. I imagine that pain is worse."

It was here that Chris had needed his Q-Tip. He remembered thinking how, for the first time in his career, he

239

would enjoy relieving this man of his burden as soon as the monk was gone. Pascal then asked the priest, "Is there redemption for me?" And the priest had said a prayer. The dream ended abruptly when Chris sprang up in bed. He called Malice. "I know who he is!"

Chapter 82.

Van Every rounded the corner as Malice grabbed his bag for the flight to Virginia. "I'm glad I caught you," he said. He reached into his pocket and pulled out the sheet of paper Malice had given him at the hospital. "Brought you something."

Malice answered, "A going away present?"

"Something like that." Van Every handed Malice an envelope. Inside were two sheets of paper, one of which was a photograph. On the top of the second page was the name Malice had given him to research. Just like on the board of All Else, Van Every had drawn lines from the name to four boxes labeled: Family, Friends, Location, Occupation. "If lives are gonna cross, they'll do it here," he'd told his team. From those boxes he had drawn a line to an empty box near the bottom of the page.

"I thought you said you had answers."

"I wanted to see the look on your face," Van Every replied. "I had to go deep for this. Used up some creds."

"I understand," Malice replied.

"Temperance is a fifty-eight year-old native of Princeville. Like most every other young person around here looking for a future, she went north. Stopped in DC. She had been there a few years when she took in a foster child. Afterwards, she left the state. The agency didn't bother looking for her. The kid had been in and out of hospitals since birth." VanEvery watch recognition crawl into Malice's veins.

"How old was the child?" Malice asked.

"Around four or five. A boy. He'd be mid-thirties today."

"Pascal's name goes in the box, doesn't it?"

"Home... Friend... Occupation. Another trifecta. But you already knew that, doc."

"No, Detective. Not till now."

"Temper—that's what they called her—was the daughter of the Pascal family housekeeper, and Joy Marie's childhood friend. Some say her best friend even though Temperance was black and a few years older."

"Did you find her?"

"Not yet?"

Malice shook his head and was silent for several minutes. "Mechisedec," he said out loud.

"You think Mechisedec killed her, too?"

"No," Malice answered, "but she could have put him in motion. The bigger question is, 'Is he finished?'"

"Then he's nothing but a vigilante?"

"He's more than that, Detective."

"What the hell is this about, Able?"

"Detective, if I told you that, I'd have to kill you."

Chapter 83.

Mechisedec slept. Dreams brought faces with demands to be heard. Some called for retribution. Fear filled the boy in his dream. Lights rolled past him on the way to one more examination. His own screams echoed down the long corridor with the sullen gray walls. He ate and slept between injections, always longing for a voice to calm him, a song to comfort him, a kiss that made it all right. Even in his sleep he cried. By the time she found him, there were no more tears to give.

"Finding you was God's will," the woman said to the child, and she cried for him. "God in Heaven; you are your mother's son. One day, I will tell you all about her. Her family must have locked her away. They took you from her; I know it. Your mother loved you from the moment you were in her womb. She would never give you up, never. But you're safe now. Wherever she is, she sent me to watch over you until she can find her way back."

But the boy's mother never came. As he grew, it became evident that something in him was wrong. At twelve, he began to change; the stark resemblance to his mother faded. He could heal from a bruise overnight, but suffered excruciating pain for no apparent reason. His mother's favorite flower had given him comfort until one day, the scent of gardenia made him sick.

The boy became curious about Temper's clothing, wearing little pieces now and then—a shirt, her underwear. Temper poured all the love she had into this child, never having a family of her own because she had no love left over. Even so, love was not enough to save him.

At fifteen, the pain was gone but confusion took its place. "Who am I?" he asked.

The torment in his question touched her and opened the door to all her stored away secrets. Secrets she hoped would free him from his demons. And so she began.

The day you were born is the day God gave me my purpose: finding and taking care of you.

Your uncle had given me the day off. I went on about my business, but later in the day, my spirit got troubled. Something told me to go check on your mother. So, I borrowed my boyfriend's old car and went back.

The help had to park in the back behind a patch of trees and walk to the main house. I was coming through the path when I saw your uncle getting into his car with a baby. I didn't know whether to run to the house to see about your mother or see if there was something wrong with you. But something about the whole thing didn't look right. So I ran back to the car and followed him. When he didn't turn off on the road that led to the hospital, I was certain something foul was going on. That old car could barely keep up. When we crossed the North Carolina line, my fear that you were being taken away became real.

"When your uncle pulled up at the hospital in DC, I was scared again that something was wrong with you, that this was some kind of special hospital. By the time I caught up and went inside, he was gone and so were you. No one would tell me anything. So, I drove back home and went immediately to see about Joy Marie. Your uncle told me she had left the country earlier that day. He said they had given me the day off because it would have been too hard for Joy Marie to say goodbye. I knew that was a lie.

I went back to that hospital the following day and waited until I saw some colored people who worked there. Sure enough, one of them remembered the mixed baby. I spent the next four years searching orphanages, hoping to find you. Praying there would be something about you that was Joy Marie and I'd know you.

The truth calmed him and life with Temper went on. He awoke one day obsessed with learning. By the time he was seventeen, school had nothing left to teach him. He began

243

absorbing on his own, reading and writing, calculating and experimenting until his keeper could no longer reach him. Every night he heard her recite two lines of prayer: "My God, I commend him to your care. May his hands and feet serve only you." One morning, he was gone.

Chapter 84.

What do you fear?

Nothing.

Then why do you question your actions?

I used two innocents.

Was it not their purpose?

Mechisedec did not answer. He considered that the specter was right; all are in the service of God. Breathing a sigh, he longed for a drink from the well of blood-red peace.

The voice continued through Mechisedec's acceptance. *I have observed and wonder. What have you become; Good or Evil?*

According to you, I am beyond either.

Yes. That is my position but not yours. So choose.

I am the hand.

The hand that kills.

The hand that redeems.

Others say you are evil and destroy what is good. I say you have arrived at your natural inclination.

My natural inclination is to judge.

You have become a will to power. Superhuman. Your will to power is natural.

I walk in the shadow of Him that sends me.

Then cease your doubt. Be that for which you are created.

Mechisedec bowed his head.

Advise my soul, Oh Lord
That these hands may not fail in service
That my feet may follow my heart in judgment
And both work to your glory.

Chapter 85.

"There is nothing more precious than family, is there?" he asked when Malice answered the phone.

"Dead or alive?" Malice immediately wished he could take it back. This was the child of Joy Marie, the mother whose bones he held in his hands, brother to one for whom the light of day never came. No father, and no family he could claim. On the day of his birth, he became laboratory dust for the curiosity of would-be gods.

Mechisedec chuckled. "I see you made the morning paper. Solving the case of the Princeville Princess. Congratulations."

Hoping the offense had passed, Malice asked. "When did you know?"

Mechisedec considered the question that held a multitude of answers, and said nothing.

Malice continued. "The first victims were just a cover weren't they? Getting to Pascal and Haiger was always your primary objective."

"You are implying the Varians were innocent, Dr. Able. They were atoned; their lives given to God's purpose."

"Why the hands and feet?" Malice asked.

"They are the instruments by which we carry out our purpose. The gifts by which every creature demonstrates its intention. They were simply given back to God."

"What now? Will you come back so we can figure this out?"

"Why? We are what we are, Dr. Able—the creation of birth, circumstance and time. Shaped by what we do and what is done to us. Despite it all, we are called to reach our highest potential; to be, to do, that for which we are born."

"When did you know?" Again, when Mechisedec did not answer, Malice said, "You've obviously considered this question: What are you?"

"The same thing we all are, Dr. Able. The thoughts of God. We add and analyze the events of our lives in search of meaning, looking for Truth. Doing in the hopes we are never forgotten. Only, the things we experience are like spider webs made of dew. Regrettably, Truth has yet to find us worthy."

"Come up with that all on your own?" Malice said.

"Feel free to think on it with your morning coffee."

"I'll do that."

Both were silent until Malice spoke. "I'm curious. What did Temperance call you?"

Mechisedec hesitated. "She called me Son."

Malice smiled. "Comedian too, I see." Assuming Mechesidec was still being literal, Malice searched his biblical memory for synonyms. It returned King, Shepherd, Prince, Emmanuel. Which would Temperance have named you, he said to himself. Only one name made sense.

Malice accepted the man's mastery at nondisclosure but made one last attempt. "You said that Fate is unpredictable. You lived, your brother died; you were found by a family friend; your mother returned from the grave, and you killed the uncle that tried to kill you. Sounds like plain ol' revenge."

"Fate unfolds God's Plan. She spared me; she spared you often, Dr. Able. What we don't know is why. The unknown is unpredictable."

"So, she hasn't taken you into her confidence, huh? Well, let me help. I predict that I will find you, and we shall see what you are."

"I look forward to it. We shall see what you become with your new purpose, Daniel St. John. Let us see what makes it through the cracks of what you hold sacred. Then, we shall meet again."

"Yes, Prince, we will."

Every Truth holds one Forbidden thing.

~Q~

*"You are what you think. Don't like it?
Change your mind."*

The mythic stories in **The Scent of Gardenia** are
available as companion books for young readers
under the titles: **Spell Me A Story and The
Keepers of Carifa.** It is a great way to share
reading with your children.

Also look for:
*Blood of Their Sons,
What I Know About God
The Keeper of Lost Things*

M E B Smith lives in Charlotte, NC.

To contact or place an order:

Online: www.FrogsHairPress.com

Postal: Frog's Hair Press
                  PO Box 34483
                  Charlotte, NC 28234

E-mail: FrogsHairPress@gmail.com

Phone: 980-428-9885

FHP welcomes your comments whatever they are. Thanks for taking the time to write.

The author is available for interviews and discussion groups in person, by phone and online.

Share comments with other readers about this and other FHP creations on Facebook. See the website for details.

www.ingramcontent.com/pod-product-compliance
Lightning Source LLC
Chambersburg PA
CBHW061609170626
46811CB00001B/374